THE TROJAN HORSE TRAITOR

AMY C. BLAKE

This publication is a work of fiction. Names, characters, places, and incidents either are products of the author's imagination or are used fictitiously. This work is protected in full by all applicable copyright laws, as well as by misappropriation, trade secret, unfair competition, and other applicable laws. No part of this book may be reproduced or transmitted in any manner without written permission from Hallway Publishing, except in the case of brief quotations embodied in critical articles or reviews. All rights reserved.

Hallway Publishing
45 Lafayette Road #114
North Hampton, NH 03870

www.hallwaypublishing.com
Contact Information: info@hallwaypublishing.com

The Trojan Horse Traitor

COPYRIGHT © 2015 by Amy C. Blake

First Edition, October 2015

Cover Art by Hallway Publishing
Typesetting by Odyssey Books

ISBN: 978-1-941058-34-3

Published in the United States of America

For the glory of Christ alone

*For my wonderful husband Charles
And for my four awesome kids: Elias, Charis, Jonas, and Lukas
I love you guys*

Chapter 1

Castle Island

Levi Prince reached the top of the sandstone steps and read the canvas sign thrashing in the wind like it desperately wanted to escape: WELCOME TO CAMP CLASSIC: YOUR SUMMER-LONG IMMERSION INTO THE CLASSICAL WORLD. Another gust of wind nearly ripped the jacket from his back. Two seagulls dive-bombed him, making Levi duck and cover.

Somehow not feeling all that welcome, Levi glanced back down the steps to the beach and the endless blue-green water stretching as far as he could see. As he watched, the waves churned higher, pummeling the red-and-white ferry he, his family, and a bunch of other campers and their families had exited not fifteen minutes earlier.

Castle Island, the tiny, castle-free (as far as he could tell) speck in the middle of vast Lake Superior, was a full three hours from the mainland. And it would be his home for the summer. His nerves prickled, half in dread of the unknown, half in anticipation of a summer spent miles and miles away from his younger sister and brothers.

Most of the time he liked homeschooling, especially when he finished his work early and got to do whatever he wanted all afternoon. Or when his friends at church told him about their hour-long bus rides to and from school and the horrors of their school uniforms. His uniform alternated between pajamas and sweats, depending on his mood.

Yeah, homeschooling was good. Except that it meant he never got a break from Abby, Zeke, and Jer.

And boy did he ever need a break. He tightened his grip on his Camp Classic invitation, the one that came in the mail back in March. His ticket to a sibling-free summer. It had taken him most of the next six weeks to convince his parents to let him go. He'd been offended they didn't think he could handle himself for a couple of months without them.

Now, though, the isolation of this place made him wonder what he'd gotten himself into. It didn't help that a purple-black mass seeped across the morning sky like a bruise, and the ferry bucked hard against its tie ropes. The whole setting made the hair rise on the back of his neck.

He adjusted the collar of his jacket, along with his outlook. So it was going to rain. No big deal. He wouldn't bail now. He needed this summer on his own.

Levi turned away from the view and toward the path between live oaks and pines he'd seen the others take earlier. He'd taken his time trudging across the sand, hoping to separate himself from his siblings. Between Abby's nonstop pouting because she couldn't stay at Camp Classic with Levi, and Zeke and Jer running in circles like monkeys on Mountain Dew, well . . . he kind of hoped if he kept his distance, the other campers wouldn't know they were related to him.

Levi had only gone a few feet along the path when he heard running footsteps from behind and somebody rammed a bony shoulder into his arm. He whirled around to face a kid who oozed disdain all the way from his perfect black hair to his brand new Nikes. Levi couldn't help but run a hand over his own hair—so red it was almost orange, and kinked into a thousand ringlets despite the super-short cut he'd gotten only two days earlier.

"Watch where you're going, runt," the other kid said with a sneer.

Runt? "Excuse me?" Yeah, Levi was scrawny, but this guy wasn't exactly the Hulk.

The kid snatched the invitation from Levi's hand.

"Hey," Levi protested as he made a swipe for his letter.

"Calm down. I'm just looking." The boy made a big show of opening and reading the letter then looked up at Levi through narrowed eyes. "Leviticus Isaiah Prince?" Disbelief flattened his tone.

"Yeah?" What had Levi's parents been thinking? Between the name and the orange afro, he might as well pin a sign to his own back: *Target*.

"You actually had the nerve to come?" The hatred in the boy's words pushed Levi backward a step. The right side of the kid's upper lip curled, exposing a single white canine tooth. A Doberman on the verge of attack.

"Um, why wouldn't I?" Levi couldn't decide whether to be mad, scared, or just plain confused. This kid must have him mixed up with somebody else because Levi knew he'd never met him before in his life.

"You don't belong here." Doberman boy let out a growl. Literally.

Levi's mouth fell open. What kind of person growled at random strangers?

Though his whole body tensed to run away, Levi forced himself to stay put. He had to get that letter. Without it, the camp people might not let him stay. "Look, I don't know what your problem is. Just give me back my—"

Doberman kid snarled, "I'm gonna make your summer a living nightmare, runt." He slammed into Levi, knocking him to the ground. Then the kid tossed the letter into the wind, spun on his heel, and raced along the path toward camp.

Stunned, Levi stared after him, half-expecting to see a dog tail sprout from the kid's rear end.

Yeah, he definitely wasn't feeling the big Camp Classic welcome.

Chapter 2

Camp Classic

Paper snapped in the wind, bringing Levi to his senses. He surged to his feet and snagged his invitation seconds before it blew off the ridge and sailed far away on the lake. He glanced over his shoulder at the trail Dog Boy had taken. Maybe losing his invitation wouldn't be such a bad thing after all.

No, he wanted to stay. He could put up with one slightly unbalanced bully. Everyone else had to be perfectly normal. He stuffed his invitation deep in his front pocket.

Levi followed the path, careful to keep his steps slow so he would avoid another encounter with the creepy kid. He came to the back of a wooden building, rounded the corner, and took in the camp area. Long, low buildings like Iroquois longhouses surrounded a grassy central area. A line of people stretched to the door of the building across the green. Levi spotted his dad a little way from the door. Alone, thankfully, which meant his mom must have taken the others somewhere to run off their hyperactivity.

Before Levi could start toward his dad, a circle of multicolored lights drew his eyes farther north to the mountain peak he had heard gave Castle Island its name, though Levi thought it looked nothing like a castle. For a split second, he thought he saw some sort of building on the cliff, backlit by the rainbow lights. Then the lights vanished, and the peak looked like . . . well, a peak.

Levi frowned. What was all that about? He hadn't heard any thunder. Not that the lights looked like lightning. More like the rainbow-filled bubbles his youngest brother Jer loved to blow from his supersized bubble wand, just hundreds of times bigger. The northern lights maybe? Did those even appear during the day?

With a shrug, Levi walked toward his dad, his gaze skimming the families clustered around nervous-looking kids near his age, all of whom he knew were being taught according to the same strict, classical education system that he was.

He passed an elderly African-American woman and a girl with her nose stuck in a book. Good grief, he liked to read, but now? As he moved past another girl, this one with waist-length, golden-blonde hair, she turned a bright smile on him. Levi tried to smile back, but the extremely tall woman with her moved between them and leveled a frown at Levi. Like some sort of bodyguard. Weird.

Levi passed Dog Boy standing alone halfway up the line. The bully slouched with his arms across his chest and his chin lifted in defiance, as if daring anybody to challenge him. Levi shook his head. The jerk must have cut in front of all these people in line. Where were the kid's parents? They needed to teach him a few manners.

Levi lowered his head and hurried to where his dad waited with Levi's duffel bag and bedroll at his feet.

Dad faced him with a smile. "Hey, I thought I was going to have to go looking for you." He waved off Levi's stammered explanations. "It's fine. You're just in time. We're next."

Levi glanced at the building. The sign above the door read DINING HALL. Good to know where the food was. At least he wouldn't starve.

His hand strayed to his pocket to make sure his invitation was still safe.

Dad gestured toward the cabin area. "What do you think of the place?"

"Um . . ." Levi's eyes roamed the grassy area he figured was for archery and fencing and all that stuff he would much rather skip. Just because the campers were classically educated didn't mean they all had to be knights in shining armor, right? Plus, that kid from the ridge would probably love to stick a sword in Levi. Why couldn't they do something normal, like soccer or even basketball or football? Something that didn't involve weapons.

The dining hall door opened. A pig-tailed girl in overall shorts, her freckled face streaked with tears, walked outside with a heavyset couple who patted her back and offered her tissues.

Not exactly reassuring. Levi cut his eyes toward his dad. Maybe he'd say this wasn't the summer camp for Levi after all.

Instead, Dad cocked his chin toward the door. "Go ahead and get registered, son. I'll wait for you out here."

Levi swallowed hard. "Oh, um, okay." He'd expected his dad to at least go in with him. Especially if the registration people tended to make campers cry.

Levi went inside alone. Tables and folding chairs like the ones his church used on potluck Sundays filled the large open room. In a kitchen area beyond the tables, undersized people scurried around. Midgets, maybe? A gray-haired man who couldn't have been as tall as seven-year-old Jer carried a tray full of paper bags. He set it on a table by the wall and brushed at the mustard smears on his white apron. Grey beard-hairs poked from a hairnet on his chin.

"That's the last of the sandwiches, love," he said to someone out of sight, his voice deep and full despite his small stature.

A tiny plump woman in a blue apron came into view. She held a package of juice boxes in her stubby arms. "All right, dear. I'll just finish off with the drinks then." She crossed out of sight then reappeared, puffing, at an open pass-through window, where she plunked the juice boxes beside a bucket of Coke cans. She hovered there, peering at Levi through thick glasses that made her look like a dragonfly.

Levi waved. She didn't wave back.

"Your invitation, please?"

The soft voice drew Levi's attention to the registration table where a white-haired lady sat in a folding chair. Wrinkles covered her face, but she held her back straight and her chin tilted upward. She wore khakis and a baby-blue Camp Classic polo that seemed too casual for her. When a shaft of sunlight shot through the window, it formed a halo around her head, reminding him of the Madonna paintings he'd seen in art appreciation class at homeschool co-op last year. Though a little intimidating, the woman didn't look the type to drive girls to tears.

She cleared her throat. He'd been gawking like an idiot. Face hot, he fished his invitation from his pocket. It looked like he'd dug it out of a trash compactor. He made a useless attempt at smoothing it. "Sorry."

"That's all right." She scanned the page. "Leviticus?" Her bright blue eyes darted to his face, and she stilled with her lips slightly parted.

"It's Levi," he finally said, partly to break the uncomfortable silence and partly because he couldn't stand the thought of being called *Leviticus* the entire summer.

When she didn't respond right away, he bit his lip. Had he irritated her? Maybe this was the part where she made people cry.

"I'm happy to have you here, Levi." Her mouth curved into a gentle smile as she returned his letter. "You may carry your things to the boys' cabin—the one to your left as you leave—and get settled in to a bunk."

"Yes, ma'am, thank you." He took a step toward the door.

"By the way," she said and he turned back. "My name is Sophia Dominic. My husband and I direct Camp Classic." She reached out a veined hand.

He took it. A shock like winter static bit his palm. Though he hadn't noticed any open doors or windows, a burst of wind shivered his hair. Mrs. Dominic's eyes widened in a look of surprise. Or was that fear?

The wind stopped as suddenly as it started. Totally freaked out—though he couldn't say exactly why—Levi yanked back his hand. "N-n-nice to meet you."

He darted to the doorway, barely registering Mrs. Dominic's murmured words, "Lest I miss it, I suppose. Though how I could, I can't imagine. He is so like him."

Levi burst outside and ran for the boys' cabin.

Before he reached it, his dad snagged his arm. "You get checked in all right, son?"

Levi managed a nod.

Dad frowned, probably trying to figure out why Levi's face was so pale. "You think you'll be okay here for the summer?"

Levi released a slow breath. Would he be okay? Had the whole thing with Mrs. Dominic been as creepy as it felt? He rubbed his palm where the static had bit. No wonder the pigtailed girl had been crying. Still, maybe it was nothing. Maybe the wind came from an open window in the kitchen. But then why had Mrs. Dominic looked so rattled? And what had she said? *Lest I miss it* or some odd thing.

Dad squeezed his arm. "Levi?"

Levi gnawed the inside of his cheek. What if summer at Camp Classic was worse than summer at home?

What should I do, God?

No answer. Not that he had expected God to speak out loud, but some sense of the right decision would have been nice.

He sighed. At least he had until after the orientation lunch to make up his mind. Maybe in a couple of hours Camp Classic would seem more normal. He met his dad's gaze. "It's fine."

"Listen, we have to leave earlier than we thought." Dad eyed him, probably watching for him to hyperventilate. "Like in about twenty minutes."

Levi's gut dropped like he was on a Cedar Point rollercoaster. "So soon? Why?"

"Storm's moving in. Shouldn't be here for hours, but the camp director said he'd feel better if we got going right away."

"Oh." So much for a couple of hours to decide. He had to choose. Should he go home with his family, basically admitting he was a big baby? Or should he suck it up and stay here with a bully, a freaky old lady, weird lights in the sky . . . oh, and a bunch of lethal weapons? Yay.

"Walk with me, son." Dad guided Levi toward the woods behind the dorm. "I want to pray for you before I go. I know God has a lot to teach you this summer."

Levi's churning gut calmed slightly.

A little later, Levi entered the boys' dorm. It smelled sour, like his bedroom last August when he had found a pair of Zeke's sweaty underpants dried stiff underneath his bed. He glanced around the long open room with rows of bunk beds to the right and to the left. Half a dozen boys were scattered throughout, including the bully, who sat on a top bunk to the left. His back was to Levi.

I'm thinking my bed's to the right.

Levi headed down the central aisle, passing bunk after bunk, each piled with somebody's stuff, when he finally spotted an empty bed by the wall—a bottom bunk. It figured. Still, it was better than sleeping near that Doberman creep. He tossed his stuff onto the cardboard-thin mattress, planning to unpack after the ferry left.

A flushing sound filtered from the open doorway at the foot of his bed. Wonderful. He got to sleep by the toilets. If it got anywhere near as hot here as it did back home in Columbus, he'd soon be wishing his bunk smelled as sweet as Zeke's dirty underpants.

At that moment, a huge kid, one roughly the size of a professional wrestler, exited the bathroom and grinned at Levi. "Hey, man. I'm Trevor Patterson. Looks like I'm your bunkmate." He pointed at the bunk above Levi's.

Two thoughts struck Levi at once. First, Trevor was massive, which meant Dog Boy would keep his distance. Good news.

Second, the top bunk was rickety, and Levi would be sleeping directly beneath it. Not such good news.

"Great." Levi forced a smile, wondering which horrible and humiliating death would claim him first: asphyxiation by toilet fumes or flattening by bunkmate.

Chapter 3

The Precipice

Levi gave one final wave at the departing ferry. With a quick swipe of his fist under his nose, he turned away. The cold wind must be making his nose run. He peered up at the clouds blotting out the sun. He hoped his family made it to the mainland before the storm hit. And he really hoped staying here was the right decision.

Too late to chicken out now.

With a sigh, he started up the hill, Trevor at his side.

"You play football?" Trevor thumped both fists against his chest like Tarzan, Jr. "I'm really good."

Levi couldn't help but smile at the grin covering most of Trevor's face.

"'Course my brother Shawn's better." Trevor's grin disappeared. "Dad says he'll probably win a Heisman next year."

Levi shrugged, one eyebrow raised. "That's cool, right?"

"Yeah, cool." But Trevor's shoulders slumped like it wasn't cool at all.

"You into fencing or archery?" Levi finally asked to get Trevor talking again.

"Never done it, but I can't wait." Trevor picked up a stick and pretended to sword fight the air, his grin back in place. "Bet Shawn's never fenced anybody before."

When they reached the cabin, Trevor threw down the stick and opened the door. The two entered as Levi's favorite bully walked in the opposite door with a spiky-haired hulk of a kid.

"Just because cell phones don't work here doesn't mean we shouldn't get to keep our PSPs. What else are we gonna do for fun? Go fishing?" The hulk cackled. His face looked like a jack-o'-lantern with a too-big mouth carved out.

"They couldn't make me send my stuff back." Doberman creep pulled an iPhone from his pocket. "Sometimes it's cool to have parents who never show—" He caught sight of Levi and Trevor, stopped short, and bared his teeth.

Levi gulped. Was that supposed to be a smile? He glanced around the cabin. Empty . . . and dark with no sunlight coming in the windows. He and Trevor started toward their bunks, but the bully pocketed his phone and blocked their path. The other kid slunk along beside him with his knuckles practically scraping the ground. Yippee. Dog Boy had a pet thug.

"What're you two losers up to?" The bully's voice was a low growl.

"Excuse us, please." Trevor's ultra-polite tone might've been intimidating if his voice hadn't cracked right in the middle.

The gorilla kid busted out laughing. Trevor's eyes narrowed to slits.

Levi's hands grew sweaty, but he figured he had better say something or Trevor might get kicked out for fighting the first day of camp. He swallowed a couple of times to make sure his voice would work. "Um . . . what's your problem? You don't even know us."

Head cocked, the bully folded his arms over his chest. "I'm Hunter."

Levi opened his mouth to tell his name, but Hunter cut him off with a sneering, "I know who you are." He looked Trevor up and down. "Who's this?"

"Trevor."

Hunter jabbed a thumb toward his friend. "He's Martin."

"Little Curly Red and the Giant." Martin let out a stupid-sounding giggle.

Levi resisted the urge to roll his eyes. *Thought you needed a higher IQ than a slug to get invited to this place.*

Hunter moved in until his chin almost bumped Levi's nose.

"Listen, runt." Hunter's steely eyes bored into Levi. "I don't like—"

Hinges squeaked, drawing Levi's attention to the door opening at the far end of the cabin. Not the bathroom door by his bunk, but the one on Hunter's side.

A hunched figure emerged into the shadows and slammed the door. It crept along the dusky aisle toward the boys, both arms extended like a vertically challenged zombie. Spine tingling, Levi watched as the short, stout figure halted beside Trevor and reached out a stubby forefinger.

Trevor flinched, but the man only flipped a switch on the wall.

A fluorescent glare flooded the room, illuminating the man's wild, salt-and-pepper hair and craggy face. "Hello, boys." The man's voice was low and gravelly. "It's getting dark. The storm must be moving in." He peered from boy to boy over a pair of reading glasses. "I'm Asa Baldwin." His gaze landed on Hunter and hardened. "Dr. Baldwin to you. Your cabin master."

When no one spoke, he held out a hand, palm up, to Hunter. "Give it to me."

In an instant, Hunter's face switched from bully mode to teacher's pet mode. "Sir?"

Levi rolled his eyes.

Dr. Baldwin's mouth tightened. "No electronic devices at Camp Classic."

Anger hardened Hunter's jaw, but he pulled the cell phone from his jeans pocket without argument.

"We're in the middle of the world's largest freshwater lake. What made you think this thing would work here?" Dr. Baldwin pointed at Hunter's backpack. "Hand over the rest."

As Hunter yanked out a neon green iPad and a Gameboy, a book clattered to the floor. Without thinking, Levi bent to pick it up, trying to read the faded gold letters printed across the washed-out purple fabric. Scowling, Hunter snatched the book and stuffed it back into his pack.

Levi frowned. What did Hunter want with a prissy purple book anyway?

The cabin master harrumphed. Levi glanced at him as a look of intense interest flitted across his features. The look disappeared as the man took Hunter's electronics. "You can have these back at the end of the summer." He turned and strode back down the aisle to what Levi figured must be his room, muttering, "Why do they always try to sneak these in? Kids. They don't use the brains God gave them."

Levi bit back a laugh. Hunter leveled a vicious look at Levi, flung open the door, and stalked outside. Martin glared between Levi and Trevor. Levi managed to keep a straight face until Martin left, then both boys cracked up.

At one o'clock, Levi and Trevor walked to the dining hall. By the time they got inside, the light rain had dampened their clothes, and the wind had whipped Trevor's dark hair into spikes. The scent of fish and hush puppies kicked Levi's salivary glands into high gear. After they filled their plates with baked walleye, fried perch, and smoked carp, the boys found an empty table and dug in without talking.

"Hi." The soft feminine voice came from directly behind Levi.

When he spun around, his fork clattered to the floor. "Oh, uh . . . hi."

The blonde girl he'd noticed earlier, the pretty one with the super tall mom, stood behind him holding a tray. Her skin was so tanned it looked golden like her hair, and her eyes were the shade of a peacock's tail. A blush pinked her skin from throat to temple. "Is this seat taken?"

"Um, no, go ahead." Levi pulled out the chair on his left, wincing as it squealed against the concrete floor.

"Thanks." She sat, placed her napkin on her lap, and bowed her head.

She was praying. And using her manners. He was such a heathen. He scrambled for his untouched napkin, scrubbed it across his mouth, and waved it at Trevor, who had a glob of butter smeared on the end of his nose. Trevor didn't take the hint.

The girl opened her eyes and faced Levi. "I'm Sara." She hesitated a second. "Sara Christopher."

"Levi Prince."

"I'm Trevor." Trevor's voice chose that moment to crack again. Levi suspected nerves brought on the squeak. He didn't blame him; the girl made him feel squeaky too. She was beautiful, polite, and so tanned she must be athletic. She would probably destroy him in all the training sessions they were supposed to do this summer.

Why would someone like her want to sit by Levi when there was a table full of girls right behind him? He'd seen at least one empty seat he hadn't dared attempt to occupy.

Since his fork was on the floor, Levi used his spoon to shovel salad into his mouth. Trevor stuffed four hush puppies in his already-full mouth. Sara stirred her food around her plate. Levi searched his brain for something to say, anything to fill the silence. Before he could ask something dumb like what grade she was going into in the fall (duh, they were all going into eighth grade), Sara spoke up.

"Sorry if I'm bothering you." Was that insecurity in her eyes? No way.

She glanced at the girls' table, and he followed her glance. Two girls—one beefy with brown hair and mean piggish eyes, the other bony with pale blonde hair and a something-stinks wrinkle to her nose—cut their eyes at Sara.

"Look at that shirt," the brown-haired one whispered behind her meaty hand.

"My grandmother has one just like it," the blonde said, and they both giggled.

Levi looked at Sara's pale pink ruffled blouse with its white lacy collar. He didn't know much about girls' clothes, but he didn't think his little sister had worn anything like it since kindergarten.

Cheeks red, Sara tugged at the collar.

Levi smiled big, not caring if he had lettuce stuck in his braces. "Of course you're not bothering us." He jutted his chin toward the girls. "You homeschooled?" He might have been wrong, but he figured she would be more thick-skinned if she was in school with girls like these day after day. The kids at his co-op and church were mostly okay, at least when it came to bullying and stuff. Not that they didn't pick on people, but they were nothing like Hunter and Martin. Those two were going to take some getting used to.

Sara nodded. "You?"

Levi started to answer when the door crashed open. He whirled around in his seat. Lighting zigzagged, backlighting a tall, broad-shouldered man in the doorway. Wind-whipped grey hair flailed his weathered face. Rainwater sheeted from the yellow rain slicker that didn't fully cover his red-flowered Hawaiian shirt. He looked like a cross between an old sea captain and a retired surfer.

He strode to the center of the now-silent room. "I apologize for interrupting your meal." Though a smile creased his tanned cheeks, worry lined his forehead. "For those of you I haven't yet had the pleasure of addressing, I am Tobias Dominic, director of Camp Classic. I'm sorry I won't be able to deliver the welcome speech I'd prepared, as I'm sure it would have delighted you." A twinkle brightened his green eyes and was quickly snuffed. "However, my staff and I thought it best to skip the nonessentials."

When he gestured toward the people who'd filed in behind him, Levi recognized the cabin master, Dr. Baldwin. Beside him stood a man equally as short and stout, who shook water from his red-brown hair and scowled. A couple with long, straight, white-blonde hair, both slender and well over seven feet tall, exchanged uneasy glances. Another tall, slim woman with the black hair, reddish skin, and high cheekbones of a Native American kept her dark eyes latched on the window.

Levi knitted his brows. Didn't this camp believe in hiring ordinary-looking people?

The director went on. "With this violent storm fast approaching, we've decided it's best to move camp to our sturdier facilities north of here."

Thunder boomed, vibrating the tables and chairs, and the lights flickered. Levi half-stood to look out a window. The trees doubled over in the wind as though they'd been sucker punched, and black clouds bunched like a street gang around a victim. Anxious voices buzzed. Someone mentioned their families, and a clump filled Levi's throat. What if the ferry hadn't made it to land before the storm hit?

"Now, don't be alarmed." Mr. Dominic lifted his hands in a calming gesture. "Mr. Drake called to say the ferry has docked on the mainland. Your families are safe, and we have things under control here. I simply need you to pack your things and meet us out front in half an hour." He raised his voice over the clamor of kids and storm. "Wear your hiking boots and rain gear."

A freckle-faced girl bumped Levi in her rush for the door. "This storm has got to be a bad omen. I knew my mom shouldn't have made me come here."

Levi's lips twisted in disgust. He didn't believe in omens.

A huge gust pounded the windows. Levi shot Mr. Dominic an anxious look at the precise moment the old man's gaze darted to his. When their eyes connected, Levi's hair bristled like it had when he was little and stuck a pair of scissors into an electric outlet.

Tiny alarms prickled up and down Levi's spine, but he shook them away. Nope. No such thing as a bad omen.

Levi forced his legs to keep trudging up the mucky path after Sara. Hunter and Martin hiked in front of them, directly behind Mr. Dominic. Trevor and the other campers trailed behind. The clouds made it as dark as dusk. The growl of thunder was almost constant. During the thirty-minute trek, Levi's hands had frozen to his gear. His backpack bit deeper and deeper into his shoulders. The path grew steeper by the second. People no longer walked side-by-side, talking. Instead, they slogged along the narrow trail, heads down against the drops bulleting their hoods.

Why were they going uphill? Wasn't that dangerous? The lightning was so close the air smelled like burnt aluminum foil. Levi craned to see the path ahead without getting a face full of rain. He halted, blinking rainwater from his lashes.

What in the world?

Trevor ran into him, grumbling about the mud splashed into his face. Levi ignored him because just ahead, through a few scrubby trees, the earth ended. Mr. Dominic stood at the edge.

Levi inched nearer. A lightning flash revealed the lake far below. Steely gray and whipped white on top, gigantic waves crashed high into the purple-black sky. Thunder blasted his eardrums. Levi cowered. What he'd taken for thunder before must have been the lake, a writhing, rumbling monster. Adrenaline spurted through his veins. He grabbed Sara's shoulder.

When she turned, he shouted over the noise. "What're we doing here? We'll get killed!"

The next burst of lightning showed her calm expression. "It'll be fine." Leaning around Martin, Sara waved a hand toward the director, who now faced them. "I'm sure Mr. Dominic knows what he's doing."

"All right, everyone." The director's serene voice somehow carried above the crash of storm and water. "We're here."

Levi stifled a squawk. Here? The only thing here was a cliff.

"My wife came early to make everything ready for us." A tranquil smile graced Mr. Dominic's lips even as spray from a particularly ferocious wave splattered his boots. "I trust cozy fires and tea or cocoa await us inside." He laced his fingers and rocked back on his heels like it was the most natural thing in the world to stand on a precipice in the middle of a violent storm.

Acid burned Levi's stomach. His duffel bag slipped from his numb fingers. There was no inside, just a hundred-foot drop into the crashing waves.

His nutcase camp director was about to lead them to their deaths.

Chapter 4

The Castle

Lightning shattered the sky. Thunder vibrated the ground. What should Levi do? They had to get away from this drop-off, and there were a lot more kids than crazy Mr. Dominic and his kooky-looking staff. Levi glanced back at Trevor, still scrubbing mud off his nose, eyes hidden by his lowered hood. Did he even see the danger?

Levi turned forward and grabbed Sara's raincoat sleeve. "Sara, we've got to get out of here."

She twisted around as lights burst behind her like Fourth of July fireworks. Eyebrows scrunched, she flashed him a half-amused, half-puzzled smile, as if she thought he was teasing. "Why? Don't you like it?" She turned and pointed north. He followed her pointing finger to where empty air had dropped away to a storm-tossed lake mere seconds before.

Now he saw a castle.

It was a huge gray stone fortress that looked like it had stood there for centuries, not mere seconds. Orange lights glowed from the windows and red pennants waved on its four towers. The waters of a moat lapped at Mr. Dominic's boots. A lowered drawbridge stretched across the moat to where Mrs. Dominic waited, sheltered in the doorway from the now-gentle rain.

Levi's sleeping bag splashed into the mud beside his duffel. Had he lost his mind? Surely he hadn't mistaken this calm moat for a violent lake. He looked around at the other kids. They didn't seem scared at all, only dazzled by the castle. Levi couldn't even see those furthest down the line, so he figured they may not have seen anything—cliff or castle.

Trevor, the mud now cleared from his eyes, squeaked, "Hey, Levi, would you look at that? Cool."

Ignoring him, Levi turned forward. Hunter's and Martin's faces were angled so he could just make out their expressions. Martin's skin was mottled white, his mouth hanging so wide rainwater splashed off his teeth. Hunter's face was a mask of boredom, except for his eyes, which glittered strangely. Had they seen anything?

Had Levi actually seen anything?

Sara squeezed between Hunter and Martin, passed Mr. Dominic, and crossed the drawbridge to the door, where Mrs. Dominic stepped back to let her in and then beckoned the rest of them. "Come inside where it's warm and dry. Dinner is almost ready."

Her comforting voice made Levi want to obey, but did he dare trust her? What if she was crazy like her husband? Or maybe Levi was the crazy one?

Trevor, who'd bounded forward at the word *dinner*, shoved Levi a few paces, not giving him time to think things through. Levi shot Trevor a dirty look and moved toward the castle on his own steam. They might be headed off a cliff, but if Sara could cross the bridge like it was no big deal, so could he.

Still, he took careful steps as he crossed, staring into the moat, expecting the rain-slick bridge to disappear and plunge him into the lake at any moment. He let out his breath when he made it to the door that rose taller than two of Mr. Dominic. As he passed Mrs. Dominic, she pushed back his hood and ruffled his curls. No static shock this time. No blast of wind. Just kind blue eyes, a gentle smile, and the faint scent of wildflowers. She reminded him of his grandmother. He offered her a wobbly smile and walked inside.

Warmth and light enveloped him the moment he entered the castle. If it was a castle. It sure looked like one. He stood beside Trevor, both of them dripping on the stone floor, and studied the high stone walls. From floor to ceiling hung brightly colored tapestries depicting people and animals from classical mythology. He picked out a picture of Zeus throwing a lightning bolt and another of the Midgard Serpent coiled around the Earth. One showed a ship full of women pirates, and another pictured King Arthur with Excalibur.

He moved further into the room, trying to absorb everything. Coats of arms hung beside tall suits of armor, and a pair of identical spiral staircases led upward beyond his view. From the center of the high ceiling hung an enormous chandelier, and across the room blazed a roaring fire in a huge hearth. He ignored the jostling of other campers and inhaled the scent of burning firewood and the aroma of fresh baked bread. He felt himself relax.

Maybe this place was a figment of his imagination. Maybe he'd fallen asleep in the boys' cabin, and his subconscious mind had substituted a daydream about this nice-smelling castle for the harsh reality of the smelly toilet so near his bed. Or maybe Trevor's bunk had collapsed on him, and he had a brain injury that made him delusional.

At a sharp twinge on his arm, he whirled around.

Trevor watched him, his grin mischievous. "I'm not dreaming, huh?"

Levi rubbed his arm. "You're not supposed to pinch me to see if you're dreaming. You're supposed to pinch yourself." The irritation seeped from his voice. "This whole thing is impossible. I mean, how can we be here?"

Trevor shrugged. "Who cares? This place is sweet!" He shook rainwater from his head.

Grimacing, Levi wiped the spray from his face. He took a step closer to Trevor and tried again. Trevor might think he was crazy, but he had to know. "There was a cliff, a drop-off into the lake maybe a hundred feet below, huge waves shooting water all that way."

Trevor scrunched his eyes. "You feeling okay, man?"

Dread punched Levi in the gut. "You didn't see it?"

"Uh . . . no."

Levi dropped his voice to a whisper. "Mr. Dominic said to come into the castle. I thought he'd gone insane and was about to step off the cliff. And then Mrs. Dominic was there . . . and this castle. And Sara . . ." He frowned. Had Sara seen the cliff or had massive Martin blocked her view? He peered around the now-full entryway. "Where is Sara?"

Trevor stared at him a second longer, blinking as a raindrop jiggled free from his bangs and splashed onto his eyelid. Then he looked around, too, even rising on tiptoes to see into the far corners of the room. "Don't see her."

"Quiet please, everyone." Mr. Dominic's call from near the fireplace brought instant silence.

Levi turned toward where the director stood with his arm around his wife. Staff members fanned out on either side of them. Some Levi recognized from earlier; others were new. All were either really tall or really short. Other than the Dominics, who looked as old as his grandparents, there wasn't a single average-looking person in the bunch.

"Welcome to our home." Mr. Dominic's voice boomed throughout the room. "Some of you will find it strange living in an ancient castle on a private island in the middle of the lake." His eyes sparkled as he shrugged. "But I hope you'll find it comfortable nonetheless."

Levi's jaw dropped. This was one strange old man.

The director lifted both arms in an all-encompassing gesture. "Please make yourselves at home here. Girls, your rooms are on the third floor, east and west corridors. Boys, you're on the fourth floor, also east and west. The dining area is just through there." He pointed to an archway on his left before indicating the staff beside him. "We will be your instructors and guides during the coming weeks. We'll help you in any way we can."

When several kids murmured to each other, Mr. Dominic raised a hand for silence. "Your lessons will go on as planned, here rather than at the cabins. But not today. Today you'll get settled. The staff will help you find your rooms, which, I'm pleased to say, have much more comfortable beds than those in your cabins." His eyebrows bobbled up and down as if in amusement. "Girls, please see Mrs. Sylvester for room assignments. Boys, see Mr. Austin. Dry off and put your things away. I'll see you in the dining hall shortly."

Everyone stood speechless and motionless. Despite Levi's worry and confusion, a touch of excitement shivered his belly. He was really going to spend the summer in a castle? Wow!

The director gave one sharp clap and everyone, Levi included, scurried to obey.

"Up here." A shaggy-haired, pimply-cheeked guy named Albert Forest, whose head maybe reached Levi's bellybutton, led Levi, Trevor, and their two roommates up one of the spiral staircases. Albert looked so much like the people Levi had seen in the kitchen down in the cabin area he wanted to ask if they were a family of midgets. He didn't dare, though, because he knew his mom would throttle him if she ever found out he'd asked such a thing.

Instead, Levi contented himself with climbing step after stone step. He gawked at the dusty portraits of ladies and gentlemen that lined the walls, careful to keep hold of the railing with his right hand and his soaked duffel and bedroll with his left. Though his left hand began throbbing in time with his calf muscles after what felt like the billionth step, he refused to change hands for fear he might miss something while he did.

Ornate stands in the wall held burning torches. Every so often they passed a window set high in the stone, but other than noticing that it was brighter out, Levi didn't stop to peer out the thick, wavy glass. At first he heard voices of people above and below them on the staircase, but after a while, all he heard was panting—his own and the others'. Though they passed several landings with closed doors, they never paused until finally, when Levi thought he was going to faint and make an absolute fool of himself (or die falling down all those stairs), they stopped before a tall door of pale wood.

Albert opened it, and Levi blinked at the bright hallway beyond. With one last glance at the stairway that continued—amazingly—higher, Levi stepped through to a corridor lined with a dozen floor-to-ceiling windows. Five doors lined the opposite side, each guarded by a suit of armor.

Levi stared at the hallway until one of his new roommates, Tommy Chen, said, "Storm's over."

So that was what looked different. The sunlight. Levi dropped his stuff on the floor with a squelch, strode to the nearest window, and stared out at a cloudless blue sky. Below, a grassy courtyard stretched to the opposite area of the castle. He smashed his cheek against the glass and strained to see as far as he could each direction, thinking there had to be at least some hint of bad weather nearby. No way could such a huge storm have passed so quickly.

But there wasn't. He couldn't even see the telltale sparkle of water droplets on the grass. He rested his forehead on the cool glass and squeezed his eyes shut, hoping things would be normal when he opened them.

They weren't. Anxiety nibbled away at his excitement.

A sharp intake of breath drew his eyes to his other new roommate, a chubby kid named Steve, who stood next to him gawking out the window from one side to the other with his face squashed against the glass like a red balloon about to pop. He pulled back and looked at Levi, his expression one of pure confusion. Levi started to ask Steve what he thought of this place—maybe Levi wasn't the only one who'd imagined a cliff—when a loud bang echoed around the corridor. Levi jumped so hard his head smacked against the window.

Steve screamed, "Gun!" and dropped to the floor in a cowering heap.

Tommy laughed. "That wasn't a gunshot."

Grinning like a crazy man, Trevor stood next to a now-headless suit of armor holding its helmet. "Sorry, but this thing is awesome. I've got to get me one."

With a roll of his eyes, Levi turned his attention to Albert, who leaned against the wall chewing a fingernail. It was time for some answers.

"Where are we?" Levi demanded. "This can't be Castle Island."

"Can't be." Steve heaved himself up from the floor. "There's this huge storm going on there. At least there was." He rubbed a hand over the wet hair still plastered to his forehead.

Albert strolled over to the last door on the corridor and fitted an old skeleton key into the lock. "Don't fret now, boys. There's times the weather's a tad different here than over yonder." He held up his hand with the index finger an inch above the thumb.

A tad different? Levi opened his mouth to ask what else was different when Albert turned the knob and released a chuckle that made Levi's scalp prickle.

Chapter 5

A Tad Different

"Come on." Albert crossed the threshold without a backward glance.

Levi stood slack-jawed a moment then exchanged looks with the others. Should they make a run for it? Close Albert inside and take off down the stairs? Try to find their way out of the castle and run back to camp? He thought somebody had said there was a telephone in the dining hall. They could call the police.

But what would they say? *Help! This place is weird! There's this amazing castle with wonderful-smelling food and warm fireplaces and nice people who look a little strange. Get us out of here!*

Maybe they should stick it out a while longer. At least see what their room looked like. Levi gathered his stuff, straightened his spine, and marched to the door. Albert wasn't very big. Trevor could probably take him if he had to.

Levi walked into the room and stopped dead just inside the door. The place looked like a ritzy hotel room or something. Not that he'd ever stayed in a ritzy hotel room. Spacious and bright with a fire roaring in the grate, the room had four beds so tall they each came with their own stepstool.

Someone's wet sleeping bag pushed into the backs of Levi's knees, making him stumble forward a few paces as Albert said, "Choose a bunk. You even get your own wardrobe." A flash of what looked like envy crossed Albert's face.

Levi walked to the nearest bed and fingered the hangings tied to the canopy. There were two sets, one a heavy red material and the other gauzy white. He wrinkled his nose. Looked like a bed for his sister.

Albert snorted. "The hangings ain't to make your beds pretty. They're right useful." He tugged at the heavy fabric. "The red ones keep the heat in when it's colder'n a witch's big toe." He touched the gauze. "The white ones keep the bugs out when it's hotter'n the blazes of Hades. We heat with fire and cool with God's own sweet breath." He hooked a bony thumb toward the window. "But you'll be glad to know Mr. Dominic got generators for the kitchen and the laundry. Also to power the hot water heaters." Albert looked from one silent boy to another before slouching to another door beside the fireplace. "Your bathroom." He yanked it open. "Stow your stuff and get changed. I'll be waiting in the hall. Don't be all day, I want my lunch."

As Albert strode to the door, a female voice trickled in from the hallway.

Levi frowned. A girl in the boys' dorm?

Albert glanced out. "Some of your neighbors," he announced with a dismissive wave. "Mr. and Mrs. Sylvester are your hall chaperones. They'll keep ya in line."

Once Albert left the room, Levi went to the only unclaimed bed—the one by the window, which he refused to look out because he'd never liked heights—and set his bag on it. He opened the wardrobe and stuffed his bedroll into the bottom. Even on tiptoes, he just managed to shove his backpack onto the top shelf. What he wouldn't give to be a couple inches taller, like Trevor.

After unloading his duffel and stacking his stuff on the empty shelves, he grabbed spare clothes and headed into the bathroom, tuning out the other boys' excited talking. He needed to think.

Inside, he closed the door, leaned against it, and shut his eyes tight. *Am I losing my mind, God?*

He opened his eyes and was immediately distracted from his confused thoughts. He'd never seen such a fancy bathroom in his life. At the center of the room stood a white vanity with deep double sinks, each with gleaming brass faucets. To his left blazed a fire that must back the bedroom fireplace, and unlit torches lined the walls. To his right stood a partial wall. He edged over and peered behind it. A plush red mat three times thicker than the carpet in his bedroom at home gave way to a huge claw-footed tub. A curtain to his left hid a shower. Thick red towels hung from a half-dozen brass hooks set into the stone wall. Across the room, two cubicles, each housing a spotless white toilet, flanked a tinted window.

This place was unbelievable. A real, live castle, all the way to the toilets fit for royalty.

At least now he knew why they called this place Castle Island.

Levi moved back to the sinks and studied his reflection in one of the two full-length, gilt-framed mirrors. He looked normal. As normal as ever, anyway. But was he going crazy? Had he imagined the cliff? The storm?

Levi shook his head, stripped down before the fire, and put on dry clothes. He took a deep breath and exited the bathroom. Whatever was going on, he would just have to deal with it. Without his parents' help.

"Next?" he called to his roommates.

The moment he left the bathroom, Albert barged into the bedroom.

"Ain't you people ready yet?" He scowled at Trevor, Tommy, and Steve still dripping beside their beds. "I'm hungry. Get a move on."

Albert stomped from the room, Levi's roommates staring after him.

Levi's eyebrow rose. *Note to self: Albert gets cranky when hungry.* "Hurry, guys." He quickly spread his wet clothes on the hot stones before the fireplace. "I'll stall him. We don't want to have to find our way to the dining room alone."

Levi stepped into the hallway where Albert tapped the toe of his grubby boot on the floor and grumbled that the food would be gone by the time they got downstairs. At least he was still waiting. Levi peered around the hall, figuring he could holler for the guys if Albert tried to take off without them.

More oil paintings covered the walls—mostly landscapes and portraits of sour-faced old people. One between the windows across from his room caught Levi's eye. He moved for a closer look. A wrecked ship in the middle of a field of flowers? Okay.

Levi turned to ask Albert about the picture but caught sight of a nearby door he hadn't noticed before. He swiveled his head and looked at the door leading to the stairs they'd come up, then turned back to the door beside him. They were identical: both of pale wood and hanging directly across from each other.

"Where's this door go?" he asked Albert.

Albert glanced over. "The other tower stairs, 'course."

"The other tower stairs?"

"Yep. Don't you know nothing about castles? Everything's got a twin.

You know, twin towers, twin halls. That kinda thing." Albert shrugged. "At least that's how this one is."

"Oh." Levi reached for the door handle.

At that moment, his roommates scrambled from their room with Steve hopping on one foot as he shoved on his tennis shoe. Not wanting to miss dinner, Levi abandoned the door to follow the group.

Levi sank into a high-backed wooden chair at a long oval table beside Trevor and gaped at the high-ceilinged room. Yet another stone fireplace filled one wall, the fire casting yellow light on the room full of identical tables, one parallel to the fireplace, the others perpendicular to it. All held sparkling white china and silverware. His napkin was of a thick gold cloth, and his glass weighed a ton. He would probably make an idiot of himself trying to figure out which of the three forks to use, but this place was amazing. When he'd signed up for camp, he'd never imagined spending the summer in the lap of luxury.

Despite the weirdness, excitement again began to overtake his anxiety. Plus, he was starved. The scents of roasted meat, fresh bread, and something sweet tantalized him. Trevor's stomach growled.

"Yeah," Levi said to Trevor's stomach. "I'm hungry too."

Trevor cast him a lopsided grin. Laughing, Levi relaxed into his seat.

Both sobered when Sara—this time wearing a plain red t-shirt instead of the awful pink blouse—approached their table with a tall African-American girl. "Are these taken?" She patted the empty chairs. A huge smile filled her face.

"Where have you been?" Levi demanded.

She bounced into a seat, still smiling, while the other girl perched on the edge of the other chair. Sara touched her arm. "This is my roommate, Monica."

Levi recognized Monica as the girl he'd seen reading in the registration line. Monica held her dark chin tilted upward and her shoulders thrown back like some sort of princess.

"Hi, I'm Levi." He jerked a thumb to his right. "He's Trevor."

"Nice to meet you." Trevor's voice squeaked on the last word.

"Charmed." Monica's chin tilted another notch. "I am overjoyed to have Sara as my roommate. I was beginning to fear I'd be lonely this summer."

Trevor's face puckered at her stilted speech. "Where are you from?"

She looked down her nose at him. "I reside in Pennsylvania but attend boarding school in Montreal. Where are you *from*?" Her emphasis on the last word made Levi think of grammar lessons about not ending sentences with prepositions. Ugh. What a snob.

Trevor's ears turned pink. "Cleveland."

"I see." Monica eased her napkin from its holder, gave it a sharp shake, and positioned it on her lap.

Sara beamed back and forth between them. Not a trace of her earlier insecurity lingered. "Isn't it great? I was afraid all the girls would be stuck up, but then I met Monica, and she's so friendly."

Levi blinked. He peeked at Monica from the corner of his eye. She picked up her butter knife, breathed on it, and rubbed it with her napkin. Well, okay, if Sara liked her . . .

Sara's smile didn't waver. "Ashley and Lizzie are our other roommates. They're nice too, aren't they, Monica?"

Monica deigned to nod.

"Oh, here they are," Sara said as two girls took seats near her. "This is Ashley." She indicated a short girl with brown braids and a liberal sprinkling of freckles. Levi recognized her as the weeping girl from the registration line earlier.

Ashley fixed her brown eyes on the tablecloth and mumbled, "Hi." At least she wasn't crying now.

"This is Lizzie." Sara pointed to the other girl, who had shiny pink lips and a big smile that showed perfect white teeth. Her dark blonde hair fell straight to the middle of her back. Teal eye shadow, the exact shade of her shorts outfit, covered the lids of her green eyes. Her perfume was so strong it coated Levi's tongue.

"Hey," Lizzie said in a Southern twang. "Nice to meet y'all."

Levi sneezed.

Sara babbled on. "Do you guys like your room? Are you on the east or west side? Are your roommates nice?"

Trevor shot Levi a look asking if Sara had gone insane. Levi could only shrug and introduce Tommy and Steve, who sat on the far side of Trevor looking shell-shocked.

A group of campers moved past the table. One bumped hard into

Levi's chair. He twisted around to see Hunter strut past, a mocking smile on his face. The jerk.

Mr. Dominic stood up at the staff table and cleared his throat for silence. "Oremus."

The director waited a moment. Several kids glanced around in confusion, but Levi understood. Latin for *let us pray*. He bowed his head.

"Holy Creator and Sustainer of all, I praise you for these children. I pray you would use this food to nourish their bodies and this camp to nourish their minds and spirits. Thank you for being the Ruler of the Universe. In the name of your precious Son, King Jesus, I pray. Amen."

Levi looked up at Mr. Dominic. He'd never heard a prayer quite like that one. The director smiled. "Eat up."

The food was delicious: roast beef, mashed potatoes, fresh bread, several kinds of vegetables and desserts, and a tall glass of milk. Levi ate until he could hold no more, thinking nothing of questions or conversation. Finally full, he leaned back in his seat. He watched Trevor pile his plate with thirds while the girls ate more slowly, chatting between bites. Now that his belly was full, the short night's sleep and the strange day caught up with him. Half-listening to the others' conversations, Levi grew sleepier by the second.

"What is the extent of this property, I wonder?" Monica said.

"Pretty big, I guess." Sara shrugged. "So, what's your family like?"

Monica told of her three sisters and her parents, who were missionaries. "That's why we attend boarding school and stay at Grandmother's estate on vacations. Her home is in eastern Pennsylvania. My parents come there on furlough." She paused and looked at the others. "Does anyone else attend boarding school?"

Sara shook her head. "Levi and I are both homeschooled. I don't know about anybody else." She glanced between the others.

Trevor said, "Private school."

"I'm homeschooled." Steve turned brick red.

Ashley mumbled something about going to a Christian school. Tommy nodded.

"Well, I go to boarding school 'cause Momma's a U.S. Senator." Lizzie lifted a pink-nailed hand and tossed back her hair. "She's in DC a lot of the time."

"Oh?" Monica tilted her head. "Is your school in Washington?"

"Sure is."

Levi's sleep-deprived mind tuned out the conversation as Sara prattled on about their hall chaperone, someone named Miss Nydia, who'd promised to teach the girls all about sewing. Who cared about sewing? All he wanted was to climb into his comfy-looking bed upstairs.

"What do you think?" A low voice from the table behind him sharpened his fading brain. "Could it have been some sort of giant projection that looked like a cliff? Like, some big screen that gets moved . . . somehow . . . so you see the castle when they want you to?"

Levi's pulse quickened. If someone else had seen the precipice, then Levi wasn't crazy. He glanced over his shoulder. Martin, his face pale, leaned near Hunter. Disappointment stole over Levi when he saw who had spoken, but he shook it away. Even creepy Hunter and his thug buddy Martin were better than nobody.

"It wasn't a screen," Hunter said in a loud voice. "These people are aliens." When several people stared at him, he grinned and spoke even louder. "It's true. I mean, haven't you looked at these people? They're not normal."

"The Dominics look normal," said a dark-haired girl. "Just, you know, really old."

"Of course they're old. That's because they're from another planet. And haven't you noticed the weather?" Hunter moved in close to the wide-eyed girl. Levi half-expected him to yell *Boo!*

The girl beside her shook her head, her face pinched. "It must be an atmospheric difference between the northern and southern portions of the island. Or some other rational explanation." Her voice grew shrill. "Because my parents looked into this place very carefully—did background checks and all that. A camp full of aliens wouldn't have passed inspection."

"Of course they would." Hunter was clearly enjoying himself. "They can do anything they want."

Levi shook his head. Some people watched too many *Star Trek* reruns.

A crash from the other side of his table brought Levi's head around. Sara stood beside her toppled chair, tears glistening on her cheeks.

"Sara?" Levi half-stood.

She ran from the room.

Hunter laughed. Levi fixed a glare on the bully.

Hunter leaned closer to the two girls, his gaze flicking to Levi. "Haven't you ever heard of the Great Lakes Triangle?" He raised both eyebrows and nodded in a way Levi figured was supposed to be significant.

The girls looked at each other then shook their heads.

Hunter stroked his chin with long, pale fingers. "Well, this is it. Aliens abduct ships and airplanes, then they take people off to other planets to perform experiments on them."

Levi grimaced. How stupid. Everybody knew there was no such thing as aliens. And everybody with any knowledge of geography at all knew the Bermuda Triangle was in the Atlantic Ocean off the coast of Florida, not in the Great Lakes.

After a couple games of ping pong with Steve, Levi sat near the unlit fireplace of the great hall and watched Trevor and Tommy shoot pool. Kids played foosball and board games in the huge room, while others kicked around a soccer ball in the grassy courtyard.

Sighing, Levi leaned his head back against the headrest of the overstuffed chair. He wanted to go upstairs to bed but didn't want to have to find his way alone. As the pool match dragged on, he let his eyes drift shut.

Levi jolted awake and leapt from the chair. Shadows filled the silent, empty room. His heart pounded. He was alone. At least he thought so.

"What's wrong, little boy?" A jeering voice came from the gloom beside the fireplace.

Levi squinted into the darkness. "Who's that?"

Hunter stepped forward, the shadows turning his face into a demon's. "Scared?" He strode closer until his nose was inches from Levi's face. "You should be." He dropped his voice to a whisper. "You know what these people are, don't you?"

A bizarre image of ET phoning home flashed through Levi's mind.

"Witches," Hunter said softly. "Wizards. Demons. Monsters." His eyes narrowed to slits. "They're going to turn you into their slave."

Mind disoriented from sleep, Levi couldn't fight off panic. He fled the room, his only plan to escape the castle. He raced along the corridor, skidded through the empty dining room, and rounded the corner to the foyer. With Hunter's laughter echoing behind him, Levi scrambled past the spiral staircase that led to his room and sped to the front door. He gripped the heavy brass doorknob in both hands, twisted hard, and wrenched the door open wide.

Before him, a deluge smashed the trees. He could barely make out streams of muddy water coursing down the path they'd climbed only a few hours before. Directly in front of him, the lowered drawbridge took a beating from the violent wind. Rainwater hit the wood with such force it ricocheted into his face.

Should he try to make it through that horrendous storm to the camp and call his dad? Or should he go back into the castle—with Hunter, clear skies, and who knew what else?

He hovered in the doorway, undecided. The wind tore at him as if to pull him from the stone shelter. His ragged breathing was so loud he didn't hear the footfalls until they were right behind him.

"Leviticus Prince?"

He froze. Now he'd never escape.

Chapter 6

Castle Island?

The sound of his name startled Levi so his already racing heart doubled its beat. The blood drained from his face, and he swayed.

"It's all right, son." The voice was barely loud enough for Levi to hear over the storm. He turned to find Mr. Dominic a foot behind him, hands raised in a gesture of peace. "You're free to leave at any time. I won't keep anyone in my home against his will."

Okay then, I'm out of here. Levi took a step toward the door.

"It's only fair to warn you, however," the director said in a slightly louder voice, "the path to the cabins is treacherous in this rain. No one is at camp, and there's no way back to the mainland."

Levi whipped around and glared at him. "What about the ferry?"

"It won't return until the storm clears." Mr. Dominic gestured outdoors. "No one in his right mind would go out on the lake in this weather. It would be suicide."

Levi glanced behind him as a tree was ripped from its roots mere feet from the castle door. It was a small tree, but still . . . Levi took a step back into the castle. "What is this, some kind of hurricane?"

"Not a hurricane, no. Just a big storm. What the old lake captains call a nor'easter'." He indicated the door handle. "May I?"

Levi forced himself to take deep breaths, trying to get enough oxygen to his brain so he could think clearly, logically. Should he try to make it to the cabins? Would the phone work if he got there? How long until the ferry returned? What could his parents do if he got in touch with them?

His shoulders slumped. Mr. Dominic was right. Only an idiot would go out in this weather.

But he had to keep his guard up because something was definitely strange here.

Yet even as he studied the old man's eyes, he felt some of his fears melt away. He shook himself. Was Mr. Dominic bewitching him? What if Hunter was right about these people?

But what choice did Levi have? He had nowhere else to go. At least for now. Was there really anything to be scared about anyway? Maybe his imagination was going haywire.

"Fine." Levi moved so the director could pull the heavy door closed.

As soon as the door shut, the sounds of the ferocious storm completely disappeared. He frowned at the director. "I don't understand."

"I know." Mr. Dominic's smile was kind, not like an evil wizard's. Then again, what did an evil wizard look like?

Sighing deeply, Levi headed for the stairs.

Fifteen minutes later, he climbed the step stool and flopped down on his fluffy bed. His legs felt like half-melted Twizzlers. Hiking up those stairs several times a day would either whip him into shape or kill him. If aliens didn't get him first.

Trevor, Steve, and Tommy were conked out in their beds, Steve's snores alternating with Trevor's in a horrible duet that echoed off the high ceiling. Ugh. Tomorrow he'd write home for a care package—one that included earplugs.

Levi woke early the next morning. Pinks and oranges painted the sky outside the window at the foot of his bed. Yawning, he scooted nearer for a better look at the castle grounds, anticipation once again replacing his apprehension from the previous night. That and a vague sense of having been an idiot to let Hunter scare him. Hunter would probably make fun of him in front of everybody at breakfast. For some reason, Sara's face flitted through his mind at that moment, sending a rush of heat through his cheeks.

When the view out his window registered, it cleared away all thoughts of Hunter and even Sara, and he let out a bellow so loud it woke the other three boys. Tommy banged his head on the wardrobe beside his bed. Trevor jumped up, missed the stepstool, and landed in a heap on the floor. Steve's muffled "Huh?" came from the bed nearest the bathroom.

Levi could only stare out the window at the glittering sunshine, though it wasn't the sunshine that bothered him this morning. On this side of the building, the one facing out from the castle rather than into the courtyard, he could see for miles. Only he didn't see what he should see on Castle Island.

There was no lake. However hard he strained his eyes, he saw no water at all. Flat meadow extended for what looked like a mile before ending in a forest that stretched long and far until it ended in mountains. From what he could see, it didn't look like they were on the sunny side of the island. From here, it didn't look like they were on an island at all.

Proof positive Camp Classic wasn't what—or at least, *where*—it was supposed to be.

The four boys piled onto Levi's bed, their faces plastered to the window, until the sun rose fully.

"The lake's gotta be just past the mountains." Tommy pointed at the distant peaks.

"That makes sense," Trevor said, picking at the single long hair on his chin. "We just thought this hill was the north end of the island when it's actually in the middle."

Levi squeezed his lips shut. He didn't think he should say too much about how he'd seen Castle Island end at a cliff and the castle magically appear in thin air. If Trevor hadn't seen anything, Steve and Tommy sure wouldn't have. Levi spouting off probably wouldn't give them a high opinion of his sanity.

"What about the weather yesterday?" Steve asked quietly.

Left eyebrow raised, Levi peered at Tommy and Trevor. How would they explain that one away?

"Well," Tommy said slowly, "if this is the middle of the island, it wouldn't get hit as hard with storms."

Trevor nodded. "Or maybe the storm turned before it got this far north."

Levi frowned. Right. It made perfect sense for a violent storm to stop at the castle door.

Then again, his roommates hadn't looked out the south door the night before like he had. And he wasn't about to tell them he'd been at the door because he was running away from Hunter like a scared two-year-old.

At the ringing of the breakfast bell, his roommates clambered off of his bed and threw on their clothes, apparently content with their explanations.

Yet as Levi dressed and hurried down the steps behind them, a question kept poking at his brain. If they weren't on Castle Island, surrounded on all sides by Lake Superior—and despite his roommates' explanations, he couldn't bring himself to believe they were—then where in the world were they?

Chapter 7

Ears

The delicious meal of pancakes and maple syrup did a lot to make Levi forget his worries, especially since Hunter didn't so much as make a face at him the whole time. Apparently whatever had bothered Sara the night before was forgotten too. She sat talking to Monica with sparkling eyes and hand motions punctuating her words.

He shook his head. Girls. They made no sense with their moods bouncing around like rubber balls. Just like his sister. She'd be laughing one minute then weeping hysterically the next. He couldn't keep up. He smirked.

"What're you thinking about?" Sara paused with her juice glass halfway to her lips, her blue-green eyes on him.

He glanced at the others. Monica was giving Trevor and Tommy a detailed account of a rugby match she'd attended in England with her grandfather, and Ashley and Lizzie were talking too quietly for him to hear.

"Nothing." Levi shrugged. "Just my little sister."

"You were smiling. You must miss her."

Levi studied his empty bowl, the tips of his ears hot. "A little, I guess. We're less than two years apart, so we've always been sort of paired up. Mom would say, 'Levi, Abby, help your little brothers get ready to go.' That kind of thing." He swallowed the lump from his throat and glanced at Sara, expecting her to laugh at him.

Instead, she worried her lower lip. "Wish I had that. I don't have any brothers or sisters."

"I actually couldn't wait to get out from under it," he said louder than he intended. "Being the oldest of a bunch of kids is pretty annoying most of the time."

Sara folded her arms across her chest. "Well, it's lonely being an only." A grin quickly replaced her scowl. "I guess I get to have lots of siblings this summer, though."

Levi smiled. "Guess you do."

Levi's brain ached. Wasn't this supposed to be summer camp?

Lessons had begun after breakfast. Levi and his roommates shared classes with Sara and hers. After a tortuous hour of Algebra review with Dr. Baldwin in one of the third floor classrooms, they'd gone next door for Latin, where Mrs. Sylvester drilled them on vocabulary and case endings for another hour. It was finally lunch time, and even the prospect of fencing seemed better than more study. At least he'd be out in the courtyard. Who knew camp would be so much like school. And he didn't even get to wear pajamas to class here.

After lunch, Levi followed Trevor and the others from his corridor through the French doors leading to the inner courtyard. The whole pack of them paused under the covered stone walkway and looked around for their fencing instructor.

"Anybody ever done this before?" Steve's eyes were so wide his eyelids disappeared into his chubby face.

Trevor shook his head. "How hard can it be, really?"

"Yeah." Tommy leaned against a column. "If you've done any sports at all, you should be able to get it."

Levi eyed Tommy's wiry arms. "Are you into martial arts or something?"

Tommy looked at him like he was crazy. "No. Hockey."

"Oh." Levi's armpits grew damp. What if he was the only one who flopped at this? His only sword-fighting experience was with his little brothers—using plastic swords.

"I bet it's a lot like ballet," said a tall, thin girl named Gabrielle who walked around everywhere on her tiptoes, her nose in a skyward tilt. "I should do fine."

Steve's face went ashen and sweat beaded his forehead. He was probably envisioning his big feet in ballet toe shoes. Levi offered him a wobbly smile, glad he wasn't the only one scared spitless.

He glanced across the courtyard. Mr. Sylvester, the seven-footer with white-blond hair, led some kids to the grassy common area and gestured for Levi's group to join them. Levi slunk along at the rear.

Oh, boy. Hunter and Martin waited beside Mr. Sylvester with ugly smirks on their faces as if chomping at the bit to slash their fellow campers to pieces. Levi positioned himself behind Steve and Trevor, leaving only the slightest peephole. He prayed he wouldn't be called on for any demonstrations.

"Fencing is a beautiful sport," Mr. Sylvester announced in a British lecture voice. "It will help you develop a strong body, a keen mind, and a renewed spirit. All of which are essential in the face of the evil surrounding us."

The face of the evil surrounding us? Levi glanced around. They were at summer camp, for crying out loud. The only evil face Levi saw was Hunter's. He grinned at his private joke. Until he caught a glimpse of Hunter's hard eyes, which had somehow found their way to his hiding place.

Come to think of it, a few fencing lessons may not be such a bad idea.

"All right, everyone," Mr. Sylvester said. "Form a wide circle around me." After they circled up, he waved to someone on the walkway. "Mr. Drake? Join me, please. We shall demonstrate the proper way to engage in a sword battle."

Mr. Drake, the ferry pilot who was also over seven feet tall and had the same long black hair, reddish skin, and high cheekbones as his wife, stepped into the ragged ring carrying two golden scabbards. He handed one to Mr. Sylvester, and the two exchanged bows. Both wore white protective suits, but neither put on the masks piled near the far walkway.

The two men sparred gracefully, thrusting and parrying while sunbeams glinted against their silver blades. Levi tried to watch the men's feet, but they moved too fast for him to follow. Then he tried to study their faces, but long black hair blended and swayed into long blond hair, masking their eyes.

After a few minutes, Mr. Sylvester caught Mr. Drake square in the chest protector, forcing him to lean back until the ends of his dark hair brushed the grass. It only lasted a second, but in that frozen instant Levi's breath caught, not over the excitement of the match, but over what he saw.

Mr. Drake's ears. His pointy-tipped ears. Not just slight points either. These were *Lord of the Rings* ears.

Bizarre.

As the men shook hands and bowed all around, Levi didn't join in the wild clapping and cheering. He could only stare, hoping for another glimpse of ears. He'd never heard of anyone having ears that pointy. At least not anyone human.

He rubbed his suddenly cold hands together. Strange castles with unusual weather and islands that didn't end where they were supposed to, all that was odd enough, but this—

Trevor elbowed him. "That was awesome, wasn't it?"

Levi forced his stiff lips to move, eyes still fixed on the fencing instructors. "Yeah."

The only other motionless person in the group caught Levi's attention. Hunter, arms across his chest and head thrown back, regarded Levi with a knowing look in his eyes.

Chapter 8

Confusion

Levi's t-shirt stuck to his sweaty body. The cool dimness of the castle felt great after baking in the early afternoon sun. He'd only dropped his sword three or four times during training drills. Thankfully all the blades were covered in some sort of foam-filled leather sheaths; otherwise he might've severed an artery.

Lizzie was nearly flawless in the exercises, at least until she chipped a nail. After that, she refused to continue until a disgusted Mr. Sylvester let her run to her room for her nail repair kit. Poor Steve, though, hadn't made it through any of the maneuvers without fumbling at least once. It probably hadn't helped that Hunter, who drilled without error directly behind Steve, kept whispering about the irresistible target made by Steve's wide rear end.

As he started for the stairs, Levi stretched. Muscles he'd never used so hard in his life protested. Time to try out that luxury shower before his roommates beat him to it. He hurried up the steps. By the time he got to the fourth floor, he had to stop with his hands on his knees and catch his breath. When he got his wind back, he reached for the handle of the door to his corridor.

The door beside it caught his eye. He knew it must lead along the north corridor like the one on the third floor that housed their classrooms. He opened it a crack and peeked inside. Empty. He tiptoed to another door in the middle of the corridor, glanced around to make sure he was alone, then turned the handle and pulled. Stepping through, he let out a tiny gasp.

Large bands of soft multicolored light swathed the room, painting rows of benches red and green, purple and blue, yellow and pink. Levi stepped further in, blinking hard until he understood he'd entered a chapel. The colors came from floor-to-ceiling stained glass windows lining the entire north wall. The rows of benches were padded pews. A raised platform at one end held a communion table and a pulpit.

Levi sat down in the first pew he came to, a center seat, since the door opened in the middle of the room. He wiped at his sweaty forehead and breathed deeply, inhaling the scent of candles and old wood smoke. He relaxed in the peaceful atmosphere. Had he been alone even once since coming to Camp Classic?

His eyes skipped to an open Bible on the communion table, and a twinge of guilt bit him. He hadn't so much as opened his Bible since he got to camp. Mr. Dominic had read a few verses after breakfast, but Levi knew that wasn't enough. His parents had insisted he read his Bible each morning from the time he'd learned to read.

Sorry, God.

A brief vision of pointy ears filled his mind, and he shook it away. Maybe reading his Bible more would keep him from being so confused. Or delusional. At this point, he wasn't sure what to believe.

"I'll do better, I promise." Levi's quiet words shattered the stillness of the chapel, making him wince. Maybe he should leave. Mr. Dominic had told them the cellar was off limits and that boys and girls weren't allowed to enter each others' dorm corridors. Other than that, they were to make the castle their home.

Still, he should get back to his room and clean up. He was stinking up the chapel.

The next morning Levi was scheduled for Literature and History, his two favorite subjects. When he arrived, he settled into a desk near his roommates and glanced around the classroom. Sara and the girls were in the class too. Unfortunately, so were Hunter and Martin.

The stumpy, brown-haired Literature teacher, Mr. Austin, glowered at the campers from beneath bushy brows. "This summer you'll study *The Iliad*," he barked as if someone had dared complain.

Levi shrank back in his seat, not sure he was going to enjoy this class so much after all. Yet the teacher's excitement about his subject became evident the longer he spoke, and Levi's hopes for the class rose.

Mr. Austin's jowls quivered and he bounced on the balls of his feet as he reviewed Homer's version of the Trojan horse tale. "Paris, the prince of Troy, kidnapped Helen, wife of the Spartan king, Menelaus. The Trojans and Spartans waged war over the woman for years. Then the Spartans came up with a sneaky idea. They built a huge wooden horse and hid inside it. But the Trojans thought the Spartans had fled. They wheeled the horse inside their gates, gloating over their great victory." Mr. Austin's voice deepened to an ominous rumble. "In the night, the Spartan warriors emerged from hiding, utterly destroyed the Trojans, and took the fair Helen home.

"Trickery!" he bellowed, making several kids jump. "Deceit! Never let down your guard for an instant! That's what we learn from this story. Don't be so all-fired sure of yourself that you give your enemy a way in. Otherwise, they'll trick you—and sometimes, destroy you."

Levi and the others stared in wide-eyed silence. This was one strange teacher.

"Now, for homework—"

Levi groaned along with the rest.

Archery class took Levi outside the castle walls for the first time—on the north side, opposite where they'd arrived from the cabins. Mr. Sylvester led Levi's group through a foyer area beyond the great hall and fiddled with elaborate locks on the giant door. His wife waited at his side.

"Man, look at that," said Luke, a kid from Levi's hall who was even smaller than he was. The kid's glasses took up most of his face.

Levi glanced from Luke to the locks situated well above Levi's head. "Yeah, pretty impressive."

Luke sucked in a breath. "I'll say."

Mr. Sylvester's words about surrounding evil flickered through Levi's brain. "Doesn't look like anyone could get in this place really easy," he said as much to himself as to Luke. So why did he suddenly feel nervous?

When Mr. Sylvester finally undid all the locks and opened the door, he raised the massive portcullis. Levi's palms dampened as he followed the teacher under the iron spikes. He sure hoped the ropes held that thing up. He also hoped he was better at archery than he was at fencing.

Mr. Sylvester lowered the drawbridge, took his wife's elbow, and looked expectantly at the campers. "Well, come along."

Levi glanced at Luke. The boy's mouth hung wide. Levi started over the drawbridge, watchful for anything Mr. Sylvester might call evil. They crossed a broad field to an archery range at the edge of the forest he'd seen from his window. A long, high mound waited behind the targets for stray arrows.

When they arrived at the range, Mr. Sylvester asked the campers to divide themselves into their usual class groupings, which meant Levi didn't have to be in a group with Hunter. He ended up next to Mr. Sylvester and overheard him ask his wife to take the west dormitory kids. She shot a look at Hunter and Martin, who were bragging to the boys from their hall.

"I took out three deer with a bow and arrow last winter. It was wicked." Hunter's lips twisted into a grin that made Levi feel sorry for the deer.

Martin popped his gum between his teeth as he fumbled with a camouflage arm-guard. "I can't wait to kill something."

Mr. Sylvester shook his head in disgust. "Never mind, dear. I'll take that bunch. You take these fellows." He cocked his chin toward Levi's group.

Levi found his mind straying from Mrs. Sylvester's lesson on the proper way to hold a bow and string an arrow. His gaze kept skipping from the bow she held to her white-blonde hair, though it wasn't her hair that interested him. It had hit him that she was tall and reed-thin like Mr. Drake. Did she have the same type of ears?

In spite of his distraction, Levi shot fairly well on his first couple of tries. One arrow actually hit the target instead of the dirt beside it. All of Ashley's arrows ended up clanking off of a target three over from hers, but Sara and Tommy both seemed to be naturals. Tommy hit right next to the mark several times, and Sara shot bullseye after bullseye with apparent ease.

Shooting a hockey puck must've helped Tommy's aim, but that didn't explain Sara's skill. He watched her line up, one eye closed, body still. Every time she let fly, the arrow soared to its mark and pinged in the target's center. Then she'd release a joyful bubble of laughter totally different from Hunter's harsh cackle on the other end of the range.

When the lesson was over, the group walked back to the castle door, Levi surrounded by a bunch of boys whose shots got closer and closer to the mark as their stories grew. He smiled and dropped back a few steps, wanting to slip to the edge of the castle and peek around it. Could he truly have mistaken the moat for a raging lake?

Levi wound up near Sara and Mrs. Sylvester. The teacher looped her arm across the girl's shoulder, and both smiled. The wind snatched at their long hair, the one pale, the other golden.

"You shot well, Sarafina, my dear." Mrs. Sylvester's tone was tender.

Sarafina? Levi peeked at the two as the lady brushed back her hair, momentarily revealing her left ear—her perfectly-formed, pearly-white, pointy-tipped ear.

Too stunned to notice what his feet were doing, Levi plunged into the cold moat.

Chapter 9

The Moat

Levi panicked. His lungs squeezed as he flailed in the murky water. After a few seconds, he forced himself to calm down and pushed up toward the light. He surfaced, splashing and spluttering, and swam to the edge where Mrs. Sylvester and Sara knelt. They reached to help him, but he hoisted himself out on his own. The laughter and catcalls from kids on the drawbridge sizzled the droplets on Levi's face.

"Are you okay?" Sara asked. At least she wasn't laughing at him.

"Yeah." Levi wrung water from his t-shirt and glared at the puddle beneath his feet.

Mrs. Sylvester took his arm. "Come on, let's get you inside."

Levi looked up at her face. It was pale, like he'd really scared her.

Her husband rushed up. "Is he okay?" He turned from his wife to Levi. "Are you okay?"

Levi's skin practically steamed with humiliation. What was the big deal about falling into the moat? Everybody had to know how to swim before coming to camp. Surely they didn't think he was so wimpy he'd drown in the few seconds he was under.

"He's fine, dear. It's nothing," Mrs. Sylvester told her husband in a soothing voice, as if she recognized Levi's extreme embarrassment and was trying to spare him more.

But Mr. Sylvester studied Levi's eyes for what felt like a long time. "You're fine? You didn't go very deep, did you?" He frowned hard. "Did you get bumped on anything?" His eyebrows shot up. "Or see anything?"

Levi shook his head. Why the third degree? He glanced at the tranquil water. Was something in there?

"No, no, of course not," Mr. Sylvester answered himself with a short laugh. "Nothing at all to see, of course. Let's stay back from the moat from now on, all right?" He slapped Levi on the back. "Don't want to get in that nasty water. Deep and dark. Not at all a pleasant place to swim."

Grimacing, Levi darted a look at Sara. She raised both eyebrows and shrugged.

Mrs. Sylvester patted her husband's arm. "He's really fine, dear. Let's go on in now and let him change out of those wet clothes." The two locked eyes a moment. She turned a bright smile on Levi, the kind his mom gave his dad when she was really worried but didn't want Levi to know. "At least it's not cold outside, right?"

"Right." Levi looked down at his sopping shorts. "Good thing tomorrow's laundry day."

Sara giggled. "Better not miss it or you'll be wearing dirty socks for a week."

Thinking of the single pair of underwear in his wardrobe, he blushed. It wasn't dirty socks he was worried about.

He walked with Sara toward the drawbridge. The adults flanked them like Levi might fall back in the moat if they got too far away. Most of the other kids had already gone into the castle, but Hunter, Martin, the piggy-faced girl who'd mocked Sara, and a broad-shouldered, buzz cut kid named Greg lingered on the drawbridge, mocking Levi for his tumble into the water. They didn't stop until Mr. Sylvester shooed them inside.

By the time Levi sat down for supper, everyone seemed to know about his little dip in the moat. He did his best to ignore Hunter and Martin, who took turns falling out of their chairs and pretending to splash around on the floor—much to the amusement of their new buddies. Levi kept his face near his bowl of chili, trying not to react as Hunter kept adding to the story. Really nice stuff like, "He was squealing like a two-year-old!"

The guys at Levi's table didn't laugh, but by the time he finished forcing down his food, Levi figured his neck would be permanently red. Heaving a sigh, he glanced up at the head table. Mr. Sylvester had his head right next to Mr. Dominic's. They cast frequent looks his direction. Great, now they were talking about him, too.

Then Mr. Drake walked up and bent to join their conversation. When he swept back his hair so it wouldn't dangle into Mr. Dominic's chili bowl, Levi remembered why he'd fallen into the moat in the first place.

Pointy-tipped ears—both Mr. Drake's and Mrs. Sylvester's.

A question throbbed Levi's temples. Was there any possible way this camp had nonhumans on staff? As his eyes slid between Mr. Drake and Mr. Sylvester, another question intruded into his mind. If they weren't human, what were they?

Should he talk to Hunter about all this? Creep though he undoubtedly was, Hunter and his mindless minion Martin seemed to be the only other people suspicious about Camp Classic and its employees.

What if Hunter was right? What if this camp was run by aliens or something? Did that mean they'd entered some alternate reality somehow?

"Scared him so bad he wet his pants." Hunter's jeering words shattered Levi's internal debate.

Levi's eyes locked on Hunter. As most of the campers burst out laughing, the bully's face twisted into a taunting smirk.

Levi broke eye contact. How could he even consider confiding in a jerk like Hunter? Loneliness and despair sagged Levi's shoulders.

Sara touched his arm. "Just ignore him."

Levi offered her a wobbly smile and glanced at his other friends. Each face reflected Sara's sympathetic expression.

Except Trevor's. Levi's John Cena-sized roommate stood up and fixed Hunter in a steely glare. "Shut up, Hunter, or I'll shut you up."

Face flushed, Hunter opened his mouth. Then shut it again. Lip curled, the bully turned his back on Levi's group as if they were beneath his notice.

Levi smiled his thanks at Trevor. Shrugging, Trevor stuffed an entire dinner roll in his mouth.

When Levi's eyes returned to the staff table, Mr. Dominic, Mr. Sylvester, and Mr. Drake were no longer there. When had they left? Didn't they hear Hunter's mean words?

Levi stared down at his half-empty bowl as he considered the situation. He was sick of worrying about cliffs and ears and abnormal stuff.

What if he'd simply been so tired and stressed his first day he'd imagined the cliff thing? It was possible. Maybe there were plenty of people in the world with pointy-tipped ears, and he'd just never heard of them. He shouldn't freak out about them. That was rude. Not to mention that it tended to land him in moats.

He straightened his spine. It was time to get beyond his idiotic obsessions and enjoy his summer off. His roommates and friends were great, really. He liked the activities and classes for the most part. His biggest challenge here, besides the class work, was Hunter. And the best way to deal with Hunter was to avoid him unless an adult was near. Because Hunter never showed his true colors around the staff.

That's the plan, Levi. Don't forget it. He gave himself a mental tap on the forehead. *You're gonna forget all the weird stuff, stay away from Hunter, and have a fun, stress-free summer. Period.*

Now if he could just keep to the plan.

Chapter 10

The Campout

The next night Levi lay in bed trying to read his Bible, but his thoughts kept straying to his horrible day. He'd overslept, forgotten his dirty laundry, and had to miss breakfast to run back and get it. He was late for Logic class, and Mr. Dominic clearly didn't approve of tardiness. On top of that, they studied logical fallacies, which his mom had neglected to teach him, so he missed all the questions the director threw at him. Then Mrs. Austin sent them from Science class with a huge pile of homework.

Wasn't this supposed to be summer camp?

Afternoon lessons were cancelled due to rain—he didn't know why he'd thought it wouldn't rain on this side of the island—trapping him in the great hall with hyper campers while he waded through his homework.

After a supper filled with more reenactments of his near-drowning in the moat and his resultant fainting spell—so went the current exaggeration—he trudged upstairs to his room. He folded and put away his clean laundry while Trevor, Steve, and Tommy threw balled socks at each other.

Now as Levi tried to concentrate on his Bible reading, a pair of oversized underwear dropped in the middle of the page. He scowled around the room in search of the culprit.

Steve stood red-faced a few feet from Levi's bed. "Uh, sorry." He snatched his drawers, snickering as he scurried away.

Levi slapped his Bible shut, slammed it onto his nightstand, and flopped down with his back to the room, hoping the others would get the message: *I'm tired! Shut up so I can sleep!*

But they kept hurling underpants, socks, and other articles of clothing, all while cackling uncontrollably. Idiots. They reminded him of his little brothers on a sugar high.

He curled into a tight ball. He missed his brothers. At least he could yell at them to get quiet or tell on them or something. Here he had no control. He buried his face in his pillow.

So much for his big plan for a wonderful summer.

The next afternoon, Mr. Drake led the campers outside the north castle door for a woodcraft lesson. The short, pimple-faced man named Albert surprised Levi by joining him as he passed under the raised portcullis.

"Hi, Albert. You help with this class?"

Albert stuck out his small chest. "Yup. I'm the woodcraft assistant. I know lots about the woods."

"Really?" Levi looked around, wishing his roommates would hurry. He didn't want to get stuck with Albert the whole afternoon, especially if Albert got hungry again. He couldn't deal with crankiness right now. He had enough problems.

"I can teach you lotsa stuff about the trees and the undergrowth and such. Help you watch out for poison ivy." Albert lowered his voice as they neared the forest. "And worse stuff."

Levi's forehead crinkled. "Worse stuff?"

Albert gave an exaggerated nod then moved over to Mr. Drake. Levi stared after him. He felt a brush on his sleeve and turned to see Sara at his side.

"Don't worry about it." Her smile dismissed his vague anxiety. "Just stick close to the group and you'll be fine."

Halfway through Mr. Drake's lecture about safety in the forest, Levi heard a rustling in the underbrush behind him. He turned his head and searched the thick leaves. The hair at the nape of his neck stood up, but he didn't see anything.

Sara leaned close. "What's wrong?"

"Thought I heard something. Must've been the wind."

"There is no wind today." She grabbed his wrist and yanked him toward Albert. "Stay near the staff, away from the thickest growth."

Levi blinked at her. Though anxiety poked at his stomach, he pushed it away. *Uh-uh, Levi. Ignore the weird stuff, remember? Keep to the plan.*

He returned his gaze to the teacher. Nothing else disturbed him for the remainder of the lesson.

Except his sweaty palms. And the red half-moons Sara's nails had tattooed on his wrist.

Levi's group assembled in the foyer the next morning armed with sleeping bags and backpacks. The Drakes and the Austins led their group for a campout in the woods south of the castle. Hunter's group would go with the Sylvesters, Dr. Baldwin, and Miss Nydia to the forest on the north side. Levi was glad Hunter and his thugs were the ones camping in the freaky north woods. Maybe something would scare the bully out of them.

As soon as he crossed the drawbridge, Levi couldn't resist a backward glance, just in case, but there was no sign of the lake.

Mr. Dominic stood in the open castle doorway calling, "I'll be here to let you in tomorrow afternoon." The director winked at Levi as if the two shared a secret.

Levi eyed him a moment. When Trevor nudged Levi, he followed the group on autopilot, not joining in the others' excited conversations.

Camp Classic is normal. Camp Classic is normal. Camp Classic is normal. Levi mentally ran and reran the mantra until Mr. Drake stopped them in a clearing with an old fire ring at its center. By that time, Levi was okay. Who cared if Mr. Dominic winked? Maybe the old man had something in his eye.

When Mr. Drake told the kids to set up camp, they divided out several four-man tents. Levi, Trevor, Tommy, and Steve pitched their tent and set their gear inside. They got done fast, mostly because Tommy went camping a lot with his dad, and went to help the others finish theirs.

Levi expected Sara and her roommates to need help, but they'd finished first and had already gone to gather wood and water. He moved near Lizzie as she gingerly picked up a few twigs, as if afraid she'd mess up her nails. He scooped up a couple of branches. "You sure got that tent up fast."

She smiled. "Why, sure, honey. Sara knows all about pitching tents."

"Really?" Sara? He glanced over at Sara laughing with Monica as they carried buckets of water from a nearby stream. Ashley, a pile of sticks in her arms, joined him and Lizzie, and the three met up with Sara and Monica near the tents.

As he added his wood to the pile, he started to ask Sara where she'd learned so much about camping, but he couldn't decide how to ask without sounding like what his sister would call a pig.

As he thought, Lizzie whipped out a small mirror and dabbed something on her lips.

Monica snatched the mirror from Lizzie's hand. "We are camping, Lizzie. One does not wear lip gloss on a camping trip."

Sara covered her mouth, and Levi smothered a snort.

Monica leveled them with a dirty look and then rounded on Ashley. "I'm right, aren't I, Ashley?"

Ashley shrugged, eyes darting for help. Clearly, she'd rather be anywhere but the middle of an argument.

Lizzie closed the gloss and dabbed her lips together. "Momma told me a lady ought always to look her best." She sent Monica a slit-eyed look. "We all know a girl ought to do what her momma says." She raised an eyebrow at Ashley. "Ain't that right, Ashley honey?"

"Um . . ." Ashley tossed Sara a help-me look.

Sara stepped between her roommates and put a hand on Ashley's arm. "Never mind, you guys. Come on, Ashley, let's go get some more firewood."

The soft whoosh of released breath was Ashley's only response as she and Sara passed Levi. Lizzie's eyes shot green daggers at Monica. Monica turned up her nose and stalked away, murmuring something about "Momma's little princess." Flinging back her hair, Lizzie stomped the opposite direction, trailing her strong perfume and drawled comments about "irritating know-it-alls."

Levi shook his head. And he'd thought his roommates were hard to deal with.

Sleeping outside wasn't all it was cracked up to be. Levi flipped and flopped as he struggled to get comfortable in his sleeping bag. Trevor and Steve's snoring duet, the many forest noises, and the adults murmuring around the fire kept him wide awake. Surely that pathetic excuse for a mattress in the boys' cabin would've been better than the ground, even with Trevor's bulk threatening to crash the whole thing in on him.

Levi shifted. Was that a stick under his ribs? He twisted. Why did they call these things four-man tents when four boys couldn't even fit comfortably?

Finally giving up on sleep, he crept from his bag, slipped on his shoes, and unzipped the tent. He stole through the flap and breathed in the cool night air. It smelled much better out here. The tent stunk like old gym shoes, as if one of the guys should've hit the showers before they left the castle.

Levi moved outside the ring of tents and tipped his head back. Maybe he'd pull his sleeping bag out here under the stars. He could fall sleep studying the constellations.

"How marvelous is your handiwork, O God," he murmured. How did the rest of the verse go? His dad told him he should study the Psalms this summer. Hadn't gotten started yet, but there was always tomorrow. Shrugging, he perched on a tree stump, his gaze on the night sky.

"We have to watch carefully, even on this side of the island." Levi sat up straight at the whispered words from the nearby two-person tent—the one he'd seen the Austins put up that afternoon.

"But surely he wouldn't come here." The high-pitched whisper had to be Mrs. Austin's. "She must be safe. She had such fun today, poor dear."

The deeper voice said, "You know he'll go anywhere. Even into the castle if he can get an invite. And don't forget he can change how he appears. We must be constantly on guard."

Levi strained to hear Mrs. Austin's response. Instead, the zing of a zipper made him jump.

A grunt and muffled creaks followed. Stubby Mr. Austin emerged from the open tent flap, paused, and peered around.

Levi froze. Who was the couple talking about? Who could go anywhere and change appearance and was so dangerous they had to keep guard against him? And who was the "poor dear"?

At that moment, Mr. Austin's gaze fell on Levi. The man reached into a pouch on his belt and withdrew a sharp-looking knife that sucked the moisture from Levi's throat.

Blade gleaming in the starlight, Mr. Austin stalked toward Levi. "I see you there, you scoundrel."

Chapter 11

Weakness

Levi swallowed hard. "It's me, sir. Levi Prince."

Mr. Austin stopped within inches of him, his head only a little higher than Levi's though Levi hadn't gathered the courage to stand. The man considered him for an agonizing moment, dagger too near Levi's heart.

Not daring to breathe, Levi fired glances around the silent campsite. Should he scream? Make a run for it? How far would he get before the short, bullnecked man caught him?

When Mr. Austin finally lowered the dagger, it shook in his hand. "What are you doing out here, boy? You should be in your tent. You could get hurt." He gulped air. "I could have hurt you."

Levi let out a shaky breath. "Couldn't sleep. Sorry."

"Well, get back to bed and stay there."

Levi stood on trembling legs. He should go. He wanted nothing to do with scary stuff. But he had to ask. "What are you guarding against? Who's so dangerous?"

Mr. Austin's black eyes flashed, his face stone. In the dim light, he didn't look human. A shiver rocked Levi's spine.

Mr. Austin's mouth relaxed into a slight curve. "Listening to things not meant for your ears?"

Levi hesitated, not sure whether to nod or shake.

"You'd best be more careful, lad. I'll not hurt you, nor will I lie to you. But there's some who would deceive you. And cheerfully kill you."

Uh, okay. This was one paranoid man.

Mr. Austin's hand shot out and gripped Levi's arm. Levi let out a startled squeak. Mr. Austin leaned in close. Levi fixated on the way the man's ears blended into his cheeks, with no lobes. Boy, did he ever want to run, but his wobbly ankles wouldn't cooperate.

Mr. Austin's gaze roved the campsite and trees before he moved in so close his beaky nose brushed Levi's chest. "The spirit world is more real here than you think," he said in a guttural whisper. "More than in your safe little world." Mr. Austin raised both wild brows. "Remember that, young Levi."

Levi's scalp prickled. He managed a nod.

Mr. Austin released him and stepped back, his voice its usual bluster. "Watch yourself. To bed, scoot."

Levi scooted.

The next afternoon, Mr. Dominic stood in the open castle doorway as promised. Levi wondered how he'd known exactly when they'd arrive, but he was too tired to ask. The rest of the camping trip had gone okay. Mr. Austin hadn't so much as looked at him funny all day, almost like they'd never had that disturbing middle-of-the-night chat. Maybe they hadn't. Maybe Levi had dreamed the whole thing. He hoped so.

Now Levi only wanted to clean up and grab some supper. Lack of sleep and stomping around outside for more than thirty-six hours had worn him out. A massive black hole had replaced his stomach.

Trevor stomped up the stairs behind him and dropped his gear on the floor of their room. With a goofy grin, he laid a heavy arm across Levi's shoulders. "We made it. Castle, sweet, castle!"

Groaning, Levi shrugged out from under Trevor's smelly pit. "I was gonna call dibs on the shower, but you need it more." He waved a hand in front of his nose.

Trevor sniffed his underarm and shrugged. "If you say so." He trudged to the bathroom, leaving his camping gear in the walkway.

With a disgusted shake of his head, Levi unpacked and sat on the edge of his bed to wait for the shower. Everybody was supposed to get to call home on Sunday afternoons, and tomorrow was Sunday. Though he hadn't seen any signs of a telephone in the castle, he knew there'd been one at camp. Wouldn't it have made more sense to use the phone today? Now they'd have to make the long hike again tomorrow.

No matter. He'd hike back right now if he could use the phone. He needed to talk to his family, his dad especially. He could use a little wisdom.

Minutes later, Trevor burst from the bathroom in his underwear. Levi scrubbed his forearm across his eyes and hurried into the bathroom, only to be met with the sight—and smell—of Trevor's filthy clothes and wet towel.

Levi sighed. *Give me strength.*

Levi squeezed into the pew beside Sara the next morning. On his other side flopped Lizzie, scratching welts on her face and arms. Levi bit back a laugh he knew he shouldn't feel. He guessed the mosquitoes liked Lizzie's perfume. What would her momma say about how she looked now?

He glanced behind him at his roommates. Trevor whispered something to Steve, and Steve elbowed Trevor. Tommy snickered behind his hand. Levi faced front with a sigh. He liked his roommates, but he was tired of their noise and goofiness. Yesterday when he'd told Trevor to pick up his dirty clothes from the bathroom floor and hang up his towel, Trevor had snapped, "Yes, Mother."

Trevor's sarcastic tone still burned Levi's cheeks. He missed his sister; together they always controlled Zeke and Jer. He could use her help with his roommates. He glanced sideways at Sara, so calm and quiet. Maybe sitting by her would soothe his nerves.

She offered him a smile as lights from the stained glass painted pastels across her features. His tight neck muscles loosened. He returned her smile.

"Welcome." Mr. Dominic's rich voice echoed from the pulpit. He rocked on the balls of his feet like he was thrilled to be there, though Levi knew some of the kids—namely, Hunter, Martin, and Greg—would never have shown up if chapel wasn't mandatory.

Levi leaned forward in his seat. Since his dad was a preacher, he'd listened to sermons all his life. What did camp directors know about preaching?

"We gather on this beautiful Sabbath morning to worship the Great Emperor and his beloved Son, High King Jesus. My wife will lead us in a hymn of worship before we open the Holy Scriptures."

Eyes shining, Mrs. Dominic stood in front and invited them to join her in singing the Gettys' "In Christ Alone," one of Levi's favorites.

Singing the words, "In Christ alone my hope is found; He is my light, my strength, my song," steeled Levi's spine.

"I know many of you are feeling a little overwhelmed with life here at Camp Classic," Mr. Dominic began, making Levi wonder if he was a mind-reader. "For some of you, the lessons and homework are piling up. For others, it's the physical activity—the fencing, the wrestling, the roughing-it. And then there's homesickness and learning to interact with new people in a strange place. You wonder how you can possibly find the strength to survive the coming weeks. You feel weak."

Levi swallowed hard. That was exactly how he felt. Weak, confused, and out of control.

Mr. Dominic's lips curved in a compassionate smile. "Believe it or not, the one and only Ruler of the entire universe understands exactly how you feel. In fact, he loves to use the weakest of all to accomplish his will."

"God must really want to use Levi." Hunter's mock-whisper and the accompanying snickers—one snort sounded like Trevor's—burned Levi's ears.

Though Sara cast him a sympathetic glance, Mr. Dominic continued, apparently unaware of the comment. "He loves to work in us when we're at our most fragile because then we're also at our most humble. We know we can't possibly accomplish the big task before us. We know our only hope is in Christ alone. He is the only one strong enough to carry us through."

Mr. Dominic picked up a worn Bible. "Let's look at First Samuel seventeen for the story of a weak boy named David who defeated a giant Philistine named Goliath." After reading the passage aloud, he looked up. "Many think this is simply another heartwarming story in which the underdog defeats the well-armed giant with only a slingshot and a few stones." His eyes roamed the campers. "But this story isn't really about David."

Levi frowned. It wasn't?

"It's about the Lord God of Israel, who worked through David's weakness to shame his enemies and proclaim his glory before the nations. He chose a shepherd boy to defeat a giant and ultimately become king. Just like he chose insignificant Bethlehem to become the birthplace of King

Jesus, a baby who became a man, the one who died and rose again to save us from our sins.

"If you find yourself tempted to despair because of your weakness in the face of strong enemies, even if those enemies are merely homework and training sessions"—Mr. Dominic smiled—"take heart. Throughout the Bible, God shows us how he uses the weak things of this world to confound the strong. All to bring glory to his name."

Mr. Dominic closed with prayer, thanking the "Emperor Father" for governing the universe and for sending "High King Jesus" to save his people.

Levi rose with the rest of the group, thinking about the director's curious names for God. Clearly God's kingship was important to him.

"Excuse me." Mr. Dominic's voice interrupted the shuffles of those preparing to leave the chapel. "I forgot one announcement. If you'll recall, we promised you an opportunity to call home each Sunday afternoon. I regret that you'll be unable to do so today."

Complaints broke out. Mr. Dominic raised a hand for silence. "I truly am sorry, but the storm knocked out the phone lines to the island. Mr. Drake took the ferry over to the mainland to request service, but due to outages in more populous places, repairmen haven't been able to come here yet."

One girl raised her hand. "Our parents are expecting us to call. They'll be worried when we don't."

Mr. Dominic nodded. "I understand. I asked Mr. Drake to contact your families via computer while he was on the mainland, informing them of the outage in case service wasn't restored before today." Mr. Dominic waited a moment. When no one else spoke, he continued. "I know you want to talk to your parents, and I feel sure phone service will be restored by next Sunday. Until then, know your families are aware of your well-being. Please feel free to write letters. Mr. Drake will take them to the post office when he next goes across. For now, let's enjoy lunch and rest this afternoon."

Levi watched the director gather his things as the others exited the chapel. He'd really wanted to call home.

After a moment, Mr. Dominic nodded to Levi, the only one still seated, reminding Levi of the man's strange wink before the camping trip. Levi managed a return nod, but queasiness slithered into his gut.

Was the phone really out of service?

Could Mr. Dominic, a man who had just preached the truth, be lying?

Chapter 12

Hunter

Later that week, Levi stood on the bank of a surprisingly deep river that cut through the woods north of the castle. He gripped the lead rope of the canoe he was to share with Hunter. Levi knew the canoe trip would most likely not turn out great for him, not with Hunter as his partner, but Mr. Drake and Miss Althea, a niece of the tiny camp cook who also taught Levi's art class, had paired the campers according to who had experience boating, and Levi—"never done this"—found himself paired with Hunter—"I've canoed thousands of times."

When Hunter flashed him a sadistic smile, Levi nearly begged off. But he didn't want to look like a baby. Going against every lick of common sense he had, Levi climbed into the front of the canoe.

He glanced around at Sara, who was paired with Suzanne, the skinny, snooty-looking girl he'd seen hanging around Hunter's husky friend Jacqueline. Sara looked comfortable with everything about her boat, except the other occupant. Monica sat in a canoe with Trevor, who'd claimed to be great with boats. Trevor looked a little nervous, and Monica looked terrified. Maybe Trevor had exaggerated a little. They'd probably end up tasting river water.

Levi didn't have much time to worry about his friends, though. Before Mr. Drake gave the word, Hunter took off, paddling farther and farther from the group.

"Hey, stop," Levi yelled. It was all he could do to hold on as they whipped down the river.

Mr. Drake and Miss Althea hollered for them to wait, but Levi was too scared of falling in to look back. Hunter laughed in his ear, sending a shiver up his neck. Where was this maniac taking him? Why had Levi gotten into the boat with Hunter in the first place? Levi glanced at his chest, reassuring himself that his orange life vest was secure.

Think, Levi! Should he whack Hunter with his paddle and wait for the others to rescue him? Try to paddle backwards? That might slow them down. But what if he tipped the canoe? He glanced around. They were in the middle of the river now, pretty far from the bank, which whipped past at a dizzying rate. Was it his imagination or was the water getting rougher?

"God, help me," he squeaked out.

Hunter cackled. "Your precious 'Emperor God' can't help you. I'm the one in control out here."

Shocked, Levi twisted to look back. Hunter's eyes glowed like molten metal.

"Stop right now, boys!"

Levi peeked behind Hunter. Miss Althea rapidly closed the gap between her canoe and theirs. Steve sat in front of her with his oar on his lap and his eyes huge.

"I said *stop*, Hunter!"

Her tone would've made Levi halt instantly, but Hunter, face twisted, paddled harder.

"I mean it, Hunter Jacobson. I know who you are."

Hunter's oar stilled as his cheeks paled.

As Miss Althea approached their craft and guided them to shore, her eyes were fierce. She beached both crafts, and with a strength that surprised Levi, pulled him from the boat and plopped him on the sand.

Next, she yanked Hunter out. "Shame on you." She glared up at him, her fists clenched, her rage making Levi glad he wasn't Hunter.

When she turned on Levi, he flinched. Thankfully, her voice and eyes softened. "Are you okay?"

At his nod, Miss Althea rounded on Hunter again, her hair slapping Levi's belly as she whipped around. "You will never, ever behave in such a way again." Even though she only came to Hunter's stomach, she clearly had the upper hand. "Your forebears would be ashamed of you."

Steve, who'd climbed out of the canoe on his own, flashed Levi a questioning look. Shrugging, Levi waited for Hunter's reaction.

Face red, Hunter opened his mouth as if to talk back, but closed it when Mr. Drake canoed around a bend and called, "Is everybody all right, Althea?"

She speared Hunter with one more glare before calling back, "Fine, Janus. Are the other kids okay?"

Mr. Drake glanced at the canoes trailing his. "Everybody's accounted for. What happened?"

"We'll need to discuss that later." She cocked her head at Hunter. "With Mr. Dominic."

Mr. Drake's brows lifted, but he only nodded.

"We'll have to change up." Miss Althea looked at Levi. "Hunter needs to ride with me."

"It was a joke." Hunter folded his arms over his chest. "The little coward needs to grow a backbone."

Levi cast him a dirty look and climbed into his canoe. As soon as he got settled, his mind flitted from Hunter to what he'd seen when Miss Althea's hair slapped him—another view of pointy-tipped ears.

Those ears sure didn't help him with his ignore-the-weird-stuff plan.

On Sunday afternoon, Levi clutched the telephone receiver to his cheek and hunkered into the rickety chair, his face close to the battered desktop.

"Dad." He fought the tears threatening to steal his voice and glanced around. The rest of the campers paid him no attention. On his left, Luke used a clunky black rotary phone, and on his right, Gabrielle chattered into a white rotary phone, her finger twisting the cord. The other campers whispered to each other while waiting their turn.

"You okay, son?" His dad's voice soothed the lump from Levi's throat.

Levi pressed the phone closer. "Yeah, I'm okay now." And he was. He'd spoken briefly with each of his siblings and with his mom—she'd cried and then laughed when he'd asked her to send ear plugs—but it was this talk with his dad he really needed.

"How's camp? You fitting in okay?"

Before the word *fine* popped out, Levi hesitated. He wanted to be straight with his dad about how things really were. Memories of the past couple weeks flitted through his mind . . . the disappearing castle, Hunter, pointy ears, Hunter, his roommates, Hunter, lessons, Hunter—

"There's this guy here who pretty much hates my guts."

"Why?"

"I don't know. Really, I don't." He heard the defensiveness in his voice and tried to tone it down. "He's just hated me from the first day. He's kind of a bully to everybody."

"Have you spoken with the staff about this?"

Levi snorted. "No way. I'm not tattling."

A sigh filtered across the phone line. "Yeah, I can kind of see why you'd say that." Silence, then, "If he does anything really nasty, though, go to the director. Bullying isn't acceptable."

"Okay, Dad." It would have to be really bad for him to snitch. Besides, Hunter had gotten a week of dishwashing duty after the canoe incident. Maybe now he'd stop tormenting Levi. Yeah, right. That was gonna happen.

"You have to use your own judgment, son. I'm not there to decide for you."

"I know." He ran a finger along the scarred desktop.

"What about the rest of the kids?" Dad's voice sounded more upbeat. "Made any friends?"

"Yeah, some. My roommates remind me of Zeke and Jer, though. Kind of messy and loud, you know?"

Dad laughed. "Well, you ought to feel right at home then." He paused, his tone more serious. "Don't try to boss them around, Levi. That's not the way to make friends, not even with your little brothers."

Levi squirmed in the hard wooden seat. "Got it."

"Okay." Dad grew quiet again, making Levi think he had more to say on the subject. Instead he said, "How's everything else? You said roommates—don't you mean cabin mates? Has your bunkmate flattened you yet?" He chuckled.

Levi smiled. "No, we actually moved to the other side of the island when that storm hit. Had to go to a stronger building, so we're living in a castle."

"You're joking."

"No, it's a real live stone castle, and it's cool." Should he mention the disappearing cliff thing? Nah. His parents would stick him in an asylum. "I'm on the fourth floor."

"You? Doesn't being up that high scare you?"

Levi thought a moment. His phobia about heights hadn't bothered him that much this summer. "Maybe I'm growing out of it."

"Maybe."

At a tap on his shoulder, Levi turned. Mrs. Drake pointed at the wall clock and held up one finger. Levi nodded.

"I've gotta go, Dad. It's the next guy's turn. I'll talk to you later, okay?"

"Sure, Levi. We love you and pray for you every day."

"Thanks. I love you too."

"Don't forget whose you are, son. You'll be fine if you remember that."

Chapter 13

Heat

Levi and his roommates sat at the back of Science class trying to listen to Mrs. Austin's lecture on the human skeleton. June was drawing to a close, and the classroom was hot and stuffy, even with the windows thrown wide.

Levi stifled a yawn. Hoping more oxygen would help him fight off sleepiness, he inhaled deeply through his nose—and wished he hadn't. Something stank. Bad. He looked around for the source of the smell but didn't see any likely suspects. He even sniffed his own pits just in case.

Gabrielle grimaced over her shoulder. "Ew, what's that smell?"

Levi shrugged and tried not to look guilty.

Snuffling sounds turned Levi's head. Tommy hung across the aisle sniffing the air. "Steve, is that you I smell?"

For answer, Steve's face turned hot pink.

Trevor looked at Steve, nose wrinkled. "Why do you stink so bad? I know you took a shower this morning when Mr. Sylvester said we had to."

Steve huffed out a breath. "I missed laundry day, okay? Sorry."

Levi opened his mouth as Mrs. Austin leveled a glare on him. Levi snapped his mouth shut. Mrs. Austin was normally a nice lady, but she took her class seriously and expected the campers to do the same. When she finally turned back to the board, Levi dared a whisper. "Haven't you ever heard of washing your stuff in the bathroom sink?"

Steve's face brightened. "I never thought of that."

Whipping around, the teacher fixed Steve in a glare. Steve slapped a hand over his mouth.

She scowled at him a second longer before asking the class, "Who can tell me how cartilage is different from bone?"

While Monica rattled off a dictionary definition of cartilage, Steve whispered, "I'll try that during break later." He beamed at Levi. "Then I'll hang my stuff out in the bathroom to dry. That's a great idea. Thanks."

Levi managed not to roll his eyes.

"Yeah, that's a great idea." Tommy pinched his nose. "But what about right now? You smell horrendous."

Steve shrugged.

Trevor sighed. "You can borrow some of my stuff after class."

"Thanks, Trevor," Steve said too loudly.

"Boys." Mrs. Austin gave them the evil eye. "I'll thank you to stop talking during lessons."

Levi scrunched down in his seat.

She planted both fists on her hips. "Since you gentlemen want to wag your tongues, who can tell me which parts of the human body are made up of cartilage?"

Levi and his roommates were silent.

Though Monica and a few others raised their hands, Mrs. Austin ignored them. "Levi Prince?"

Levi met her eyes. He'd told himself he would let it go, stick to the fun-summer plan, but . . . "Ears," he blurted.

Mrs. Austin's stubby hands grew still.

Levi ran his forefingers along the cartilage on his ears. "The parts on top." He waited. What would she say to that?

The teacher's face reddened as she flattened the hair over her ears. "Um, yes, ears are made up, in part, of cartilage." She turned abruptly back to the board.

Ha! I knew something was going on here. Levi's triumph seeped away with his breath. Mrs. Austin's self-conscious reaction was not good. It most definitely did not fit in with his ignore-the-weird-stuff plan.

July arrived. With it came sand flies, and Albert. Levi couldn't decide which was worse. He used the gauzy white curtain around his bed to keep the insects from disrupting his sleep, but it wasn't so simple to keep Albert away.

Mr. Dominic gave Albert permission to sleep in the empty room next to Levi's because, according to Albert, "My brothers were about to drive me nuts." Now Albert constantly dropped into Levi's room, parked it on one bed or another, and chattered away for hours. It was nearly impossible to get homework done or even have a quiet moment to think.

One muggy afternoon, Levi sat on his bunk doing Latin homework while his roommates played flag football in the courtyard.

Albert came in, climbed onto Tommy's bed, and started a monologue, which Levi tried to ignore. "There was this one time when I was cuttin' firewood out north, and don't you know that ornery Deceptor tried to trick me. He was pretending to be a—"

Pen drooping, Levi stared at the little man.

Albert stared back. "What?"

"What did you say?"

Albert's eyes widened, then his face blanked. "Nothing."

"You mentioned somebody called Deceptor. Who's that?"

Albert stood up fast. "Nobody. Not supposed to say nothing. Gotta go."

He rushed to the door, paused, turned back. "Things is different here. You'll see stuff you ain't used to seeing. If you pay attention."

He lifted both hands and tucked his wild mane behind his ears.

Levi's jaw dropped. But Albert was gone, leaving Levi with more unanswered questions—and another view of pointy-tipped ears.

"What in the world does it all mean?" he asked the empty room.

Chapter 14

The Cliff Returns

In archery class that week, Levi chose a bow and quiver from the rack, turned, and walked straight into Hunter, who was about to discharge an arrow.

"Sorry," Levi said.

Hunter whirled around, sharp arrow tip an inch from Levi's chin. "Watch it, Prince."

Heart thudding, Levi stepped back. He'd avoided Hunter since the canoeing fiasco, but now he'd managed to get himself on the wrong end of the creep's arrow. Why hadn't Levi looked where he was going?

Hunter cut his eyes meaningfully toward Sara, Monica, and Trevor, who stood nearby. "Never can tell who might get hurt with these sharp tips." He touched the arrow point. "Accidentally, of course."

Levi narrowed his eyes. "You better not—"

"Places, boys." Mr. Sylvester stepped between them. "It's time for your lesson."

"Yes, sir, of course," Hunter said to the teacher. Once Mr. Sylvester moved away, he whispered to Levi, "You better learn your lesson, runt."

"After final exams at the end of August, we'll hold the Camp Classic Olympics," Mr. Dominic announced at breakfast a few days later. "You'll be required to compete in at least three events. You must register by the last day of July or be assigned whatever is left." He grinned at the campers' groans. "Sign-up sheets are posted on the back wall. I'd suggest you spend any free time practicing for your events. We'll give out medals at our farewell luncheon with your families. You'll want to make the best showing you can."

Levi couldn't think of a worse way to end camp.

Later that day, he and Trevor stared at the blank sign-up pages. Fencing, archery, canoeing, running, wrestling, boxing. Even javelin throwing, which Mr. Austin promised to demonstrate the next day.

He still didn't understand what this camp had against soccer. Levi could handle that. Or flag football or basketball. At least he'd done those before. "What're you signing up for?"

"Don't know." Trevor pulled out a dining chair, turned it toward the back wall, and plopped down. "You?"

Levi turned a chair and extended his pitifully short, scrawny legs next to Trevor's long, muscular ones. He sighed. "I don't know. Why can't we just be spectators? I'm pretty good at that."

Trevor laughed.

"What? I'm serious. Why not offer Armchair Olympics? I could win the gold in that one."

Trevor laughed harder, earning a glare from Levi. When Trevor collapsed in a giggling heap on the dining room floor, Levi couldn't help but laugh with him.

The next Sunday marked the fourth time the campers got to call home. Trevor decided not to go, claiming his dad wouldn't want him to call and interrupt the Indians game. Both Monica's and Steve's families were on vacation. Sara and Tommy didn't want to go either, so that left Levi to walk down with Dr. Baldwin and a handful of other kids.

Nobody said much as they hiked to the cabins. Levi kept wiping sweat from his upper lip and wishing he could swim in the river with his friends. Skipping the phone call home wasn't an option, though. His mom would freak if she didn't hear from him weekly.

When they got to the cabins, he called home and spoke to each member of his family, Abby last of all.

"So how's it going?" she asked, but rushed ahead before he could answer. "We just finished swim lessons, and I passed to Dolphin level. Zeke didn't, so he's kinda mad. Mom said she'd give him extra lessons when we're at Grandma's next week." She barely paused for breath. "You're gonna miss out. Grandpa's taking us fishing. Then we've got Vacation Bible School after that."

Abby rattled on for five solid minutes before he cut her off to say he had to get off the phone. It sounded like his family was perfectly happy. Without him.

Levi stomped up the trail, glaring at the dirt his boots kicked up. He didn't want his family to be miserable, but it bothered him that even Abby didn't sound teary when she'd said goodbye.

A swooshing, splashing sound drew his head up. He'd reached the top of the hill where the castle usually waited with a smiling Mr. or Mrs. Dominic at the door. He'd grown so used to it being there he'd pretty much decided the cliff thing was a fantasy. But now, neither of the Dominics was here . . . no door . . . no drawbridge . . . no moat. Levi inched forward. Earth fell away to lake. Waves crashed into rocks a hundred feet below.

"Somebody, come look!" Where was everybody? "Hello!" Panic skittered through his veins. He couldn't look away or the cliff might disappear again. "Anybody?" No answer.

He risked a quick glance around. Apparently, he'd left everyone else behind.

Then Dr. Baldwin emerged from the trees, and his eyes widened at the sight before him. He met Levi's gaze, and his lips twitched . . . into a grin?

Before Levi could demand an explanation, light like a million rainbows shattered the air. He whipped around as the cliff disappeared and the castle reappeared. Mrs. Dominic stood in the doorway apologizing for the delay.

Levi could only stand there, slapped speechless by the proof he'd worked so hard to deny.

Levi was not in a good mood that night. He could no longer pretend Camp Classic was normal. In fact, it was the opposite of normal. It was downright freaky. Neither Dr. Baldwin nor Mrs. Dominic had said a word about the cliff incident that afternoon. None of the other campers had seen a thing, not that he'd asked. Levi faced—all alone—evidence he didn't know how to handle. Between that and the ubiquitous ears, Levi's fun, stress-free summer plans had been smashed to smithereens.

When Levi exited the bathroom, furious that Trevor had used Levi's towel (again) and thrown it on the floor (again), he stormed past Tommy's bed, tripped over a pile of dirty clothes, and landed on his rump. Albert, sprawled across Levi's bed eating Doritos and drinking Pepsi, snorted soda out of his nose all over Levi's pillow. Tommy, Steve, and Trevor fell all over themselves laughing at Levi's graceless landing on the stone floor.

Not at all interested in a late-night party in his room—not to mention crumbs in his bed— Levi snapped, "Ha ha. Let's all laugh at Levi falling over our junk. If you slobs would clean up after yourselves occasionally, people wouldn't hurt themselves in here."

Trevor smirked. "Yeah, Tommy, can't you pick up your stinky socks so Levi doesn't fall on his poor bottom?"

All but Tommy laughed.

Levi's blood pressure rose. "It's not just Tommy, Trevor. I'm sick of you using my towel and leaving it wadded up on the bathroom floor. Use your own!"

That stopped Trevor laughing and got Tommy going, but Levi wasn't finished yet.

"Steve, quit eating in here all the time! Your open packs of chips and Twinkies are just asking mice to move in."

That wiped the smile off Steve's face.

"And Albert—" Levi rounded on him— "for someone who moved upstairs to get a room alone, you spend an awful lot of time in here." Levi stomped over to his bed and wiped chip crumbs from his comforter. "Get off my bed!"

With a reproachful glare at Levi, Albert stood, muttered good night, and swept from the room. While his roommates cleaned up, Levi flopped onto his bed, heart drumming.

"Hey, Levi," Trevor called from the open bathroom doorway. "Happy?" He pointed at the neat row of towels.

Levi faced the wall. "No."

Neither Albert nor any of Levi's roommates were speaking to him the next day, so he sat with the girls at breakfast. Sara's wide-eyed "What's up with you guys?" didn't help his mood. Especially when Tommy muttered something about bossy people being a pain in the neck.

By the time Levi got to Logic class, he'd about had it with Camp Classic. Nothing made sense here, even his own attitude. He liked his roommates—Albert, too. He'd never before had friendships like he did here. But here he was, rabidly angry with the whole place and everyone in it, himself included.

At the front of the classroom, Mr. Dominic cleared his throat. The campers quieted. Levi looked up from the desktop he'd nearly scorched with his glare.

"Many of you have yawned your way through our previous classes." The twinkle in the director's eyes took the sting out of his words, but Levi didn't care one way or the other. Why shouldn't Mr. Dominic be rude? Everybody else was.

"Most of you figure you have no intention of becoming lawyers or statesmen who need the ability to argue a case without fallacious reasoning," Mr. Dominic went on. "Yet I'd like to explain why logic is important in other areas of life, areas that deeply affect you."

Despite his irritation, Levi felt his interest rising. Most teachers never bothered telling students how their subjects would be useful in real life. Levi's mom did sometimes, though usually she just told him to learn the material.

"All of you were selected from classical school settings." Mr. Dominic walked around his desk and leaned against it. "You are all learning according to a particular educational system—one that says the early years should be spent in memorization, the middle years in connecting the whys and wherefores of what you've memorized, and the final years in learning to interact with your knowledge and with the world around you."

Levi nodded. Yeah, he knew about the trivium.

Mr. Dominic's eyes roamed the campers' faces. "You are all in those middle years—what we call the Logic Stage. That means you should be training your minds to make logical connections . . . to discover the reasons behind events. I've been teaching what faulty logic looks like so you'll learn to see beyond your prejudices and preconceived notions, beyond appearances, to what is true. When you make those connections, you can learn from history to avoid making the same mistakes in the future.

"You've all studied ancient civilizations in the Grammar Stage of your learning." Mr. Dominic rested his arms across his stomach. "You learned about the Egyptians, the Greeks, the Romans, and the medieval people. You read literature about them, studied their histories, learned some of their languages." Eyebrows arched and chin tilted, he smiled. "It's time to put your knowledge to use. What can you learn from mistakes the ancients made? What can you learn from what they did right? Why did they do what they did? And what does that have to do with you?"

Mr. Dominic waited. Levi glanced at his silent classmates. Did the director expect one of them to answer? Levi didn't know the reasons why the ancients did what they did, but he did know one thing. He wanted a logical explanation for Camp Classic and its staff.

What was the deal with the disappearing cliff? What about Albert's and Mr. Austin's warnings about things being different here? And what about all the strange ears? None of it was logical, and it was really getting on his nerves.

Levi's jaw set. He was supposed to start asking why, huh? Well, maybe he'd do just that.

Chapter 15

Logic

When class ended, Mr. Dominic asked Levi to stick around a few minutes.

Levi slowly gathered his stuff as the others filtered from the room. Had he done something wrong? Despite his irritation, he hadn't spoken one word in class, and he'd tried to keep his face blank.

When the room emptied, he said, "You wanted to see me, sir?" His voice squeaked like Trevor's still did sometimes.

Mr. Dominic looked up from the papers on his desk and smiled, the twinkle again in his eyes. "Don't worry, young man. You're not in trouble."

Levi sighed.

"I thought you might have something on your mind? You looked like it during class." The director studied him, waiting.

"Um . . ." Now that he had the chance to ask questions, Levi didn't know what to say. His mom always said he'd argue with a tree, but this was different. Way different.

"You seemed to want to voice a disagreement or ask a question. It's okay to do both." Mr. Dominic leaned nearer, voice low. "That's actually what I want you to do, you know. That's how you learn." He winked as if sharing a funny secret, an act that reminded Levi of the time weeks before when Mr. Dominic winked at him from the castle door.

The memory brought Levi's agitation rushing back. He jammed his arms across his chest. Did Mr. Dominic really want to know what he thought? Levi knew from experience adults didn't like it when kids came off as disrespectful.

Careful to keep his voice level, he said, "Well, it's just . . . I'm trying to understand some things about Camp Classic . . . I mean, things aren't logical." He hesitated. "This place is . . . well, it's strange."

Mr. Dominic leaned back in his seat. "Okay. How so?"

Levi watched the director's face. He didn't look mad. "Well, the castle itself for one thing. I know for sure it disappears, and what kind of place disappears? What's the deal with the cliff? Where's it go when you or your wife are at the door? How can this castle and the land to the north possibly fit on Castle Island? Who's Deceptor? What's the evil you're trying to keep out by hiding this place?" He stopped and sucked in a much-needed breath. "And what's the deal with all the strange ears?"

Mr. Dominic surprised him by chuckling. "My, my, so many questions. You're paying attention to what's around you. No wonder you looked like you were about to burst during class."

Levi waited. "Are you going to answer?" He softened his tone. "Sir?"

A frown crinkled the director's forehead. "Yes, I will."

"You will?" Levi's heart skipped a beat.

"Yes, but what shall I answer first?" Mr. Dominic glanced at his wristwatch. "You have another class in about two minutes. Perhaps it would be best to meet together and discuss your questions when we have a reasonable amount of time in which to do so."

Eyes on his shoes, Levi nodded. He knew when he was getting the brush-off. He hefted his backpack and turned to go.

"Leviticus." The director's firm tone drew Levi around.

"I'm not ignoring your questions. Come to my office after supper this evening. Let's say around eight."

Levi nodded again, this time with a smile.

Mr. Dominic nodded back. "Good. We'll seek answers together then."

At eight o'clock, Levi knocked hard on Mr. Dominic's office door. He'd thought all afternoon about what answers the director might give. He'd entertained all sorts of ideas, ranging from crazy to semi-rational—everything from government conspiracies to UFO landing sites to geographical phenomena. Now, he couldn't wait to find out the truth.

Mrs. Dominic opened the door.

"Hello, Levi." Her face looked paler than usual, the lines around her eyes etched deeper. "I'm so sorry, but Mr. Dominic won't be able to meet with you tonight as planned."

Levi's jaw clenched. Obviously, the director didn't think he was important enough to bother with.

"He really wanted to keep your appointment." She gave him an understanding smile. "Mr. Dominic was called away from the castle on important business but asked me to tell you he'd meet with you at the first opportunity."

Levi nodded. "It's okay. I can wait." And he could. Mr. Dominic hadn't told him he was a lunatic or totally dismissed him. He'd get answers soon. He'd just have to be patient a little longer. After all, how long could this "important business" take?

Mrs. Dominic's eyes brightened nearly to their usual sapphire. "You're a good boy."

His cheeks warmed. "Thanks."

"You're so like your namesake." Her expression turned dreamy, as if she'd gotten lost in a memory.

"Huh?"

Mrs. Dominic blinked. "Never mind, dear. Go enjoy your evening." She fluttered her hand in dismissal. "My husband will let you know as soon as he can reschedule your meeting." She closed the door before he could answer.

Puzzling over her reference to his name, Levi turned away and headed to his room. How could she know anything about the person he was named for? He'd died a long time ago.

When he opened the door to his room, all thoughts of his namesake fled as something whacked him square in the face.

His hands flew up to cover his face. "Hey!" When nothing else hit him, he peeped through his fingers.

From various points of the room, Trevor, Tommy, Steve, and Albert laughed, hugging pillows to their chests. He'd walked into a pillow fight. Perfect.

"Sorry," Tommy said through giggles that proved he wasn't sorry at all. "You stepped right into the line of fire."

Fingering his bloody lip, Levi looked down at the pillow by his feet . . . his pillow. He looked toward his bed . . . a rumpled mess. Not his mess.

The Trojan Horse Traitor 83

He was going to explode at these guys like he did last night if he didn't get out of here fast. He whirled and left without a word, careful not to slam the door. He stood in the corridor. Drew several deep breaths. Paced back and forth. Stalked to the nearest window.

A few streaky patches of orange and purple colored the darkening sky. He glanced at his watch—nearly nine. He needed to get out of here, but where could he go? Room check was usually about nine thirty. That gave him half an hour.

He strode to the nearest door, headed for the chapel. Maybe there he'd find a little peace.

Yet when Levi opened the door to the chapel corridor, he heard voices, and the last thing he wanted was to see anyone. He veered around and started up the steps. He'd never gone upstairs before.

The stairway was jet black. Too bad he hadn't brought his flashlight.

He started up. A strange smell hung in the tower, stale like a mix of old smoke, dust, and . . . something he couldn't identify. Something that raised goose bumps on his arms.

Teeth clenched against the irrational fear, Levi kept climbing. He wasn't about to go back to his room, not now anyway, and the chapel wasn't available. He would not let some odd smell dictate his steps. He hugged the rail, blind in the now-total darkness. The higher he climbed, the more a bunch of icy moths fluttered in his stomach.

He glanced over his shoulder to the vague shadow of light on the landing below. He was really high now. Had he come to any more landings without realizing it? How high did these steps go? He hadn't thought the castle was this tall.

By the time he fumbled into a closed door, his hand ached from gripping the rail. He kept clinging to it with one hand, though, while he felt around with the other. He grasped a cold doorknob. Did he dare turn it? What would he find on the other side?

Almost against his will, his hand twisted the knob. It let out a squeal. He winced. Then shoved. The heavy door opened with a banshee scream.

Levi froze. Full-blown fear like hyper bats attacked his belly. He strained his ears. Who—or what—might he have disturbed?

Nothing, of course. Don't be such a coward.

Giving his head a disgusted shake, Levi moved past the door.

He'd found the tower roof. The night air cooled his cheeks. Freaky tower stairs and irritating roommates forgotten, Levi crossed the stone roof and stood in the middle. The stars spread across the blue-black sky, their pinprick lights dazzling his eyes. With a sigh, he sank onto the hard floor and lay back to enjoy the celestial show.

A creak from behind jerked Levi from his relaxed position. His head whipped around. Something large separated itself from the doorway and crept toward him.

Chapter 16

The Tower

Levi's heart battered his chest. He wanted to scream like his little sister but couldn't make a sound.

"Levi?" His name started out deep then rose several octaves.

"Trevor!" Breath whooshed from Levi's lungs. "You scared me half to death. What're you doing up here?"

"Following you. To see if you're okay." Trevor crossed the roof and sat next to Levi. "Why did you come up here? Those stairs are . . . wow."

Levi laughed. "Yeah, but look up there." He tipped his chin toward the night sky.

Trevor looked up. "Sweet."

A moment later, Trevor cleared his throat. "Um, listen, I'm sorry about hitting you and all. I know you hate when we use your stuff without asking. We shouldn't have messed up your bed or stole your pillow."

Levi ran his tongue over his fat bottom lip. It felt like a plump grape tucked under the skin. It would probably be purple by morning. But even in the dim light, he could tell Trevor really was sorry.

Levi looked back up at the huge canopy above them. Pillows, towels, crumbs, even a busted lip didn't matter so much in light of that hugeness.

"It's okay. I shouldn't let it bother me so much." He lay back down.

Trevor sprawled flat on his back, cushioning his head with his hands. "So why does it? Bother you, I mean? You have brothers and sisters. Shouldn't you be used to having people in your stuff?"

Levi traced his finger over the stone. "I think that's exactly why it bothers me. I mean, they're always there and in my junk. How hard is it just to leave my stuff alone?"

"Oh."

Levi sat up, suddenly angry again. "Something wrong with that?"

Trevor sat up and scowled. "I didn't say anything. It's just you have a family that gives a rip." He raised a finger. "Siblings who want to play with you." He raised a second finger. "A dad that cares what you do." A third finger. "A mom who loves you enough to stay home." His voice cracked. "You have no clue how good you've got it. Some of us don't have anybody. Just a brother who's better than they are at everything and who hates their guts." His hand closed into a fist. "And a dad who couldn't care less about them, just ships them off to school and summer camp and anywhere else to get rid of them." He smacked his fist into his palm.

Levi flinched at the smack. What could he say to that? He'd sure never felt like his family didn't care, not really. "Sorry."

"Doesn't matter." Trevor flopped back against the stone floor. "Man! You could've picked a softer spot to stargaze."

Levi snorted out a laugh. "Well, next time carry the pillows up here instead of hitting me with them."

They both laughed, and Levi lay back down—careful not to flop.

A while later, Trevor broke the silence. "I thought you had some meeting with Mr. Dominic tonight. You weren't gone long."

"He wasn't there. Mrs. Dominic said he got called away on business."

"That's kind of weird, isn't it?" Trevor glanced at him. "I mean, where would he go? We're on an island."

"Maybe he had to go to the mainland."

"This late? He was at supper."

"Don't know. I just know that's what she said." Mrs. Dominic's words about his name returned to his mind. "She said something else . . . something strange." His voice dropped. "She said I was like my namesake."

"What's strange about that? She would've seen your dad the first day of camp. Maybe she meant you look like him."

"But I'm not named after my dad." Levi thought a moment. "She didn't sound like she meant my looks so much anyway. More like my personality maybe."

"Well, who are you named after? Maybe she knows him."

"No way." Levi's eyes tracked a shooting star. "He's my great-great-grandfather. Died long before I was born."

"Oh. She must be confused then. Has you mixed up with somebody else."

"Yeah."

They watched the sky a few more minutes.

"So what was he like? Your great-great-grandpa, I mean. Your folks must've told you about him if they named you after him."

Levi's smile turned wistful. "My dad loved him. Papa Levi—that's what they called him—used to tell these fantastic stories when Dad was a kid. Dad would sit listening to him for hours while the rest of the kids played. They thought my dad was goofy because Papa Levi was so old, and they thought he was boring. But I don't blame him for listening. Dad told me and the others the same stories at bedtime when we were little. Still does for Jer sometimes."

Levi's voice softened. "I listen to him when he does. I think he knows I do, but he doesn't mention it. They're great stories—all about this land filled with elves and dwarves and dragons and water sprites. I always wished I could go there."

"Sounds cool."

"Yeah, Dad said Papa Levi sounded like he'd really been to that place. He described every inch of the castle and the way everybody looked. He talked about going to a summer camp type thing and meeting centaurs and minotaurs and all these bizarre creatures." A laugh surfaced as he remembered one of the stories. "My favorite was about a time he went camping and brought sandwiches along for lunch. Papa Levi was just about to take a big bite of his ham and cheese on rye when something snatched it right out of his hands. He wound up chomping down on thin air while this long-haired bird woman flew off with his sandwich. Found out later she was a harpy. Crazy, huh?"

Trevor chuckled. "Sounds like here."

Levi froze, startled.

Trevor shrugged. "Except the mythical creatures, of course."

Levi turned unseeing eyes on the night sky. Could that even be possible?

"What? You look so serious." Trevor half-laughed. "I'm just saying about the summer camp thing and the castle and all."

"I know, but the way he described the castle, it was a lot like this one.

With the four towers and symmetrical sides . . . and the inner courtyard. And I know it was someplace north and surrounded by water. Plus . . ." He fell silent, not ready to mention the staff's strange ears.

Trevor didn't seem to notice. He was craning his neck, studying the sky. "Do you see the Dippers? I've been looking all over for them. And Orion and the others? I haven't found a single constellation I know."

Frowning, Levi twisted his head and scanned another portion of sky. "Now that you mention it, I can't pick out any of them either. Strange."

"Yeah." Trevor pointed. "The North Star should be there, but it's not. You'd almost think this wasn't the night sky over North America at all." His short laugh sounded forced.

Levi tried to laugh, too, but it fell flat. Should he voice the suspicions that had nagged him since his first day at Camp Classic? At least he wouldn't be alone with his fears anymore. Alone with Hunter and Martin, that is. He sat up, hoping he'd sound rational—or at least not like the average lunatic. "Actually, I've been wondering a lot about that."

Trevor sat up, face scrunched. "What?"

Levi hesitated. Last chance to back out. If he spilled his theory, what would Trevor think of him? But still, he needed somebody to talk to, and Mr. Dominic had bailed on him. Besides, he wasn't even sure he could trust the director, and he was tired of worrying alone. "Okay, here goes. I know you said you didn't see the cliff that first day when we came to the castle. And you haven't acted too worried about how the weather's sometimes different here. But something's bizarre about this place." He eyed Trevor's serious expression. So far, so good. "I think we're in some other land." Even as he waited for Trevor to fall over laughing, Levi felt more certain than ever he was right.

When Trevor didn't so much as giggle, Levi rushed ahead. "It's some place that doesn't fit on Castle Island. The land should've ended at the castle, but here it is." He waved his arms toward the dark land stretching miles beyond the castle. "That should all be water, not earth."

Trevor's nod was slow, his expression thoughtful. "I've wondered about that. This place is awfully big for a small private island in the lake—even one as massive as Lake Superior. And then there're the stars." He looked up again as if checking whether they'd moved to normal positions. "Where do you think we are?" Trevor's voice squeaked on the last word.

Levi shivered. If Trevor was scared . . . "I don't know."

Trevor nodded, his eyes huge.

After a moment, Levi said, "Have you noticed the ears on the staff?"

Trevor's guffaw broke the heavy silence. "Ears? What're you talking about?"

Irritation lifted Levi's chin. "They're pointed on top. At least Mr. Drake's and Mrs. Sylvester's are. Albert's and Miss Althea's too. I saw them."

Trevor's mouth fell open. "You're serious?"

"Yeah. And Mr. Austin's are weird, too. They're not pointy, but there aren't any lobes on his. I mean, the floppy parts at the bottom where he should have lobes connect directly to his jaws." He touched his own ear lobes. "It's creepy."

"So what're you saying?" Trevor's voice fell to a whisper. "You think they're not human?"

"Well, yeah . . . I mean, maybe . . . I don't know what I'm saying." Levi flapped his hands. "I just know Papa Levi's stories sound a lot like this place. With elves and dwarves and stuff."

Trevor's eyes bugged out. "Are you telling me you think Mrs. Sylvester is an elf? And Mr. Austin's a what? A dwarf? What's that make Albert and Miss Althea? They're not built the same."

"Fairies." Levi breathed the word. "Pixies. Sprites."

"Okay." The way he stretched the word into three syllables showed how nuts he thought Levi was.

Levi didn't care. Saying it out loud convinced him his theory was right. Crazy or not.

Disbelief sagged Trevor's jaw. "You're not just messing with me, are you?"

"I'm serious. I didn't want to see it at first, but now I'm sure." Levi gripped his hands together. "Besides, Mr. Dominic practically proved I'm right this morning when he didn't tell me I was nuts."

"What do you think Mr. Dominic is? If you're right about this place, I mean." His voice squeaked on every other word. "You think he's, like, a wizard or something? Gandalf the Grey meets Lord Voldemort? Does that make him good or evil?"

"No . . . I don't know." Levi's voice firmed along with his resolve. "But I do know this much: as soon as Mr. Dominic gets back, I'm gonna ask him."

Chapter 17

Mafia Beatings?

By the time the boys crept back down the dark staircase, the grandfather clock on their corridor chimed midnight. When they slipped into their room, Steve and Tommy both sat up.

"Where've you been?" Steve demanded. "It's way past room check."

"On top of the tower. Why? Are we in trouble?" Levi tried not to sound anxious. What would Mr. Sylvester deem proper punishment? Did elves have some horrific disciplinary measures for their naughty children?

Tommy shook his head. "You lucked out. Albert said Mr. Sylvester was gone somewhere tonight, so Mrs. Sylvester just knocked on the door at ten for lights-out."

Relieved, Levi tumbled into bed. He slept hard, dreaming all night of fairies and dragons. It wasn't until morning that he was struck by the oddity of Mr. Sylvester and Mr. Dominic leaving the castle on the same night.

Though a little worried when Mr. Dominic and Mr. Sylvester didn't return over the next several days, Levi had the most fun he'd had since coming to camp. He and Trevor spent hours coming up with ways to prove Levi's "Castle Island Theory," as they called it. They were so busy stalking the staff for proof that they were nonhumans Levi didn't have time to get irritated with his roommates even once.

Levi and Trevor spent one entire afternoon hanging around the infirmary, hoping to catch Dr. Baldwin in something that would reveal his true identity. At least until he shooed them away with a gruff, "Unless you're sick, be gone!" In canoeing class they shadowed Miss Althea, but quickly backed off when she threatened to dunk them in the river. On Tuesday after supper while Tommy and Steve were in the great hall, they cornered Albert in their room and asked to see his ears. He gave them a look like they were insane and took off. When Albert steered clear of them the rest of the week, not even showing up for Spades night on Wednesday, Levi told Trevor, "See. That proves he has something to hide."

When it came time for fencing class Thursday afternoon and Mr. Sylvester still hadn't returned, Mrs. Sylvester filled in. She began class with a lecture about the ways girls could use their smaller frames to advantage against larger opponents.

Near the rear of the group, Levi nudged Trevor. "Think she knows where her husband and Mr. Dominic are?"

Trevor shrugged. "Ask her."

"No way. You ask."

"Nope." Trevor narrowed one eye in a wink. "But I'll keep a close eye on her. I still haven't seen those ears you keep yapping about."

Before Levi could reply, Mrs. Sylvester pointed their direction. "You'll do, Mr. Patterson."

Levi glanced at Trevor, who tapped himself on the chest in question.

Mrs. Sylvester nodded. "Come here and suit up. We'll demonstrate the techniques I've described."

Trevor cast Levi a helpless look. Levi shrugged. Maybe they should've been listening to the lecture.

"While Mr. Patterson gathers his gear, the rest of you divide out so you can practice what we show you. Girls on the left; boys on the right."

As his classmates moved, Levi edged into the boys' group and glanced around self-consciously. All the boys except Luke were bigger than he was. Greg, Martin, and Trevor towered over him. He was even smaller than most of the girls. What if he got paired against Hunter's huge friend Jacqueline? She'd flatten him.

"You should probably go on over there with the other little girls, runt," Hunter whispered from Levi's left.

Levi frowned, partly in irritation, partly because Hunter was right. Pretending he hadn't heard, Levi watched Mrs. Sylvester's demonstration with Trevor. But Hunter's words rankled. It was true Levi was horrible at fencing. He had no bulk to throw around against an opponent.

He could barely swing a sword without chopping off his own head. Even though Hunter wasn't much bigger than Levi, the creep was really good.

If Levi ever had to face Hunter in a duel, it would be David and Goliath all over again. Maybe Levi should learn to fight like a girl.

When Levi sat next to Trevor at supper that evening, Tommy and Lizzie were still teasing Trevor about his fencing display. In a single move, Mrs. Sylvester had felled Trevor like a tree.

"I was distracted," Trevor insisted for the tenth time as he grabbed his full-to-the-brim milk glass and took a swig. He widened his eyes meaningfully at Levi.

Levi bit back a smile. He knew Trevor really had been distracted trying to see Mrs. Sylvester's ears. Not that Trevor could explain that to anybody else. Still, Levi had to admit it looked funny when the toothpick-thin teacher swept Trevor's muscled legs out from under him.

A slight commotion at the staff table drew Levi's attention to several adults clustered around somebody. When the group parted, he spotted Mr. Dominic and Mr. Sylvester seated in their usual places, their heads together in quiet conversation.

Levi elbowed Trevor.

"Oof." Trevor's hand, the one holding his full glass, jerked into the air. Milk splattered everywhere. Lizzie got splashed square in the face. Milk drowned Steve's ham and beans. Several people shrieked.

Levi didn't notice the commotion because Trevor's yelp drew the men's heads up, giving him a clear view of Mr. Sylvester's black eye and the livid purple bruise on Mr. Dominic's forehead.

Where had they gone to get those bruises? What had they been doing?

Mr. Dominic met Levi's eyes, grinned at him, and then turned back to Mr. Sylvester.

"Why'd you dig your bony elbow in me?" Trevor's indignant words brought Levi's gaze back to the milk disaster.

"Tell you later."

By the time they cleaned up the mess and Trevor changed to non-milky clothes, it was nearly nine. Knowing he shouldn't knock on the Dominics' door so late, Levi instead sat beside Trevor on Trevor's bed.

"What do you think?" he whispered.

The Trojan Horse Traitor

Trevor shook his head. "I don't know. It's kind of hard to think, much less see, when I've got milk in my eyes. Next time you want to show me something, keep your bony elbows off."

"Sorry, but be quiet." Levi jabbed a thumb toward Tommy, who'd looked up from the lines he was learning for the summer play.

Trevor's lips puckered in disgust. "So what'd you see?"

Levi told him about the men's battered faces.

"Who do you think hit 'em?"

"Don't know."

"It's like a mafia beating or something." Trevor's eyes were the size of golf balls.

Levi rolled his eyes. "You watch too much TV."

"Oh, yeah." Trevor's face reddened. "Well, you're the one who thinks we're in some fairyland!"

Levi slugged Trevor on the arm—not too hard, but hard enough. "Shut up, already."

"You asked for it." Trevor's fist drew back for a return slug when a tap on the door saved Levi.

The door opened, and Mr. Sylvester stuck his head in. "Lights out, boys. Better enjoy your beds tonight."

Stifling a groan, Levi nodded. He'd forgotten tomorrow was another camping trip.

Steve exited the bathroom, tugging his pajama top down over his big belly. "Hi, Mr. Sylvester. Glad you're back." He stopped and gawked at the man's bruises. "What happened to your face?"

Levi exchanged a look with Trevor. Leave it to Steve to ask the question. At least Levi didn't have to do it.

Mr. Sylvester's smile was guarded. "Oh, I had a little run-in with a nasty creature when I was helping Mr. Dominic." He waved a hand in the air. "I'm fine. It isn't as bad as it looks."

"Oh, sorry you got hurt." Apparently satisfied, Steve climbed into bed as Mr. Sylvester left.

Levi couldn't dismiss the bruises so easily. He tossed for what seemed hours after Trevor and Steve's snoring contest began. Now he wasn't just facing the possibility of spending the summer on some strange mythical island.

Now he had to worry about what else was here.

Because what "creature" on this island could do that much damage to two grown men?

Chapter 18

Fire!

The next day's camping trip started out much better than Levi expected. Though only the second time Levi had camped on the north side of the castle, nothing bad had happened the first time. He and his roommates had gotten as good as Sara at pitching their tent. Plus, they got to fish for their supper in the river they always canoed in. Levi was actually pretty good at fishing.

They cooked their fish over the campfire—Levi had caught seven—and ate beneath the stars. Afterward, he sat around the fire with his friends and toasted marshmallows. This was how summer camp should be. Friends, campfire, s'mores, no weird ears . . .

Levi and the others talked and joked until Mr. and Mrs. Austin told them to get some sleep. Hours later, a blast of wind shook Levi's tent, startling him awake. He sat up and sniffed the air. Something was wrong. There was way too much smoke in the air. Surely the adults had put out the campfire. He slipped from his tent despite Mr. Austin's warning about staying inside after dark.

Fire snaked toward the tents from some nearby bushes.

"Fire!" he yelled then ran to grab the water bucket they always kept close in case the campfire got out of control. He snatched the nearly-full bucket, trotted to the fire, and dumped it on the flames nearest the tents. Sara, Monica, Lizzie, and Ashley piled out, but he was too busy to pay much attention.

Mr. Austin ran over, stripped off his jacket, and smacked at the fire. "You okay?" he called to Levi.

"Yeah." Levi sprinted to the river, scooped a bucketful, and raced for camp.

Miss Althea, barreling toward camp from a side path, nearly crashed into him. "What's going on?"

"Fire." He wheezed the word and kept on running.

After a moment, Miss Althea ran alongside him, snagged the bucket, and took off ahead. He staggered after her, clutching his side.

By the time he got back to the tents, the fire was out. Kids clumped together in shocked silence. Mrs. Austin and Miss Althea walked among them checking for injuries and calming fears.

Mr. Austin stalked over to Levi and hissed near his ear, "You see anyone?"

Levi twisted around to see the man's face. "*Anyone?* You think somebody did this on purpose?"

Mr. Austin lifted thick eyebrows and gave the charred path a meaningful stare. Levi saw what he meant: the fire had burned in a straight line—unnaturally straight—from a clump of bushes that showed no signs of charring. Someone had definitely started the fire. In a direct path to the tents.

"Who would do such a thing?" Visions of Hunter's evil face crept into his mind, but he shook it out. No way would a kid do something like this.

"I told you, boy," Mr. Austin said in a low rumble. "The spirit world is more real here than in your world."

In your world? Did that mean what Levi thought it meant?

Before he could ask, the man barked out his own questions. "Well? Did you see anyone? Or anything strange at all?"

"No. The wind woke me, and I thought the air smelled wrong . . . too smoky for our campfire. Then I came out here and saw the fire." Levi shrugged. "Don't know how it started."

Mr. Austin narrowed his eyes. "No wind now." He peered toward the bushes. "Be back later." Loosening the sheath on his belt, he stomped into the underbrush.

Mrs. Austin and Miss Althea finally got the kids settled in their tents, Levi included, but he didn't sleep. He sat at his tent flap watching the women watch the trees by the light of the campfire they'd rekindled. Long after his tent mates' snores filled the cramped space, Levi sat. He couldn't sleep until Mr. Austin returned.

He watched Mrs. Austin wring her hands as the night passed with no sign of her husband. Sometimes, Miss Althea offered soothing murmurs and pats on the arm. Still, nothing changed.

As the sky darkened before dawn, dread hollowed out Levi's gut. Mr. Dominic and Mr. Sylvester together had gotten beaten up by a creature loose on this island. Mr. Austin was alone—and much smaller. What would he look like when he came back?

If he came back.

Tired but relieved, Levi slogged along the trail to the castle behind Mr. Austin. Levi had never been so happy to see the crotchety Literature teacher as when Mr. Austin returned to camp unhurt a few minutes after sunrise. The man hadn't said a word about where he'd been or what he'd found. He'd simply shaken his head at his wife's unspoken question and hurried the kids into taking down camp with the promise of breakfast at the castle.

Now Levi trudged along, his back weighed down with gear, his brain cloudy from lack of sleep, and his stomach grumbling with hunger.

His ears perked up when Mrs. Austin murmured to her husband, "Was it him?"

"Had to be. I saw his tracks." Mr. Austin's voice was husky. "At least I think it was his tracks. Depends on the shape he took, but we've trailed this track from him before." He scrubbed both hands through his hair. "And then there's the fire. You know how he likes fire."

The shape he took? One glimpse of Mrs. Austin's pale face and trembling mouth raised the hair on Levi's neck. What was this creature that liked setting things on fire?

"Why do you think he did it?" She lowered her voice. "Do you think he knew she was in that tent?"

"I don't know." Mr. Austin took his wife's stubby hand. "All we can do is report it. Tobias and Sophia will know what to do."

Mrs. Austin nodded. "I pray they do."

Swallowing the fear clogging his throat, Levi prayed the same.

Chapter 19

Friends

All through breakfast, Levi thought about the night before. His head ached. He wished he could talk to Trevor about what he'd seen, but he didn't dare. Too many people might overhear.

Levi looked at the staff table. The Austins and Miss Althea were still absent, as were the Dominics. Others were missing, too, but that wasn't unusual since the campers generally stayed out until late afternoon on Saturday. He wondered what the Dominics thought about the fire. Would they know what to do?

A new person settled into the end seat of the staff table. His tired eyes drifted to her. Levi sat up straighter and shook his head to clear it. Was that Sara's mom? She looked just like the super-tall woman he'd seen with her the first day. What was she doing at camp? And why was she at the staff table instead of with Sara?

Frowning, he leaned around Tommy and tapped Sara on the shoulder. When she turned, he pointed toward the staff table. "Isn't that your mom?"

Her eyes tracked his finger. A wrinkle formed between her brows. "No, I don't see her."

He pointed again. "There on the end. Isn't that the woman who brought you to camp?"

Sara stood up to see better, and the line between her brows erased. "Oh." She laughed lightly. "No, that's not my mom. That's Miss Nydia. You know, the Sylvesters' daughter. Our hall chaperone."

Now Levi's brow scrunched. "Why did she bring you to camp?"

"She didn't. She just stuck close to me since my parents couldn't." Her face flushed. "So I wouldn't be alone."

That really cleared things up. "Well, if she works here, why haven't I seen her at meals?"

"She's kind of shy, eats in her room or in the kitchen a lot." Sara peered at the young woman. "I'm surprised she's here now."

At that moment, Miss Nydia lifted her eyes from her plate and spotted Sara. Her eyes filled with tears and she flashed Sara a smile Levi thought was ridiculously sappy.

Sara waved at her.

With his roommates in the courtyard playing volleyball, Levi spent the rest of Saturday morning in bed. He had no energy. Telling Trevor what he'd seen the night before would have to wait until he'd had a nap.

Later, he startled awake to a disturbing close-up of Trevor's sweaty face.

"Aaahhh!" He pressed a hand to his heart. "What're you trying to do, Trevor, give me nightmares?"

Trevor snickered. "Sorry, just thought you might want to get up for lunch."

After lunch, Levi joined the others in the great hall to play games. Tommy and Steve took turns beating each other at pool. Ashley was the millionaire tycoon at Life, and Trevor beat them all at Clue. Monica was in the middle of skunking Sara, Lizzie, and Levi at Scrabble when Sara asked if everyone had chosen their events for the Olympics.

Levi groaned. Steve echoed him. No one else spoke.

Sara said, "Come on, guys, it'll be fun. Just pick something you like."

"That's easy for you to say." Levi shuffled his tiles around. "You're the best archer in the whole camp, and you're good at fencing. You canoe great and probably everything else too."

"All of y'all are better at every single solitary thing than me," Lizzie said from her seat next to his. "I'm hopeless."

"I have the same problem," Monica said, "though Tommy and Trevor are both athletic. They'll do well at any event."

Both boys twisted their pool sticks in silence.

"Doesn't matter which ones I do," Levi said, knowing he sounded like a pathetic loser. "I don't have a chance."

Steve grunted his agreement.

Monica fingered a letter tile. "I have to be honest with you. The thought of competing before an audience makes me panic."

Sara patted her arm.

As Levi studied Monica's vulnerable expression, he realized she hadn't used any six-syllable words lately. Maybe she'd acted so snooty earlier in the summer because she was unsure of herself. Maybe her snootiness was like Trevor's squeaking—it only came out when she was scared or uncomfortable.

Monica put down *z-o-o-p-h-y-t* on the *e* in *ear* he'd just played. With her triple word score and the fact that she'd used all her letters, she earned one hundred and sixteen points. Double his current total. Okay, so maybe she really was a know-it-all.

"All I know is we'd better sign up soon or we'll get stuck with what's left," a white-faced Ashley said.

Levi looked at her; he'd never heard her say so many words at one time.

She had a good point though. He imagined getting his nose smashed flat in a boxing match against Martin or his head stuck in Greg's hammerlock hold. He shuddered.

"We should all sign up for the same three events, so we can practice together. Those of us who do better at certain events can help the others." Sara tucked her bottom lip between her teeth.

Levi figured the self-conscious look was Sara trying not to brag about her abilities, though she had plenty to brag about. Still, there was something to her idea. "You realize we'd probably wind up competing against each other," he said slowly.

"True." Trevor tapped his chin. "With eight of us, we should fill most of the spaces."

The others considered the idea in silence.

Steve shrugged. "I'd rather be beat in every event by you guys than by Hunter and his thugs. At least I'd know you weren't trying to kill me."

"Good point, honey." Lizzie touched Steve's arm. He turned a brighter pink than her nail polish.

Levi pushed back from the game table. "Let's do it."

They hurried to the dining hall. After some debate, they signed up for archery, fencing, and canoeing. Levi wasn't too happy with their choices,

The Trojan Horse Traitor

but Sara promised to help with all three. Trevor's fencing was pretty good, and Tommy was great at archery. Lizzie had turned out to be decent at canoeing. Levi would've preferred foot racing over anything else, but Steve looked horrified at the mere thought of huffing around a track. Not even Trevor wanted to face Greg or Martin in a boxing match.

"We'll start practicing tomorrow afternoon," Sara told them, both hands on her hips as if to prevent arguments.

Nobody said anything, but Levi complained plenty in his head.

Levi tossed and rolled in his bed that night. Why had he slept all morning? Now he couldn't make his brain quit spinning. After an hour, he gave up, crawled from bed, and stuffed shoes on his feet. He'd go back to the tower rooftop for a while. Maybe he'd get sleepy in an hour or so. Snagging his pillow, he sneaked toward the door when a low whisper about made him leap to the ceiling.

"Where ya going?" Trevor clambered down the short steps by his bed.

"To the tower." Levi glanced at the still-sleeping Tommy and Steve.

"Can I come?" Trevor pulled on tennis shoes and grabbed his pillow.

"Guess so."

They tiptoed from the room, Trevor just remembering to snag his flashlight. They left the light off until they entered the dark stairwell, then Trevor clicked it on. Levi threw frequent glances behind him at the shadowy steps. He was glad Trevor brought a light. Even with it, Levi's palms left sweat smears on the rail. Would they get in trouble if someone caught them out of bed? Surely not. It's not like they were leaving the castle.

Once on the roof, they settled back on their pillows to stargaze. A few wispy clouds marred the night sky, but the beauty still struck Levi. He lay motionless, inhaling the breeze that smelled faintly of rich earth, flowers, and grass. The absence of the lake smell reminded him of all he hadn't told Trevor.

After rattling on for ten minutes about the fire, Mr. Austin's suspicions, and the sudden appearance of Miss Nydia Sylvester, Levi waited for Trevor's reaction.

"Bizarre" was all he said. Then, "So this really is . . . like . . . some other world?" Trevor's face was pale in the moonlight.

Levi gave a slow nod. "Sounds like it."

"Who's the girl the Austins think somebody's out to get?"

Levi shivered, though it wasn't cold out. "I don't know."

"Well,"—Trevor propped up on one elbow facing Levi—"whose tent was the fire aimed at? You said it went in a straight line. The line would've headed for the target, right?"

Levi closed his eyes to picture the scene. The fire had raced directly for one particular tent, but whose? He remembered running for the water bucket then dashing to the fire. And out of the corner of his eye, he'd seen four girls exit a tent.

His eyes popped open. "It was the girls' tent."

Trevor's forehead wrinkled. "Which girls?"

"*The* girls." Levi made himself not yell. "Sara, Monica, Ashley, Lizzie—the girls." He paused, frowning. "But why? Who'd want to hurt them?"

Trevor's mouth, which had fallen open, now closed into a hard line. "Sounds like the Austins think it was just one of them, but which one?"

Levi stared at a planet pulsing in the distant sky. "Monica's folks are missionaries where Christianity's against the law. Maybe someone came after her to get at them?"

"Maybe. Seems like they'd go after the parents there, though. But I guess she's an easier target here by herself."

"Not if I can help it," Levi said with more bravado than he felt.

Trevor nodded. "It may not be her. What about Ashley? Where's she from again?"

"Sara said Ashley's parents are farmers in Missouri, so I doubt she's the target." Levi flopped back on his pillow.

"I don't know. She's so quiet it's hard to guess what's going on with her."

"Yeah." Levi tapped a finger against his temple. *Think, Levi.* "Now, Lizzie . . . her mom's a U.S. Senator from Louisiana or someplace like that. Politicians always have people after them."

"What about her dad? What's he do?"

"I think she said he's a lawyer." Levi lowered his voice. "But I think he left them when she was little. I doubt he has anything to do with it."

Trevor grunted. "What about Sara?"

Levi thought back to the few times he and Sara had talked about their families. She'd never told him much about her folks. "I think she's from somewhere near Superior, and I know she's homeschooled. I get the idea she lives with both parents, but she doesn't have any brothers or sisters." He shrugged. "That's all I know."

"Interesting," Trevor said in a serious tone.

"Interesting?" Levi laughed. "What are you, Sherlock Holmes?"

"Well, it *is* interesting." Trevor's voice rang with irritation. "Any of the girls could be somebody's target."

Levi sobered as he remembered what the Austins said about the creature shifting shapes. Humans couldn't do that. "Or *something's* target."

Chapter 20

Answers

The next morning, Levi and Trevor had a terrible time waking up. They missed breakfast and yawned their way through the chapel service. Trevor decided to rest awhile that afternoon, but Levi knew he had to stop napping or he'd never get back on a normal sleep schedule. Besides, he had promised his mom he'd call even though his family was at his grandparents' house for the week.

Yet when he called, nobody answered. He left a message on the answering machine and stomped back to the castle, ranting to himself. "Made me waste an hour hiking down to the telephone just to talk to a stupid machine."

To make matters worse, Hunter had been in line behind him for the phone. When Levi hung up after mere seconds, Hunter smirked. "Nobody loves poor little Levi."

Hunter's friend Suzanne—blonde, bone-thin, and horrible—cracked up.

Levi's face burned at the memory. "Jerk." He stomped up the final hill, eyes on his hiking boots. "They're both jerks." He didn't bother looking around even when they arrived at the castle. Who cared whether the cliff made an appearance or not?

When he reached the entryway, still stomping and grumbling, someone's hand landed on his shoulder. *Hunter!* He glared at the hand, ready to smack it away. Instead, he saw a man's work-roughened fingers. He looked up at Mr. Dominic's weathered face.

"Hello, Levi." If he'd noticed Levi's initial urge to slap his hand away, Mr. Dominic didn't show it. "I believe we have an appointment to make up. Is this a good time for you?"

Levi nodded. So the director hadn't forgotten him after all.

He followed Mr. Dominic to his office. When Levi stepped inside, his mood lightened.

Bookcases crammed with old leather volumes filled every inch of wall space. Levi's eyes flitted hungrily from spine to spine. At home he devoured books, something he didn't get to do at camp.

Mr. Dominic smiled. "A fellow book lover, I see. You must seek out the castle library on the other end of this floor. I think you'd enjoy it."

Levi was too busy gawking at the room to answer. To his right sat a huge antique desk. Directly behind it, sandwiched between another pair of bookcases, hung two large maps—one a world map and the other of a place he didn't recognize. Tiny green pinheads stuck in various spots on the world map, while red ones marked places on the other map.

In the center of the room stood a massive unlit fireplace, dividing the two halves. Beyond it, Levi glimpsed another desk, this one also framed by bookcases. Flower-filled vases rested on stands in the corners and a large portrait of a golden-haired baby hung on the wall behind the desk. Must be Mrs. Dominic's side.

Mr. Dominic strolled to his desk, offered Levi one of the matching wingback chairs across from it, and sank into his office chair.

"I hope you like lemonade. I've asked Mrs. Forest to bring us a tray." The director smiled at Levi's nod. "She should be here momentarily. We can address your questions after that."

Levi twisted his hands in his lap, trying not to stare at the strange map above Mr. Dominic's head.

Mr. Dominic watched his silent struggle. "Do you like my world maps?"

Levi blinked. World maps . . . plural?

A sharp knock sounded at the door. Mr. Dominic called, "Come in," and Mrs. Forest bustled into the room carrying a tray almost bigger than she was. Levi recognized the tiny woman he'd seen his first day of camp, the one that reminded him of a dragonfly. Puffing as if winded, she moved to Mr. Dominic's desk and set down the tray of lemonade and cookies. At the director's quiet word of thanks, she left, closing the door behind her.

When both were settled with a drink and a napkin full of cookies, Mr. Dominic said, "Well, what shall we discuss first?"

Levi sat silent, his mouth full of peanut butter cookie. Which of the many questions swirling around his brain should he ask first? He swallowed, choked on a crumb, swigged some tart lemonade—which made his eyes water—and gasped. "What is that a map of?" He pointed at the strange map.

What made him ask that question first?

"Ah." The director glanced at the map. "An excellent question . . . the answer to which, I think, will answer many of your other questions." He quirked his lips as if in apology. "And raise many more, I'm afraid." He studied Levi through serious eyes. "Are you sure you want to know? The answers may very well change the way you look at life."

Did he want to know? The truth had to be better than his and Trevor's wild guesses—Area 51 part two, Atlantis risen again, an old KGB training site. All ridiculous. "Yes, sir, I want the truth."

"Very well. That is Terracaelum."

Levi's brow wrinkled. "Never heard of it."

"No? Never? Break it down. You know your Latin. Many names find their roots in that ancient language. What does it mean?"

"Terra. Earth or land." Levi's gaze drifted toward the open window. "Caelum. Heaven or sky." He hesitated. "Earth Heaven? Land Sky? That doesn't make sense." His eyes returned to the director's.

Mr. Dominic traced one finger along the edge of his desk as if he had all day for Levi to figure it out.

Levi wondered if the director had a dunce cap in Levi's size. He blew out a breath. "Okay, come on. Mix it up a little. Heaven land? Skyland?"

The director beamed at him.

Levi pumped his fist in the air. "Yes, I got it." Confusion squashed his joy. "That doesn't make sense." He pulled at his bottom lip. "You mean like, land *of* the sky? Land *in* the sky?" He sagged against his chair. In his mind he pictured the earth end in sky, the cliff drop away to the lake below, the castle suddenly appear in the void. "Do you mean to tell me," he said slowly, "that this castle is in the sky? Literally? We're, like, on some land suspended in thin air? Above the lake?"

By the time he finished, his voice was squeaking like Trevor's and his head was pounding. What made it worse was the look on Mr. Dominic's face—like a proud papa watching his child take his first steps. "Wonderful! You figured it out even faster than I did when I was your age."

"But—"

"You did suspect, didn't you? That's part of what you wanted to discuss with me, am I right?"

Levi's mouth opened, closed, opened. "Well, yeah, but nobody else seems to notice the weird stuff." Even Trevor had never seen the ears Levi described. If they'd gone much longer without proof, Trevor probably would've given up on Levi's Castle Island Theory too. But now Mr. Dominic was telling him it was all true?

Mr. Dominic waited in silence, probably giving him time to process it all.

Levi frowned as everything sank in. How dare Mr. Dominic bring Levi and a bunch of other kids to some alternate reality hanging in thin air? What if the whole place fell and dropped them in the lake? What if it floated away or something? Finally, he snapped, "I have some questions."

Mr. Dominic steepled his fingers and waited.

"How come everybody in the world doesn't know about this place?" Levi pointed at the map of the world—the *real* world.

"Because one may enter only if invited by the rulers of this land." Mr. Dominic watched him with raised brows.

"You mean like by a king and queen?" Levi raised both palms. "Wait." No way. "You mean you . . . and Mrs. Dominic?"

Mr. Dominic gave a slight bow. "Prince and princess, actually."

Levi took another sip of lemonade and swished it around his mouth. Maybe a sugar rush would clear his brain. Prince and princess? Rulers? Of a separate world from the universe God created in six days?

Levi sat up straight and slapped his glass on the desk, narrowing his eyes at the would-be prince. "Are you trying to make me believe I'm in some world outside of God's control? Someplace under some other ruler? Because I'm not buying it. God's in charge of all things—my dad's taught me that since I was a baby. And the Bible says it too." Panic blurred the edges of his vision.

When a broad smile creased Mr. Dominic's face, Levi blinked. Maybe the old man really was crazy.

"You're absolutely right, son. The entire universe belongs to the God of the Bible, and Terracaelum is but one small part of it."

Levi's ears heated as he realized he'd falsely accused Mr. Dominic. And that the man was thrilled with him for it. "But . . . but, why? What's the point in this place?"

Mr. Dominic leaned forward in his seat and perched his chin on his fingers. "You know God created all things, you've already said that. You're aware our first parents sinned, and the consequences of that sin wreaked havoc on all parts of creation, even the smallest."

Levi thought of how little kids told lies from the time they could speak, of the pollution in the air he breathed, of the cancer that had attacked his Aunt Marcy's cells, eventually killing her and leaving his cousins motherless. He nodded.

Mr. Dominic smiled sadly. "You've heard myths and legends all your life, have you not?"

Levi blinked at the shift in subject. "Sure."

"Many of the creatures in those stories are based on real beings."

Something clicked in Levi's brain. "You mean like elves and dwarves and all that?" A vision of Mr. Drake's pointy ears flashed across his mind's eye. "I was right." He sat in stunned silence. "There really are mythical creatures here." He shivered as his own words sank in. "Right here in this very castle." He'd actually been rubbing shoulders with non-humans all summer.

"Well, yes . . ." Mr. Dominic's chin puckered. "Though you can hardly call them mythical when they exist in reality."

Levi refused to be distracted with logical arguments. "But why are they here? Why don't they live in the world?" He pointed at the first map. "With us, I mean?"

The director sighed. "Levi, you know what humans are like. Think of the amazing creatures you've read about, many of whom have what we'd call magical abilities or are simply bizarre or helpless. How long would they last there?" He turned his eyes on the map of Earth.

Thinking of child abuse, toxic waste dumps, and extinct animal species, Levi nodded. Of course people would exploit fairies and dragons. They'd want to steal their abilities. And water horses or centaurs—what zoo wouldn't kill to capture them?

"So why are you here?" He looked into the man's green eyes, so bright and sometimes so strange. "You are human, aren't you? You and your wife?"

"Yes, we're quite human." Mr. Dominic held out a palm as proof. "You remember another part of the Great Sovereign's creation mandate? Mankind was set as overseers of the earth and its inhabitants."

Levi nodded.

"So, too, the land and inhabitants of Terracaelum must always be ruled by humans—one man and one woman."

"That's you and Mrs. Dominic? You really are the rulers here?" Levi heard the awe in his own voice. "Should I call you Your Majesty or something?"

The man chuckled. "Mr. Dominic will do just fine." His face grew serious. "Really, young man, I meant it when I said my wife and I are more prince and princess of Terracaelum. We are certainly not king and queen. God is the only Emperor, and Jesus is the only King."

"But," Levi started, not sure how to phrase his question without sounding rude, "don't you sin too? I mean, all humans sin, so how can humans rule Terracaelum without taking advantage of its creatures?"

Mr. Dominic nodded. "Mrs. Dominic and I are sinners saved by grace through faith in King Jesus. And yes, sinful more often than we'd like. That's why God has provided training and safeguards for us."

"Oh." *O-kay.* "And that means . . . ?"

"The spirit world is more—shall we say—*physical* here than in the human world."

Levi's brow furrowed. Wasn't that what Mr. Austin said?

The director offered a sympathetic smile. "I know it's confusing, but bear with me, and I think you'll understand." At Levi's nod, Mr. Dominic went on. "Both good and evil in the spirit realm are more actual here, more *felt*, you might say. And so the Spirit sent to comfort and guide us is also more tangible here." He tapped himself on the chest. "He still lives in us, but He actually meets us sometimes. He speaks with us."

"Uh huh, and what does he say?"

"He gives me wise counsel, convicts me when I sin, admonishes me to obey."

Levi turned his head, giving the director a sidelong stare. "What does he look like?"

The director shook his head. "I don't know. He usually appears as a gentle breeze brushing my cheek or a soft whisper in my ear." His voice dropped. "Sometimes as a gale screaming in my face, but that's only when I'm particularly foolish and disobedient."

Levi frowned. "Is that why the big storm forced us to the castle when we first got here? Because you did something wrong?"

Mr. Dominic shook his head. "No. Sometimes a storm is simply a storm. Other times, someone . . . else . . . causes them. I've learned to tell when it's something beyond the natural."

Levi popped to his feet. He needed to move . . . to think. He paced back and forth, paused at the open window, strode behind Mr. Dominic's chair, and finally stopped before the map of Terracaelum.

Studying the jagged green oval of Terracaelum, he spotted a small castle symbol on the southern tip. Farther north he saw symbols for trees, a river, more trees, and what looked like hills or mountains, then more trees and mountains at the northern tip. A pale gray edged Terracaelum on the south, while the rest of the green oval ended abruptly in blue. "Is Terracaelum a peninsula off of Castle Island?"

"Not really. It's an island with the castle acting as a bridge between lands. The inhabitants of both places are prohibited from accessing the other without permission from my wife or me."

"So we can't get into the castle without you or your wife letting us in." Levi thought of the time he'd returned from using the phone and found no castle. Of Mrs. Dominic's flushed face when she—and it—appeared. A sudden, terrifying thought drew his eyes to Mr. Dominic. "Can we get out without you?"

"Certainly."

Relief sagged Levi's shoulders.

Mr. Dominic joined Levi at the map and placed his finger on the castle symbol. "You're free to return to Castle Island whenever you wish; however, you may not reenter the castle without invitation."

Levi's gaze drifted to the red pins marching from the northern tip of Terracaelum to the castle. Something about those pins prickled the base of his spine. "What do the red pins mark?"

His expression grim, Mr. Dominic faced Levi. "Places we know Deceptor has appeared in the last six months."

"Deceptor?" That was the name Albert let slip. An evil name. "That means . . . deceiver or liar, right?"

"Correct."

Levi's breathing quickened. "And he's bad, right?"

"Very."

"You mean he's Satan?" His pulse raced. "Like the devil himself?"

"Not the Prince of Darkness himself, no, but an agent of his."

"An agent of Satan is on the loose in Terracaelum?" Levi thought of the strange fire he'd fought the other night. "What's he look like?" He dreaded the answer.

"That's part of the trouble." Mr. Dominic sighed. "He's a shape-shifter. He takes different forms depending on what suits his needs."

Did that mean he'd been close to Deceptor, with only a thin tent wall between them? "Wait," Levi said as an even more horrifying thought occurred to him, "he's the only evil being here, right? I mean, you and the rest of Terracaelum's . . . uh, inhabitants are good?"

The lines on Mr. Dominic's face deepened. "Unfortunately, as in the world you know, many are happy to align themselves with evil."

"Why can't you just wipe out Deceptor and be done with it?"

Mr. Dominic drew in a slow breath. "Imagine a great chess game with Deceptor as the black king, and I as the white. Each of us has an army fighting for our side—battling over Terracaelum. Deceptor is under orders from his master to gain control of this land and its citizens. I am under orders to protect and govern it for God's glory."

"But who's on Deceptor's side?" Levi couldn't imagine any of the staff helping him.

"Think again of the classical myths you've read. Think of the creatures that haunted your dreams afterward, the ones that turned them into nightmares."

Images of ogres and trolls, hags and werewolves, witches and monsters filled Levi's mind. "Those creatures are here?" He couldn't suppress a shudder.

Mr. Dominic nodded, mouth tight.

"Let me get this straight." Levi folded his arms across his chest, half in fear and half in growing anger. "An evil sorcerer with an army of monsters is beating a path to this castle?"

Again the director nodded.

"Then why in the world did you bring a bunch of kids here?"

Mr. Dominic rested calming hands on Levi's shoulders. "There's some consolation for us, son. Deceptor can't enter this castle without invitation. It's off-limits to him. He can come to the door, but not inside, not unless my wife or I invite him."

"He's prowling around outside trying to get in?" Levi's voice shrilled. "Can't you ask for a legion of angels to fight him?"

"Certainly Terracaelum has an assigned angelic protector who sometimes aids us. He—"

At a loud rap on the door, Mr. Dominic's gaze flicked towards the sound. His hands dropped from Levi's shoulders.

The banging grew louder, and Levi's hands tightened into fists. What if it was Deceptor?

Chapter 21

Beyond Fear

"Come in," Mr. Dominic called.

Levi's eyes bulged. Shouldn't the director at least ask who—or what—was there before inviting it to enter?

The door burst open, and Mr. Sylvester rushed inside. He stopped short, mouth ajar, at the sight of Levi. "Er, sorry to interrupt, sir." He dipped his head.

Mr. Dominic waved away the apology. "May I help you with something?"

"I need you to come now. It's important." His eyes widened, flitted to Levi, returned to the director.

With a nod, Mr. Dominic marched around the desk, tugging Levi along with him. "I do apologize, Levi, but I'm afraid I must cut our conversation short." While his tone was nothing but pleasant, he practically shoved Levi into the corridor. "We'll chat again another time."

Wait! Levi spread his hands. "But sir, if I could—"

"Goodbye, now."

"Okay, yeah. Bye." Levi moved a few steps along the corridor, tossing back a glance as the two men hurried to the stairwell and started down.

Deflated and disturbed, Levi started up the opposite steps. His thoughts whirled tighter than the spiral staircase. For a second, he thought he might puke. It was one thing to imagine—or even suspect—he was in another world populated by mysterious and magical creatures. It was altogether another to have that suspicion confirmed by an adult.

He should find Trevor and tell him what he had found out, but somehow he couldn't bring himself to talk about it just yet. Instead he climbed the tower steps and stumbled out onto the roof, glad for the breeze that soothed the whirlwind in his brain.

Levi strode across the tower and halted at the short stone wall that came only to his waist in the middle but extended above his head on either side. Hands braced against the rough stones, he leaned forward, fighting the dizziness he'd always felt in high places. When he climbed Marblehead Lighthouse last summer, he barely made it to the top. Then he'd dug in, refusing to move one step to enjoy the view. He had never even looked up from the floor at his feet.

Now Levi shoved aside the temptation to fear. He couldn't be a coward over nothing when real danger lurked outside these castle walls—a danger threatening one of his friends. Because although the director hadn't said as much, he knew Deceptor was after one person in particular—Ashley, Sara, Monica, or Lizzie. Levi just didn't know which one.

Peering down into the courtyard, he glimpsed several campers outfitted in fencing gear, all but one paired off and sparring. A glance at his watch told him the group's identity, even though they all wore protective helmets. He was supposed to meet his friends at four o'clock for practice. Now one of them was without a partner.

He squinted at the lone person on the side. Was it the girl threatened by Deceptor? His gut clenched at the thought. Ever since he was little and slapped his baby sister Abby for knocking down his block tower, his dad had taught him to protect girls. Dad always said boys who hurt girls were the worst sort of bullies because God intended men to protect women. Although Levi couldn't claim never to have hit Abby after that, he'd always been uncomfortably aware that he shouldn't. And he would never let anyone else hurt her.

A surge of adrenaline coursed through his veins now as he thought of the threat to one of his female friends. He would do his best to keep her from harm—even though the mere thought of a real-live, shape-shifting demon scared him stiff.

At that moment, something silver shot into the air above his friends. One of them whipped off her helmet, golden hair bright in the sunlight as she grinned up at the buffered blade she'd just knocked from her opponent's hands. Sara. Trevor plucked off his helmet, then reached over and shook Sara's hand. Levi laughed. Okay, so maybe at least one of the girls was more fit to do the protecting than to need it.

But he'd stick close just in case.

"We need to tell the others about this," Trevor whispered to Levi as they walked to Logic class later that week. Levi had told Trevor all he'd learned from the director, and ever since, they kept coming back to the same argument: Trevor wanted to tell the others, Levi didn't.

"No." Levi shook his head. "There's no point in worrying them when the bad guy's outside the castle." How could the girl in danger enjoy her summer in the safety of the castle if she was worrying all the time about what was going on out there?

Trevor's eyebrows drew together in a scowl. "If Mr. Dominic disappears for another week, something might happen. She should at least be on guard."

Levi folded his arms across his chest. "So we keep a close eye out. We're not telling."

They kept up their glaring contest until the bell rang, at which point Trevor stormed into class and flopped down at his desk. Levi strolled inside and sat calmly in his own seat. Trevor could be so childish.

"Good morning, class." The unexpected voice drew Levi's eyes to the teacher's desk. There stood Dr. Baldwin, who ran the infirmary and taught Levi's least favorite class, Mathematics. "Mr. Dominic was called away from the castle today," he announced, "so I'll be filling in until he returns."

Levi exchanged a worried glance with Trevor, who no longer looked like he wanted to throttle Levi. Who had time for anger when something might be seriously wrong with the director?

"Choose a partner and a chess set." Dr. Baldwin swept a stubby hand toward a tableful of boxes.

Levi's eyebrows shot up. Chess? In Logic class?

"You'll find that playing chess helps you think strategically," Dr. Baldwin said as the campers paired off. "You have to have sharp skills in logic to win against a chess master." He stumped forward and lifted an old wooden chess board. "If you can learn to think, you can learn to fight any battle."

Levi and Trevor placed chairs on either end of a desk and set out the pieces, as did the rest of the campers. With twenty-five kids in the class, Dr. Baldwin played against Ashley, the odd one out. Her freckles looked darker than ever against her ashen face. Levi offered her a reassuring smile, which she attempted to return.

Levi loved chess. He'd played his dad since he was five. He'd even gotten to the point earlier this year where he could put his dad in checkmate. It took him no time to beat Trevor, who'd only played a few times in his life.

After their game, he and Trevor watched Dr. Baldwin and Ashley, who was so nervous she kept dropping pieces. The teacher issued instructions every so often, things like "Watch out for my knight, girl!" or "Protect your queen!" or "Don't move there!" Sweat shone on Ashley's upper lip by the time he took mercy and finished her off.

"All right, Prince, you won your match. Now you play me." Dr. Baldwin gestured for Trevor to play Ashley and instructed the rest of the class to pair off the same way as they finished their games.

Levi's palms dampened as Dr. Baldwin set up his pieces. Somehow he suspected the doctor would be harder to beat than Trevor. A short time later, his suspicions were more than confirmed. He struggled to anticipate the doctor's moves while planning his own strategy, barely keeping out of check. It didn't help that his eyes continually drifted from his opponent's hairy knuckles to his broad, swarthy face. What sort of creature was Dr. Baldwin? A dwarf probably, given his short stature and barrel chest. But then maybe he was just an unusually short, hairy human. Mr. Dominic hadn't exactly been specific when Levi asked about mythical creatures in the castle.

Dr. Baldwin's beady black eyes flicked to Levi's, pulling his mind back to the game just in time to hear, "Checkmate."

The bell rang.

Levi's face burned as he put away his pieces. He'd played awful.

Dr. Baldwin slapped him on the back. "Well played, boy. You had me hopping a time or two."

Levi checked the doctor's face. He had to be joking.

"I'm serious. You have the makings of a great player." Dr. Baldwin tutted. "Much better than your skills as a mathematician."

Levi bit back a groan.

The doctor flashed a crooked smile almost hidden behind his thick salt-and-pepper mustache. "I tell you what, next time you decide to skulk around the infirmary, I'll challenge you to a game. Give you something better to do with your free time." His right eyebrow lifted in a knowing gesture that made Levi gulp. Had he and Trevor been that obvious?

Neck hot, Levi stammered his thanks, snagged his backpack, and hurried from the room. He'd be happy if he never had to play chess against the doctor again.

With the end of July coming fast, Levi and his friends spent most of their spare time practicing for the Olympic events. And with Deceptor lurking, Levi figured he'd better learn all he could. He might need the training for something more important than games.

Getting in practice on the canoe was the most difficult since the campers weren't allowed outside the castle walls without an adult. Albert accompanied them sometimes, but he didn't have as much free time as before. "Got me a special job from the big boss hisself," he told them in a snotty way that made Levi glad to be rid of him.

The girls convinced their shy hall chaperone, Miss Nydia, to go when Albert couldn't. Levi hadn't quite decided what he thought of the tall, willowy, blonde woman, but the girls clearly adored her. He and Trevor had classified her as an elf, secretly, of course. Levi held to his resolve not to tell the others about Terracaelum. So far, Trevor had kept quiet as well.

One day when Miss Nydia was canoe-sitting them, Steve toppled the boat he shared with Levi. Deciding to dry out before another attempt, Levi plopped onto the grass beside Miss Nydia.

"Good thing the sun's out." Grinning, he squeezed water from his t-shirt.

She didn't look up from her embroidery.

"You're good at that." Levi pointed at the neat stitches. "What's it for?"

"It's Lizzie's costume."

Levi nodded. Lizzie had won the lead part as Helen of Troy in the camp play. She milked the prima donna role every chance she got. "How long's it take to make something like that?"

"Awhile." She angled her body away from him.

Levi shrugged. *Guess she doesn't want to chat.* He turned his attention to the others. Lizzie scolded Trevor for dribbling river water on her favorite shorts. Monica and Ashley paddled in circles while Tommy stood on the bank laughing at them. Levi shook his head. They had this event in the bag, no question.

His eyes drifted to Steve, now paired with Sara, who patiently instructed him on how to position his paddles and how to relax into the water's rocking so he wouldn't tip the canoe.

"I always like being Sara's partner," Levi said, forgetting Miss Nydia didn't want to talk. "She's so smooth. It's almost like we're flying on the water."

"Of course, my Sara's good at everything."

Levi looked at her. *My* Sara? Before he could ask what she'd meant or even get a glimpse of her face, Miss Nydia rose and walked away.

Man, she was an odd one.

But she was right. Sara did seem to be good at everything. She was the best archer, along with Tommy. She'd even managed to teach Levi how to shoot an occasional bullseye. But she still hadn't gotten him that comfortable with fencing. He could hang on to the sword and generally keep from getting stabbed, but unless he was paired with the weakest of the others, he always lost.

He'd fight hard against the boys, but not the girls. His dad's teaching about protecting girls wouldn't let him. Trevor got to where he could beat Sara some of the time, but not Levi. He just couldn't do it, and Sara would shake her head as time after time his sword flew from his grasp.

"You have to get over it, Levi," she'd say. "Girls can be just as good as boys at fencing, and girls can be evil. Believe it or not, a girl's sword can kill you as easily as a boy's."

Chapter 22

The Library

One hot day at the end of July, Levi and his art class pounded nails into the wooden horse they were building for the summer play. Before long, his head pounded in time with his hammer. After an hour of torture, he told Miss Althea he didn't feel good and asked if he could go in for a drink. She peered into his flushed face, felt his hot forehead, and sent him to Dr. Baldwin.

Levi dragged himself to the second floor infirmary and tapped weakly at the door. When the doctor yanked it open, Levi nearly fell into the cool, dim room.

"Ah, my chess player." Dr. Baldwin led Levi to a white-sheeted bed in the corner. "Not feeling so great today, I see." He gave Levi's shoulders a gentle push, and Levi sat. "Guess you won't be up to a game of chess this afternoon. Too bad."

After taking Levi's temperature and giving him a dose of Tylenol, Dr. Baldwin tucked him into bed. Levi dropped instantly to sleep, and when he awoke later it was dark. Peering around at the empty cots, he remembered his pounding head from earlier. He eased to a sitting position. His headache was gone, but his nose felt puffy and his throat burned.

Levi looked around for a sink to get water. He decided the closed door at the far end of the room must lead to Dr. Baldwin's room, but on this end a door stood ajar, a faint light within. He pushed to his feet and shuffled over. *Bingo. A bathroom.* He found a glass and guzzled some water.

Satisfied, Levi returned to bed, sat down, and realized he wasn't sleepy. According to his watch, it was only three in the morning. He had come to the infirmary a couple of hours after lunch, meaning he'd slept more than twelve hours. Despite his sore throat, he grinned. He was, quite possibly, the only one awake in the entire castle.

"Well, what should I do then?" he whispered to himself.

He was on a different floor than usual. If he'd been in his room, he'd have climbed to the tower roof. But he was on the second floor. The staff floor. The Dominics' floor.

The library floor.

He popped up and headed for the corridor. Mr. Dominic had given him permission to visit the library anytime, and he hadn't gotten there yet. Maybe the director hadn't meant the middle of the night, but still . . . What else did Levi have to do?

He snatched up a flashlight but didn't click it on as he crept from the infirmary. Through the hall windows, he saw a full moon pushing through the shredded clouds. Images of howling werewolves crept into his mind. Were there werewolves in Terracaelum?

Levi cast anxious glances around the empty corridor. He knew Mr. Dominic had said nobody could enter the castle without his or his wife's permissions, but what if they'd admitted a werewolf without realizing? Or what if they'd hired a werewolf intentionally, like that professor in *Harry Potter*. Dr. Baldwin was pretty hairy.

He rolled his eyes. *Don't be stupid, Levi. This isn't a book.*

Still, he hurried past the dark staircase, not liking the way his whispery footfalls echoed off the stone steps. By the time he reached the south corridor entryway, sweat dampened his t-shirt. He wrenched open the door and listened. All was silent. He sneaked to a door midway along the hall, opened it, and slipped inside, closing it quietly behind him.

Moonlit floor-to-ceiling windows revealed tall bookcases on every wall. Hanging ladders allowed access to the upper shelves. A huge double-sided fireplace cube sat in the middle of the room, like in the Dominics' office, with a group of plump reading chairs arranged on this side. Beyond the fireplace sat several study tables and more rows of bookshelves.

Levi turned to the shelf beside the door and ran his hand along the smooth leather spines, inhaling the musty aroma of old books. Despite the dust, his breathing calmed, and his throat felt less sore.

"This is one awesome library," he said softly.

As his finger shifted to switch on the flashlight, a snuffling sound came from among the far rows of bookcases. His finger stilled.

"W-who's there?" A werewolf sniffing him out?

The snuffling ceased. *It's probably a mouse, Levi. Chill. Find a book.* His finger again sought the switch.

Faint footsteps trickled from among the stacks. Levi held his breath, ankles quivering. He raised the flashlight in both hands, his mighty weapon for fighting off werewolves in dark libraries.

Yeah, right. I'm toast.

A slight, pale form emerged from the shadows, one with no fangs, no claws, not even any fur. Levi lowered his flashlight, feeling foolish. It was Miss Nydia, a skinny elf lady without so much as a book in hand. Maybe she hadn't noticed his overreaction.

Miss Nydia cleared her throat. "What are you doing here in the middle of the night?"

He could ask her the same question. "I couldn't sleep. Thought I'd look for a book." Hang on, were those tears on her face?

"You shouldn't linger out of bed for long." She stepped past him, reached for the doorknob. "You can't tell who you might meet. Could be dangerous."

"Yes, ma'am." Wow, she was paranoid. Okay, so he'd nearly brained her with a flashlight.

With one of her sad smiles, she slipped from the room. When the door swung shut, Levi's gaze pulled to the dark stack from which she'd emerged. He had to check it out. Tiptoeing among the stacks, he shone his flashlight up and down each perfectly ordered row. What was the woman doing back here in the pitch dark? Creepy.

Finally, on the bottom shelf of the back row, he spotted a book jutting from the orderly shelf as if it had been stuffed there by someone in a big hurry. Stooping low, he ran his light over the title, *Creatures of the Darkness.*

Was that Miss Nydia's idea of a good bedtime read?

Levi awoke from a heavy sleep with his neck aching and his throat raw. Bright sunlight streamed in the windows. He was curled up in the overstuffed chair he'd chosen the night before, a heavy volume of classical myths at his feet and the flashlight in his lap, the batteries long spent.

"Leviticus Prince!" The sound of his name being called, the sound that must have woken him, propelled Levi from the chair.

As he reached the library door, it burst open. Mr. Dominic and Dr. Baldwin jumped back at the sight of him, then rushed forward and grabbed for him. Levi nearly fell over in his instinctive attempt to fight off their grasping hands, but the agitation in their faces made him go still.

"Where have you been, boy?" Dr. Baldwin's face was the color of some beets Levi's mom had once tried to make him eat.

Levi struggled for a response. "Uh . . . here."

"Levi." Mr. Dominic's face was colorless, in sharp contrast to his lime-green Hawaiian shirt. "We've been scouring the castle for an hour now." He raised both brows as if waiting for Levi to explain his bad behavior.

Levi stared at him, completely clueless.

The director jabbed his finger under Levi's nose. "We were looking for you. What made you think you could leave the infirmary and wander at will in the middle of the night?"

Oops. "I'm sorry." Levi tried to free his arm from the doctor's vice-grip. He looked at the director. "You said I could visit the library whenever I wanted." He indicated the dropped book beside his chair and the flashlight still rolling across the floor. "I couldn't sleep, so I came to find something to read."

The doctor's face went from red to purple. Levi cringed. He was about to get yelled at.

Thankfully, the director shook his head at Dr. Baldwin. "Levi," he said in a soft tone that didn't quite hide his anger, "you know danger lurks, do you not? We talked about that not long ago." His voice rose a notch. "You are more aware of the dangers in Terracaelum than almost any other camper here."

Dr. Baldwin shot the director a sharp look, but Mr. Dominic didn't take his eyes from Levi's. "You should've known better than to sneak off in the night. We're responsible for your safety."

"I'm sorry," Levi said to his bare feet. "I meant to borrow a book and take it back to the infirmary with me, but I must've fallen asleep." He glanced up at the director. "And, sir? I thought the danger was outside the castle, not inside." He searched the man's face. "I thought I'd be safe in here."

Sighing as though weary, Mr. Dominic led Levi to the chair he'd vacated moments before. He gestured for Levi to sit and crossed to a nearby chair then turned to Dr. Baldwin. "Asa, please tell Aubrey and Cadmus we've found him. You may all return to your usual tasks. I'll deliver this young man to the infirmary myself in a short while."

The doctor turned another disapproving glare on Levi, nodded to the director, and swept out, banging the door shut behind him.

"It appears you need more information again." Mr. Dominic's grayish skin and tired eyes dribbled guilt into Levi's stomach. "As you may have noticed, Mr. Sylvester and I have been required to leave the castle several times lately. We've had to deal with some difficulties with Deceptor."

Levi shivered at the name.

Mr. Dominic scrubbed both hands over his face, whiskers crackling in the quiet room, then set his hands in his lap. "I'll spare you the details. It all comes down to this: we suspect a member of our staff may not be as loyal as we'd hoped."

Levi's mind reeled. Was Mr. Dominic saying what he thought?

That there was a spy in the castle?

Chapter 23

A Spy

Levi's throat burned more from fear than sickness. The only reason he hadn't been scared to death in the weeks he'd known about the threat was because he thought they were all safe within the castle grounds. "Who is it?" His fingers knotted together. "Who's the traitor?"

"We don't know. We're on the watch for suspicious activity, but so far . . ." Mr. Dominic closed his eyes a moment. "It's hard for my wife and me to imagine anyone we've trusted all these years betraying us."

Levi nodded. He couldn't imagine it either. Not that he could imagine ruling a bunch of nonhumans either. Maybe they had a different concept of loyalty.

Mr. Dominic drew in a deep breath and straightened his shoulders. "Thankfully, Deceptor is still held by the same law governing the castle's inhabitants: no one may enter without Mrs. Dominic or me admitting them." He gave Levi's knee a quick pat. "That means he can't come in, but until we find out who his spy is, you must not wander around the castle after hours. You must be on guard."

This was it . . . his opportunity to ask the question he and Trevor had gone round and round about. But should he ask? The poor man looked exhausted, and Levi hadn't helped by disappearing this morning. Finally, he said, "Who's he after? I know it's one of the girls—Monica, Lizzie, Sara, or Ashley. But which one? And why?"

Mr. Dominic's mouth formed a small circle. "How did you—" He closed his mouth and shook his head. "Levi, you've heard people say walls have ears." He let out a heavy sigh. "I can't answer your questions right now. Just . . . stick close to your friends. Please."

Levi scanned the room, half-expecting to see eyeballs peering at him from between the books. Of course he saw nothing. Though more questions flooded his mind, the weariness and pain in the director's eyes kept him quiet. Instead, he said, "I'll try," and followed Mr. Dominic back to the infirmary.

Mr. Dominic paused outside the door. "Goodbye, young man. Stay in bed today and recuperate. No more wandering."

"Yes, sir." Levi's hand rested on the doorknob. "Can I ask you something else?"

The director's lips twitched in a half-smile, his eyes brighter. "It certainly seems that you *can*; however, you *may* ask me a question as well."

Though his ears heated, Levi smirked at the director's little joke. "I've been wondering about something your wife said, something about me being like my namesake."

Mr. Dominic inspected Levi's face until Levi thought he'd die of embarrassment. With a nod, the director said, "She's right. At first I wasn't so sure, but now I think you may be very like him."

"How can you say that?" Levi tossed his hands. "I'm named for my Papa Levi. He died when my dad was a kid."

The director smiled. "Your Papa Levi was my best friend. We met here at Camp Classic when we were your age."

Levi spent the rest of the day in the infirmary. In his mind, he went over and over the director's statement that he'd attended camp with Papa Levi, but he couldn't make everything fit together. Mr. Dominic was old, yeah, but he couldn't possibly be that old. Maybe Levi had misunderstood. Or maybe the director had gotten confused. After all, it didn't look like he'd gotten much sleep lately.

Levi finally forced the whole thing from his mind, chalking it up to a misunderstanding. Throughout the day, Dr. Baldwin, who appeared to have forgiven him for sneaking out, gave him cups of tea and chicken noodle soup, and the two spent several hours playing chess. Dr. Baldwin gave him pointer after pointer. He insisted that Levi watch the whole board and think ahead to his opponent's next several moves, all while plotting his own future moves and paying attention to the current move. It made Levi's brain ache.

"Your mind has to be everywhere at once." Dr. Baldwin gave the board several sharp taps with his hairy forefinger. "There's no room for laziness in games of strategy. You'd do well to learn that in a safe game like this one. In others, like fencing, for instance, you can lose your head if you don't stay constantly aware." The doctor eyed him meaningfully.

Levi cringed. Had the doctor noticed how pathetic he was with the sword?

Determined to improve at chess at least, he focused on the game and tried to obey the doctor's instructions. By the middle of the second match (he lost the first), the light faded from the room. Levi glanced toward the window. Dusk was falling.

He peeked over at his opponent, who was studying the board. The dim lighting made his swarthy features appear even darker. The doctor's wild eyebrows formed a black slash, and his thick thatch of gray-streaked hair melded with his wild gray beard, almost covering his odd-shaped ears. Beetle-black eyes darted up and pinned Levi.

Levi drew back, suddenly very aware that this creature could not be human. How had Levi allowed this . . . whatever he was . . . to doctor him? His eyes flew to the doctor's mouth. Thick, flat teeth gnawed his lower lips.

But night was coming soon. What if the full moon grew those teeth into fangs?

Bile burned the back of Levi's throat. He coughed.

Dr. Baldwin's eyes shifted to the window. He clicked on the battery-operated lantern on the nightstand, and the lighter room normalized his features. "Getting dark," he said in a casual tone.

Levi watched his every move, ready to bolt.

"It must be about time for your supper tray to arrive." The doctor touched a cool palm to Levi's brow. Levi managed not to flinch. "I'm afraid I've kept you playing too long. You look pale. Why don't you rest until time to eat?" The doctor gathered the chess pieces.

Levi shifted on his pillow and watched the doctor pack away the game.

"You're a dwarf, right?" *Please say yes, please say you're not a werewolf.* Hold on, what if the stories were wrong? What if dwarves were worse than werewolves? Levi gnawed the inside of his cheek. Why had he asked that question? He should've made a break for the door while he could. Because if the fangs came out now, while Levi was alone and weak, he was done for.

The corners of Dr. Baldwin's eyes crinkled into a smile. "I am. And you're a human, correct?"

Levi nodded, his irrational terror slipping away in a goofy giggle. "Touché, sir."

"Touché, indeed."

After a good supper and a solid night's sleep, Levi was deemed healthy enough to return to his regular activities. In their room, Trevor, who'd supplied the doctor with Levi's clothes for his time in the sickroom, waited for a report. He'd been worried ever since Mr. Sylvester and Mr. Austin had burst into the boys' room the morning before and awakened everyone in their frantic search for Levi.

Levi filled Trevor in, careful to keep his voice low so the others wouldn't overhear. He and Trevor had a long whispered discussion about Mr. Dominic's relationship with Papa Levi, but Trevor didn't know what to make of it either. They finally decided it was all a big misunderstanding, because the director couldn't possibly have been boyhood friends with Levi's great-great-grandpa.

Then Trevor filled Levi in on the classwork he'd missed and told him all the camp scuttlebutt. Levi was thrilled to hear Martin and Greg had gotten in trouble for cheating on a Latin test, but he wasn't happy to learn their canoeing lessons had been suspended for an unspecified time.

"I wonder if that's because of what Mr. Dominic told you," Trevor said quietly from his spot at the foot of Levi's bed. "You know, about the traitor in our midst."

Levi smiled at his friend's melodramatic word choice but soon sobered as he realized Trevor was probably right. "Think they'll cancel this week's camping trip, too?"

Trevor shrugged. "Don't know." He released a yawn so huge his jaw popped. "May not be so bad if they do. I'm getting a little tired of sleeping on the ground. I don't rest well."

Levi laughed, thinking of his friend's loud snoring—snoring that hadn't lessened on any of their camping trips. "We wouldn't want poor, itty bitty Twevy to miss his beauty rest."

Trevor elbowed him. "You'd better be glad you're still recovering, or I'd have to beat you up for that one."

"Yeah, right. I'm shaking."

Levi closed his eyes moments after sunrise the next morning, the first day of August. He'd been bothered by strange dreams all night and was hoping to fall back to sleep a little longer. His mom had always told him dreams were important. She said some were the product of too much pizza and chocolate ice cream, but others were the subconscious mind's way of communicating some fact to the conscious mind—some important link it had missed. With a weary sigh, Levi forced himself to revisit his dreams before dropping back into slumber.

They had been filled with chaotic, swirling visions of elves and fire-breathing dragons, Latin verbs and banshees, swords and wooden horses. In his mind, he ran to the castle library searching book after book for some answer, while Ashley ran screaming through his brain waving maps of foreign worlds. All that was weird enough, but Hunter kept appearing in every disjointed segment, cackling as he shot arrows at Sara and chased Monica with a sword. Then Hunter set a bound Lizzie adrift in a canoe, mere yards from a waterfall that dropped off the edge of the earth.

Levi's eyes flew open. Hunter?

Could Hunter be Deceptor's spy inside the castle? Cruel, haughty Hunter who somehow seemed to recognize Levi's name that first day of camp.

Wait! He sat up straight in bed. Could Hunter himself be Deceptor? The sorcerer could change his appearance, after all. What better plan than to become one of the campers? Then the rulers of Terracaelum would admit him to the castle without question.

And Deceptor would have the invitation he needed to get to his target.

Chapter 24

The Dream

Convinced his dreams had revealed the true culprit, Levi stumbled from his bed to Trevor's and pounded on his friend's arm.

"Hmph?" Trevor opened one eye, pillow creases on his cheek. "What time is it? Get off me!"

"Shhh!" Levi stopped pounding. "I've got to talk to you. It's important."

Trevor sat up, and Levi glanced around. Steve mumbled something in his sleep, rolled toward the wall, and resumed snoring. Tommy didn't budge.

"What do you want?" Trevor rubbed his arm.

"It's Hunter."

"What about him?"

"It's him. Hunter is Deceptor."

Trevor stared at Levi, one eyebrow raised. "You've been dreaming."

Levi kneaded his knuckles into his thighs. "Well, yeah, but it's not like you think. Remember? Mr. Dominic said Deceptor could change forms. He took the shape of a camper so he could get into the castle."

Trevor rolled his eyes. "Just because Hunter's a bully doesn't make him a demon."

"No, but why else would he act like such a creep?"

"Hmmm. I don't know. Maybe because he *is* a creep?" He snorted. "Besides, I've never even seen him talking to any of the girls. He mostly picks on you, Steve, Luke, and a couple others." Trevor's eyes slid from Levi's.

Levi's ears sizzled at what Trevor had so kindly left unsaid. Levi, Steve, Luke . . . the weaklings. He added a dose of sarcasm to his words.

"Well yeah, he wouldn't be so obvious about it. He's trying to be sneaky. He's not gonna let on he's after one girl by targeting her. He's gonna be mean to everybody but her."

Trevor screwed up his face. "Maybe."

Levi thumped the mattress with his fist. "Definitely."

"Okay, let's think this through." Trevor slumped against the headboard as if he could easily fall back to sleep. "If you're right, then that means Deceptor is already inside the castle." Awareness of what he'd just said pulled Trevor out of his slouch.

"That's what I'm trying to tell you."

"But if he's already in the castle, it'll be really easy for him to get to the girls." Fear erased the last traces of sleepiness from Trevor's eyes. "Like with the fire when we were camping."

"Exactly." Levi's pulse pounded in his temples.

"Then we have to tell Mr. Dominic." Trevor pushed back his covers, swung his feet from the bed. "He thinks one of the staff is the spy. We've got to set him straight."

Levi froze. Wait, whoa. "Tell Mr. Dominic?" What if he was wrong? He huffed under his breath. He couldn't be wrong, though. His gaze drifted to the window. But what proof could he offer? A dream? The fact that Hunter was really, really mean? A gut feeling? Levi had already caused enough problems sneaking out of the infirmary. Why would Mr. Dominic believe him on such flimsy evidence? At the least, he'd say Levi's conclusion was illogical. "Uh-uh. No."

Trevor stared at him, one pajama-clad leg halfway in a pair of jeans. "Why not? Don't you think he ought to know Deceptor's in the castle?" His voice squeaked.

Levi shook his head. "It's not time yet." Not until he had proof. It was no small thing to tell the Prince of Terracaelum a shape-shifting demon sorcerer had sneaked into the castle under his very nose—disguised as a thirteen-year-old kid, of all things.

"You're serious?" Trevor's jeans crumpled to the floor. At first Levi thought he was going to argue, but then he heaved a sigh. "At least let's tell Steve and Tommy so they can help us watch. I mean, we don't even know which girl Hunter's after. A couple more pairs of eyes would be useful."

"I don't know." Levi peered at the whiffling lump that was Steve.

"Come on, man. Think. We need help. We can't be everywhere at once." Levi's gaze drifted to Tommy. "Maybe."

"Great." After a moment, Trevor leaned forward, his eyes intense. "I've been wondering something else. Why would a sorcerer from Terracaelum be interested in a senator's daughter from Louisiana of all places? Or a missionary kid? Or a farmer's daughter from Missouri? And Sara, she's from northern Michigan. The other day she told me her dad's in government. Maybe he's some bigwig, but still . . . Michigan, how normal is that? It's just, you'd think he'd be more interested in somebody from here, you know?"

Levi massaged his temples. "Well . . . if he's working for Satan, then creating chaos is his job. Of course the devil wants to hurt missionaries so they can't tell people about Jesus." He sank onto the stepstool by Trevor's bed, his sleepless night catching up to him. "Imagine the stink the Dominics would face if a senator's daughter got hurt—or even killed—at their home. And Sara—if her daddy's a government bigshot and something happens to her, Camp Classic could get shut down. As for Ashley? Well, I don't know, but nobody wants to hear that a nice girl like her got hurt at camp." He shook his head. "Think of what a big investigation could do to Terracaelum."

"Good point." Trevor snatched up his jeans, purpose hardening his jaw. "We need help."

"Now what?" Trevor jerked his chin toward Albert, who shuffled cards on Tommy's bed at nine that night. All four roommates had shown up for the talk Trevor wanted to have. Albert hadn't been invited.

Tommy and Steve tossed questioning glances at Levi. Levi could only shrug and watch with rising irritation as Albert dealt four hands for Spades.

Trevor whispered to Levi, "Why not just tell them anyway? Albert could help. Besides, if he's from here, he can back you up."

Levi's eyes darted to Trevor's. *He can back* you *up. Not he can back* us *up.* Sometime in the course of the day, Trevor had begun to doubt. Levi's shoulders sagged. Why shouldn't Trevor doubt with only Levi's word for everything? Albert had never even shown Trevor his ears.

The Trojan Horse Traitor

Levi blew out a breath. "Okay, fine." This was not going to work, but what could he do? Without Trevor . . . without his roommates . . . he was totally alone with way too much weirdness. "Guys?" Levi moved over and sat on the edge of Tommy's bed. "Trevor . . . I mean, *I* was wondering if you'd noticed anything . . . odd about camp."

Tommy shrugged. "You mean about the island being bigger than we thought? And the weather and stuff?" His eyebrows bunched. "Didn't we figure that out already?"

Steve nodded. "Yep, we settled it."

"No. I mean, yeah." Levi sighed. "That's all part of it, but there's more. This place is a lot . . . stranger than we thought."

Tommy and Steve exchanged confused glances. Trevor's index finger tapped a constant rhythm against the footboard.

Albert froze with his eyes on Levi. "What do you know about it?"

Levi tried for a confident expression. "I know a lot, Albert. I've talked to Mr. Dominic."

Albert's eyebrows shot up.

Levi nodded. "About Terracaelum. And Deceptor."

Albert's pimples stood out against his pale skin.

"Terra what?" Steve crinkled his face at Tommy. Tommy shrugged.

"We need your help," Levi told Albert. He glanced at the other two boys. "All three of you."

Trevor's finger-tapping started grating on Levi's nerves.

"We know there's a threat to one of the girls." Levi's eyes riveted on Albert. "We know who's after her. He's inside the castle right now."

"What!" Albert nearly fell off the bed, sending cards fluttering to the floor.

Tommy shook his head, hands spread. "What're you guys talking about?"

Levi kept his focus on Albert. "You know. Take off your hat." His heartbeat thrummed in his throat. Trevor's tapping ceased. This was it. If Albert didn't prove Levi right . . .

Albert pressed his lips tight for a long moment. Then he plucked the hat from his head, pulled back his shaggy hair, and showed his ears.

The boys and Albert stayed up late into the night discussing Terracaelum, Deceptor, and Hunter, all with Trevor making it sound like he'd never doubted for an instant. Though Tommy and Steve didn't want to believe they were anywhere than an island in the Great Lakes, Albert's confirmation—especially his ears—finally convinced them of the facts.

"Albert's a fairy," Levi told Tommy and Steve.

Albert's eyes blazed. "Ain't! I'm a pixie, thank you very much."

"Oh, sorry." Levi bit his lip to hide a smile.

Albert glared at him another second then said flatly, "No way a camper's Deceptor. The Dominics wouldn't allow for that."

"That's what I told him." Trevor said. So much for loyalty. Why had Trevor pushed Levi to enlist help from these guys if he was gonna bail on him so quickly?

"It has to be Hunter." Levi smacked a hand against his thigh. "Why else would he be so evil?" Why couldn't they trust him on this one? He'd been the brunt of Hunter's nastiness enough times to know.

Albert just shook his head.

"Besides," Levi said, deciding on a different tactic, "the girl Deceptor's after needs guarding no matter what. Even if I'm wrong, you can't argue that Hunter's plenty mean enough to be worth watching."

"That's true," Steve said.

"Do you know which girl Deceptor's after?" Levi asked Albert.

"Nope." Albert scrubbed short fingers through his scraggly hair, his eyes distant. "A girl used to live in the castle. A human girl. Don't know if she was the Dominics' kid or niece or what. Never saw her. I never set foot in the place before camp, but that Sylvester woman—not the mother, the daughter—she was the girl's nurse. Took care of her and all."

A girl? The Dominics' niece? Or even daughter? But they were so old. Maybe she was a granddaughter or something.

At midnight, a sharp rap at the door brought an end to their meeting. Mr. Sylvester poked his head in. With a chiding look at Albert, he told them to get to sleep.

Levi's whisper followed Albert from the room. "Watch out for Hunter and the girls."

Later that week, Levi and his roommates decided to take advantage of a free hour before fencing practice with the girls to spy on Hunter. While playing a half-hearted game of Frisbee in the field, they kept an eye on

Greg and Martin's wrestling match as Hunter, Suzanne, and Jacqueline watched from outside the makeshift ring. After twenty-five minutes, Greg pinned Martin, and the five suddenly took off in different directions.

Steve fumbled the Frisbee. "Whoa, where're they going?"

Levi shook his head. "I don't know, but I'm going after Hunter." He cocked his head toward Hunter's friends. "You guys follow the others."

Without waiting for a response, Levi jogged toward the castle, which Hunter had just entered. Inside, Levi peered around. No Hunter. The sound of running feet echoed down the hallway. Levi ran that direction on tiptoe. He glanced into the kitchen and dining hall as he flew past. Still no Hunter.

When Levi reached the entrance to the south foyer, he hesitated. Hugging the wall, he peered around the room. His eyes snagged on Hunter's black-shirted back next to the outside door. What was he up to now? At that moment, Hunter opened the south door then turned with a smirk and crooked a beckoning finger at Levi. Hunter stepped through.

Levi froze. Should he follow?

Don't go, his mind screamed. He ignored it and went.

Levi stepped out into the sunlight. Before his eyes could adjust, something smashed into his nose. Sharp pain shot across his forehead and through his cheekbones. He squeezed his eyes shut, hands cupped over his nose. Something hot oozed from his nostrils and squished between his fingers. His mouth flew open for air. Metallic-tasting blood flowed in. He gagged.

Someone cackled behind Levi. Then came a loud bang. Levi threw out his hands in self-protection. Nothing happened. Twisting around, he forced open his eyes and caught a blurry glimpse of the closed south door.

Levi stumbled forward and grappled with the doorknob. It didn't budge. He was locked outside of the castle.

And Terracaelum.

Chapter 25

Locked Out

Levi's heart thumped frantically against his ribcage. How could he get back inside? What was happening to the other boys? They'd obviously been separated for a reason—a sinister reason. What was Hunter doing now? If he really was Deceptor—and the blood gushing from Levi's nose made him even more certain he was—then he had free run of the castle. Why hadn't Levi told Mr. Dominic his suspicions sooner? Then at least he'd know to watch out for Hunter. Now who would watch over the girls?

Levi lurched out from the castle door and crossed the drawbridge, hoping to catch the attention of someone at a south-facing window. By the time he turned and looked up, the castle disappeared in a flash of light. He was on the edge of a cliff. Lake water splashed cheerfully far below.

"No!" Levi stomped his foot then instantly wished he hadn't as blood gushed down his t-shirt. Why hadn't he stayed on the doorstep? Now he couldn't even see the castle.

After staring for what seemed an eternity at the space he knew held an invisible castle, he sat on the ground under a huge tree. He prayed, harder than he'd prayed in a long time. *God, please get me back into Terracaelum.*

He sat for another eon with no change except for the receding light, his rising hunger and thirst, and the growing pain in his nose. Tears stung his eyes, but the knowledge that Hunter and his buddies probably watched from the south-facing library window made him keep his bloody pulp of a face firm.

As the sun cast red streaks across the western sky, Levi stood. He couldn't sit on the edge of a precipice all night long. He'd hike down to the cabins and try to find an unlocked door or window. At least he'd have shelter and hopefully something to eat and drink. What he wouldn't give for some Tylenol.

Levi stepped into the shadowy woods. His balloon nose and swollen eyes made it hard to see where to place his feet. He tripped on something and landed hard on both bare knees. With a groan, he pushed back to sitting. Hot blood oozed from his cuts. His throat ached. He should just give up and sit out the night in the woods. Maybe something would eat him. At least then he'd be out of his misery.

A breeze touched his cheeks. He breathed in, breathed out. *Come on, Levi. Don't give up.* He shoved to his feet. Blood trickled down his shins. Full darkness smothered the forest. He shuffled along what he hoped was the path, both hands outstretched, body hunched against another fall.

A branch cracked on his left. He drew up short, eyes straining into the darkness. All was silent.

It's nothing, Levi. Just the wind. Chill.

Another crack shook Levi into motion. He lurched headlong down the path. Something big crashed through the trees not far behind him. He didn't look back. *God, help!*

Several panicked moments later, Levi blundered into the camp clearing. He flew to the dining hall, scrambled around the building. Yanked doorknobs. Tugged windows. *Please, God, let something be unlocked.* A panther-like scream dragged Levi's eyes to the woods. In the brush not six feet away twin yellow eyes flashed. Terror spurted through his veins.

I'm gonna die! I'm gonna die!

Shoulders tensed against claws he knew would strike any moment, Levi swiped at the kitchen window.

It opened.

Levi froze for a shocked second. Another scream propelled him through the window. He fell onto the kitchen countertop, slammed and bolted the window. He dropped to the tile floor, crouched with arms over his head, and waited for the monster to crash through the glass and gobble him up.

After several long minutes, he dared peek at the window, half-expecting to see some hideous face. He saw nothing but tree branches waving against the star-strewn sky. He melted into a quivering heap. Thank God.

When his breathing settled into rhythmic puffs, he stumbled around the kitchen, running into things in the unfamiliar room. When he finally found the light switch, the room flooded with welcome light.

In a bathroom he washed up and discovered a first aid kit mounted on the wall. Staring at his battered face in the mirror, he applied antiseptic cream to the cut on his fat nose, but he couldn't do anything for his purpling eyes. After bandaging his bloody knees, he grabbed a packet of Tylenol and left the bathroom in search of food.

With frequent glances at the window in case the creature returned, he downed a glass of water, scarfed a can of tuna and some stale saltines, then swallowed the two pain relievers. Should he borrow a flashlight and try getting into one of the cabins to sleep? No way. That monster was probably waiting for him.

Hang on, could that thing be Deceptor, or should he say, Hunter? He glanced toward the window. Still nothing there, but a shiver swirled up his spine. A wild animal was bad, but Hunter/Deceptor with his opposable thumbs was worse. What if he broke in while Levi slept?

Levi double-checked all the locks.

Once the building was as secure as he could make it, he made a bed from a relatively soft chair in the telephone room, a jacket someone had left on the coat rack, and a small pile of kitchen towels. He blockaded the door with another chair then curled up with his eyes on the phone. Should he call his parents? He really wanted to. He wanted his own safe bed at home and his little brothers' quiet breathing as they slept.

"You can't call," he said aloud. His parents would yank him home faster than he could say *Terracaelum*. And then what would become of his friends?

Ears pricked for sounds of danger, he fell asleep praying help would come in the morning.

Help came in the morning all right—furious, blazing-eyed help. Levi had the misfortune of being found by Dr. Baldwin and Mr. Austin, the two most irritable males among the camp staff.

When Levi told them Hunter had hit him and locked him out of the castle, Mr. Austin snapped at him, "What kind of blamed-fool notion made you follow that boy anyway?"

Levi turned to Dr. Baldwin, half-hoping the pity factor for his bruised face would make the doctor take his side.

"Don't look at me like that, boy," he said, smashing Levi's hopes. "You of all the campers ought to have known you couldn't get back inside without the Dominics there to open the door."

Their scolding didn't make his sore nose and pounding head feel any better, so Levi trudged up the hill to the castle telling himself he should've called his mom to come get him. At least she'd have felt sorry for him. Even babied him a little.

Mrs. Dominic helped when she let them in the castle. She patted his back and asked how he felt.

"Miserable," he said.

She brushed back his hair with a sweet smile. "I'm so sorry."

Then she turned to Dr. Baldwin, her tender smile long gone. "Take him straight up to the infirmary and do something to help the poor child feel better. I'll go tell my husband where he is."

With a quick nod, Dr. Baldwin hustled Levi toward the stairs while Mr. Austin mumbled something about telling the others to call off the search party.

"Second time this week you've disappeared and made us all drop everything and go looking for you." Dr. Baldwin's cheeks were a deep red as he stomped up the steps beside Levi. "Of course I can't be blamed for not coddling you right off."

Levi followed him into the dark infirmary. Even though the pain in his face made him feel wretched, he couldn't help but ask, "Why's it so dark in here?" He pointed at the drawn drapes.

Grunting, the doctor whipped open the curtains. "Only keep them open for the humans."

"Don't dwarves like sunlight?"

"It's not the light we don't like, it's the height." He turned back from the treetops visible through the glass, his face green. "Now, sit. Let me see that nose."

Levi sat. "Why do you live upstairs?" He winced as the doctor manipulated his nose.

"Because there isn't room on the ground floor for the infirmary." Dr. Baldwin glared at him over his reading glasses. "And I don't think you'd much enjoy visiting the cellar when you're sick or hurt."

Levi opened his mouth to ask another question but shut it at the grumpy expression of the creature handling his sore nose. The doctor cleaned his cut, stuffed his nostrils with cotton gauze, and taped his nose tight. Levi gritted his teeth against the pain. When the doctor finished, Levi slumped into the same bed he'd slept in a few days before, exhausted and miserable.

"I'll give you something to take the edge off, but not until after you talk to Mr. Dominic. I don't want you too groggy to explain yourself." Though Dr. Baldwin's tone remained gruff, his expression had softened.

With a nod that made his entire face throb, Levi closed his eyes, thankful the doctor had closed the curtains once more.

"Levi." Mr. Dominic stood over him with both hands on his hips. "What happened to you, boy? Dr. Baldwin says they found you down at camp. What were you doing there?"

"Deceptor attacked me," Levi said without meaning to.

Mr. Dominic stiffened. Dr. Baldwin sucked in a breath, fingers fumbling the gauze he was rerolling.

"At least, I think it was him."

"I was told you said Hunter did this." The director shot a questioning glance at the doctor.

"Oh, he did," Dr. Baldwin said quickly. "Didn't say a word about Deceptor."

Mr. Dominic frowned at Levi. "Explain."

"I think Hunter is Deceptor."

Mr. Dominic's right eyebrow shot up. Dr. Baldwin snorted.

Levi's ears heated. "You said Deceptor could take different forms, and that he can't enter the castle without invitation, right? So he took the form of a kid and you invited him in."

The director shook his head. Levi couldn't tell whether the headshake indicated disbelief or that he thought Levi was a complete idiot. "Why Hunter, may I ask?"

"Because he's evil. He's done nothing but torment me since I got here and none of the teachers seem to realize it because he's such a con artist."

The Trojan Horse Traitor 147

"And you've been following him, this boy you think is a shape-shifting demon?" Something like admiration flittered through Mr. Dominic's eyes and was instantly replaced by stern disapproval. "Levi, simply because someone isn't nice to you doesn't make him Deceptor."

"I know." Levi was starting to feel foolish but rushed ahead anyway. "The first day of camp he snatched my letter and saw my name and acted like he knew me. It was weird. I mean, how would he know anything about me?"

"I don't know, son," Mr. Dominic perched on the edge of the bed, "but don't you think Mrs. Dominic and I considered Deceptor might try the very trick you're suggesting? Don't you think we guarded against it before we invited all these people into the castle?"

Dr. Baldwin mumbled, "Upstart kid thinks he knows more than our rulers."

Levi stared at his dirty fingernails. "Sorry."

Mr. Dominic nodded. "I can assure you, while Hunter may not be a very kind young man, he is most certainly not a demon."

"Then why'd he hit me?"

"Good question." Mr. Dominic leaned forward and inspected Levi's swollen nose and purple eyes. "He claims he never touched you. Says he saw you walk through the foyer and out the door but didn't pay much attention because he was on his way upstairs."

"He's lying!" Levi popped upright, shooting pain through his skull.

The director nudged Levi back against the pillow. "That may be, but there are no witnesses on either side." He raised both palms in a shrug. "I can't take disciplinary measures without proof."

"What about Trevor and the other guys?" Levi's voice came out a croak. "They followed some of Hunter's thugs." He stopped at the disapproving look in the director's eyes. "I mean, Hunter's friends."

Mr. Dominic's lips twitched. "Your friends are fine. In fact, it was your roommates who burst into my suite late last night claiming Hunter had killed you. Apparently they searched the castle themselves before coming to me." He shook his head. "Shame they didn't come sooner or we could have found you before you had to spend the night alone and hurt."

"I'm glad they're okay." Levi let himself relax into the pillow. "It was all my idea anyway. They were just helping me."

"Well, everyone's safe now, so we'll let it go." Rising, Mr. Dominic fixed Levi with a no-nonsense look. "Still, you leave Hunter alone from here on out."

Levi nodded. Okay, fine. So maybe Hunter wasn't Deceptor. He was still a malicious creep.

"Asa." The director turned to the doctor. "Why don't you give this young man something for his pain and let him sleep? He's had an exhausting night."

Twenty minutes later, Levi lay beneath the cool sheets, his mind fuzzy from the medication. Soft voices outside the door, left open half an inch, filtered into the haze. He forced himself to focus.

"You have to admit his deduction was a good one." Levi knew the deep rumbling whisper belonged to the doctor.

Mr. Dominic responded softly, "Yes. He couldn't know we'd already set up safeguards against Deceptor posing as a camper."

"That he couldn't."

Silence fell. Levi thought the men had finished their conversation, but the doctor's low rumble came again. "Are you sure he's not right? Maybe Deceptor found a way around your safeguards. What better person to use than Hunter? You know what his forebears were."

Another silence, then the director said, "Impossible. Put it from your mind, Asa." Another pause. "But keep an eye on him just the same. And on young Leviticus Prince here. You know his forebear as well."

Chapter 26

Pure Evil

Levi returned to his room that evening to find his roommates and Albert in deep discussion. The instant he walked through the door, they swarmed him, all talking at once.

"Where were you?"

"What happened?"

"Did Hunter kill you?"

Levi answered every question, filling them in on all he'd learned from the doctor and the director. Once they were satisfied, he asked what happened to each of them. Steve told of Suzanne and Jacqueline luring him to a storage room, hitting him with a tennis racket, and locking him in. Tommy said Greg ambushed him behind the archery range and pounded on him awhile. It was Trevor's report that made Levi's blood ice over.

"Martin tried to throw me off the roof," Trevor said in a matter-of-fact tone.

"What?"

"Yep, I followed him to the northwest tower roof, and he tackled me. We were wrestling right by the edge when he gave me a shove. I caught hold of his arm, though, and popped him a hard right." Trevor punched the air. "I didn't wait around for him to hit me back."

"I don't blame you." Levi sank down on Tommy's bed, shaking his head at what could have happened to Trevor. He could've been killed—murdered.

No matter what Mr. Dominic said, Hunter and his friends were pure evil.

"What in the world happened to you guys? You look like refugees from some war or something." Sara slammed her breakfast tray onto the table, glaring at each boy in turn. "And you." Her blue-green eyes pinned Levi. "Where were you this weekend? All of you missed practice Saturday. Levi hasn't been at meals in forever. You even missed chapel."

She flopped down and stared at Levi, both brows raised.

Before he could answer, Monica, Lizzie, and Ashley showed up and blasted them with questions of their own. The boys sat silently through the barrage. When the three girls ran out of air, they plopped down beside Sara, chests heaving.

Once Levi thought it was safe to open his mouth without getting yelled at, he said, "Hunter and his thugs happened to us. They attacked us." This got the girls' attention. "Hunter shut me outside the castle, so I had to spend Saturday night down in camp." He wasn't about to mention Deceptor or Terracaelum.

"Honey, he did not!"

"That creep!"

"He should be expelled!"

Levi nodded, glad their anger had shifted from him to Hunter.

Something like determination flicked across Sara's face, making Levi nervous. "Well, what're we going to do about it? It's clear the jerks didn't get in trouble." She gestured toward Hunter and his buddies laughing at their table. "They should've gotten kicked out of camp."

Her words were loud enough that Hunter looked her way. He inclined his head in a mocking bow.

Levi shot him what was supposed to be a menacing glare, but which probably wasn't very effective given the state of his nose. With a scornful smile, Hunter turned back to his friends.

Levi glared at Sara, sweeping his hand to include all the girls. "You aren't going to do a thing." He pointed from himself to the boys. "We can take care of it just fine."

"Obviously. You did such a marvelous job the last time." Monica's sarcastic tone wasn't lost on Levi.

Lizzie flipped her hair in Steve's face as he took a bite of pancake. "That's right, y'all. We little gals would just get in the way of you big, strong boys." She batted her lashes.

Trevor rolled his eyes. Steve picked strands of dark blonde hair from his syrupy teeth.

Levi shifted in his seat. It was probably time to change the subject. "So how's training?" he asked Ashley.

She pursed her lips and looked away.

"Fine." Sara crossed her arms over her chest. "Don't let us help."

Levi inspected her angry face. Would she and the other girls stay out of it? His eyes slid to Hunter. The bully was talking quietly to Greg and Martin, whose cheek sported a bruise the size and shape of Trevor's fist. Levi smiled at the sight.

Then Hunter caught Levi's eye and ran one finger across his throat.

Levi swallowed hard. He had to make sure the girls stayed far away from Hunter.

Chapter 27

The Boss

After supper that night, Trevor, Tommy, and Steve cornered Levi.

"If you were the girls, wouldn't it upset you to find out your friends knew you were in this strange world and hadn't told them?" Steve's cheeks reddened.

"Not to mention if they knew some evil sorcerer was after you and didn't bother to clue you in?" Tommy demanded.

Trevor's biceps bulged as he crossed his arms over his chest. "It's time to tell them, Levi."

Eyes skipping between his roommates, Levi felt his blood pressure spike. After the way the girls reacted at lunch, he'd thought about telling them himself, but not now. Who did these guys think they were, ganging up on him?

"It's not the right time." Levi swiveled away, stalked to his wardrobe. He yanked open the door and shifted his stuff around, his roommates' glares burning holes in his back.

"Not the right time?" Anger swelled Trevor's voice, but Levi refused to look at him. "Who says you get to decide what the right time is?"

"Yeah, we're their friends too," Steve snapped. "We're all in this."

Levi snorted. It's not like they'd been the ones to stop Deceptor from burning the girls alive in their tent. They hadn't faced Hunter and gotten locked out of the castle, chased by some monster, and forced to survive alone for a night. It wasn't them who'd figured out about Terracaelum.

Someone gripped the back of his t-shirt, then wrenched him around and up.

"Hey!" Levi raised both fists, toes scrabbling against the stone floor.

"Hey, yourself!" Trevor's face was inches from Levi's. "I don't know who you think you are, but last time I checked nobody died and made you king."

He released Levi, letting him stumble against the open wardrobe door.

Without a word, Levi stomped into the bathroom, refusing to rub his bruised back.

Levi spent a lot of time on his own over the next few days. Since the girls acted snotty toward all the boys—not just him—Levi figured the other guys hadn't told them anything despite their argument. Levi's roommates wouldn't even speak to him, except when Trevor whipped him at fencing and hollered, "I dethroned the king!"

On top of that, every time Levi went anywhere near Hunter's gang, they whispered threats. Levi learned to stay close to the teachers. Besides Hunter's usual goody two-shoes routine around adults, the eyes of the staff were on Hunter more often than before. This fact told Levi the director believed his story over Hunter's.

One thing bothered Levi, and now he didn't even have Trevor to discuss it with. If Hunter wasn't Deceptor, as Mr. Dominic insisted, how did he know so much about the workings of this place? If he wasn't aware they were in a different world, how did he know Levi couldn't get back inside the castle when he shut Levi out? Was there any way Hunter had been to Terracaelum before? Levi didn't see how since this was the first Camp Classic in, like, a hundred years. But Mr. Dominic and Dr. Baldwin had mentioned Hunter's ancestors—was he descended from someone who'd lived here? Like Levi and his great-great-grandpa, Papa Levi? Not that he understood that either.

Or was Levi right about Hunter after all? Was Hunter actually Deceptor, broken through the director's defenses?

Levi couldn't be sure, not with Mr. Dominic and Trevor so certain that Hunter was just a camper, but Levi didn't plan to give Hunter a chance to do more harm. Not if he could prevent it.

That evening, he sat in his room talking to Albert, who, annoying as he could be, was one of the few people not angry with him.

"Albert, fairies aren't afraid of heights, are they?"

Albert shot him a dirty look from his perch on Trevor's bed. "I'm a pixie."

"Right, sorry."

"That's a special class of fairies."

"Okay." Touchy, touchy.

"Why in tarnation would we be afraid of heights?"

Levi shrugged. "I know dwarves don't like heights, so I just wondered—"

"Fairies like heights fine. Some of us can fly." His small chest puffed out. "Pixies can fly."

"Wow." Levi's jaw dropped. "I thought that was just make-believe. Can you fly?"

Albert's chest deflated. "Nah. Not old enough yet."

"You have to be a certain age to fly?"

"Yeah, I'll be two hundred and sixty-seven soon." Albert shrugged. "Should be flying any year now. You oughta see my dad fly." A wistful look crossed his beardless face. "I can't wait."

"I can imagine," said Levi, trying not to sound dumbfounded. "So what about elves? Do they fly?"

"Nah, but they're not scared of heights neither." Albert waved a stubby hand at the high ceiling. "Elves like it bright and airy. That's why they don't mind babysitting you guys way up here."

Choosing not to comment on the babysitting line, Levi cocked his chin toward the open window. "What other creatures are out there?"

"All kinds." Albert's lower lip jutted. "There's some nice dragons over near the mountains yonder—some not-so-nice ones too, mind you. Gotta be careful you get the right kind or they'll roast you and eat you for lunch. All depends on how they're raised, ya know."

Seriously? Levi studied Albert, who plucked at his lip without a hint of teasing in his eyes.

"'Course, there's lots more elves and dwarves and fairies. Pixies too. I got some kin out west." Albert waved a hand toward the left. "A pair of harpies live over near the eastern edge of Terracaelum. You gotta watch them, they'll steal the food right out of your hands. There's some centaurs and minotaurs in the deeper pockets of the forest. A colony of leprechauns too. Tricky little buggars, them leprechauns."

Albert paused, chin puckered. "What else? Oh, there's a few griffins and a sphinx further out. Some real nasty creatures, too. A few hags and werewolves. Even a basilisk or two in the tunnels under the mountains." A shudder rocked his small shoulders. "I don't like them basilisks. The tunnels neither for that matter." His bony thumb poked into his chest. "I like fresh air and sunlight. Keeps the nasty creatures away. They can't stand the light."

Basilisks, hags, minotaurs, harpies, werewolves. Levi's troubled gaze drifted to the window as a welcome breeze touched his hair. His eyes strained to penetrate the dark patches of the forest. He wasn't so sure he liked Terracaelum. "That's why I'm trying to keep the girls out of all this," he said softly. "There's too much danger and darkness out there. They don't need to get caught up in it."

Albert moved over and leaned against the foot of Levi's bed. "That really why you don't wanna tell 'em?"

Levi frowned. Not Albert too.

"I ain't pickin' on you, so don't get mad at me." Albert raised both hands. "It's just, what with being the oldest at home and all, I think you're used to being the boss. My big brother Andrew's just the same." One knobby shoulder lifted. "You was pretty hard on me and the boys earlier this summer. I know you been trying to do better, but old habits die hard."

Levi stared down at his knotted fingers.

"Can't help wondering," the pixie said quietly, "if you'd have told the girls everything by now if it'd been your own idea? I mean, if the boys hadn't brought it up first."

Heat climbed from Levi's neck to the tips of his ears.

Albert shrugged. "Won't hurt none to think on it."

A few days later, after Levi and Sara beat Ashley and Lizzie in a canoe race, he and Sara dragged their boat up out of the water and turned it upside down. Sara returned to the river to give Ashley and Lizzie tips on their technique while Levi sat down near the trees.

The others still weren't exactly friendly to him, but at least they'd put their anger aside long enough to practice. As Levi watched, Trevor and Tommy's canoe sped around a bend in the river. Miss Nydia hurried that direction, shading her eyes as she peered after them. Levi gave his head a little shake. It must be tough on her to keep track of everybody. At least the director had given permission for them to practice again as long as they stayed with an adult.

With a sigh, Levi lay back in the soft grass, eyes closed against the sunlight. Time passed in a haze.

"Get her now," a low voice hissed.

Levi's eyes popped open. Without moving his head, he scanned the nearby area. He didn't see anyone, but a heavy cloud had drifted before the sun, shrouding the world in shadows.

"I can't," whispered a voice so soft Levi couldn't tell whether it belonged to a male or female. "Too many are with her."

The girls! Levi sat up straight, eyes darting to the river where his friends still practiced, oblivious to the voices.

"Do it," the hissing voice commanded.

Levi jumped to his feet. It must be Hunter! He really was Deceptor, and he'd just issued an order to one of his thugs. Levi had to get help. He needed to find Miss Nydia. He opened his mouth to holler for the chaperone.

"Nydia," someone else yelled before he could.

Levi spun around as Miss Althea emerged from the trees, face red and eyes blazing. He ran toward her to warn her of the danger. But she barreled right past him. He drew up short and stared after her.

Fists on her hips, Miss Althea halted in front of Miss Nydia just outside the tree line near the bend in the river.

"Where have you been?" The pixie woman's angry words carried easily to Levi.

The color drained from Miss Nydia's already-pale face. "What do you mean?"

"I mean I came out here to give you a message and you were nowhere in sight." Miss Althea clearly had the upper hand over the cowering Miss Nydia, even though the pixie's head was barely level with the elf's thighs.

"You're supposed to be watching out for these kids." Miss Althea's glare flicked to Levi. She lowered her voice. "A storm's brewing."

"I was about to call them in." Miss Nydia's eyes were bright with unshed tears.

"Well, do it then." Miss Althea grasped the other woman's wrist. "I'll help you get them back to the castle."

The Trojan Horse Traitor

Moments later, Levi and Sara double-timed it down the path after the others.

"What's the deal with Miss Nydia and Miss Althea?" Levi looked at Sara. "Miss Althea seemed really mad."

"I don't know." Sara's eyes widened. "They've always been nice to me and the other girls, but it seems like Miss Althea is always snapping at Miss Nydia over one thing or another."

Before Levi could respond, a low hiss seeped from the bushes they'd just passed. Levi's mind jumped to the voices he'd heard near the river, voices he had forgotten to mention to the adults because they'd been in such a hurry. Now everyone else was far ahead of him and Sara.

"What was that?" Sara breathed.

Levi grabbed her hand. "I don't know." He put himself between Sara and the source of the noise even as a faint whisper in his brain asked if he was insane.

The hissing came again, this time accompanied by a low growl. Sara's nails dug into Levi's hand.

"Run!"

Sara ran. Levi sprinted a step behind, not releasing her hand. She tripped over a fallen branch. He yanked her up and dragged her on. He couldn't hear any sounds of pursuit, but then his breathing was really loud.

When they burst from the forest into the castle clearing, Sara bent double, hands on her knees. Levi sucked in great gulps of air as his eyes scanned the trees. He didn't see anything unusual.

"Anybody there?" His voice wobbled.

No answer, not even a growl. Maybe it was a bobcat or a mountain lion, some creature that wouldn't dare come into the open. Anything but a demon sorcerer.

"Must be gone." Sara tugged his hand. "Come on. Let's catch up with the others."

Levi searched the woods one more time then allowed her to pull him toward the castle. As they walked away, he darted wary glances over his shoulder.

His spine tingled a warning that something still lurked.

Chapter 28

Uncle Filbert

Once he and Sara were safely inside the castle, Levi rushed to Mr. Dominic's study to report the voices he'd heard in the woods. He hadn't quite decided whether he'd tell about his and Sara's wild run from . . . well, absolutely nothing. At least nothing he'd seen.

Though he banged several times on the Dominics' door, no one answered. With a huff, Levi spun around and nearly knocked Mr. Austin to the floor.

"Sorry, sir." A drop of sweat fell from Levi's temple.

Mr. Austin grunted. "Where are you going in such a big hurry, boy?"

"I need to talk to Mr. Dominic. Have you seen him?"

"Gone. Don't know when he'll get back."

Levi felt a strong urge to stamp his foot. "It's important."

The dwarf regarded him a moment, as if weighing out the probable importance of Levi's problem. "Maybe I can help."

Levi launched into his story, leaving out his suspicions that the creature was likely Hunter/Deceptor in some scary, sharp-toothed form. Because the more he thought about it, the more convinced he became that Mr. Dominic was wrong about Hunter, while Levi was right. Not that he could say as much to Mr. Austin. He also couldn't say who he thought the second voice belonged to—Greg? Suzanne?

When he finished reporting the voices he'd heard in the woods, Mr. Austin closed one eye and cocked his head. "Think you could've fallen asleep? Dreamed it maybe?"

"Of course not," Levi said quickly then hesitated. He had shut his eyes a minute. But no, he was sure he'd been awake when he heard the voices. Besides, something had chased him and Sara. He hadn't been asleep then. Not that he'd told Mr. Austin that part.

But what if it was only their overactive imaginations?

Mr. Austin's tongue rested between his teeth as he thought. "We do have plenty of folks watching in the woods, you know, those whose sole job is to ensure the safety of you children. You might've heard a couple of them talking and mistook their meaning."

Levi nodded, though he hadn't known about the watchers and he doubted he'd mistaken the voices' meaning. Even so, he couldn't be absolutely sure it was Hunter. What if it was some other evil being? Mr. Dominic—and Albert—had admitted there were plenty of those in Terracaelum.

Mr. Austin rubbed his whiskery chin. "Tell you what. I don't know what you heard, but next time you go to the river, I'll tag along just in case."

"Thank you, sir." Levi worried his lower lip. He'd gotten the impression from Albert that dwarves didn't much like water. How much good would a dwarf do in a river?

His impression was confirmed the next afternoon when Mr. Austin watched them from a position well back from the water's edge. Levi hoped no one needed rescuing because he seriously doubted the stout dwarf could even doggy paddle.

The night before, Levi had swallowed his pride long enough to warn his roommates about the voices and hissing. Though it was clear they still weren't happy with Levi, they'd agreed to be on high alert, for the girls' sake. Clearly fed up, Trevor hadn't even asked why Levi continued in his stubborn refusal to tell the girls what was going on. Levi didn't know why anymore himself, but he did know he was sick of being on everybody's bad side.

Now Levi's eyes darted all around the river and surrounding forest. What if the voice from the woods came back? What if its owner didn't stay hidden this time? Mr. Austin had his long knife strapped to his belt and would certainly be more of a match for some evil creature than Miss Nydia. Still, Levi had trouble paying attention to his canoeing.

Though practice was uneventful, Levi hung back and walked to the castle beside Mr. Austin at the rear of the group afterward. He could keep a better eye out from there. While he and the dwarf hiked silently along the trail, the others walking in pairs ahead of them, Levi wondered about those watching over them in the woods. What sorts of beings were they?

When the castle came into view, Levi relaxed. No one would dare attack them there. As he and Mr. Austin approached the moat, dull in the hazy August heat, Levi slid an assessing glance at the teacher. Since the dwarf was whistling a tune, Levi decided he must be in a good mood, at least good enough for Levi to ask a question.

"What's in the moat?" Levi had never forgotten the Sylvesters' panicky expressions when he'd fallen in all those weeks before.

Mr. Austin shot him a strange look. "What do you mean?"

"I mean, why does the staff keep warning kids to stay away from it? Like it's dangerous or something."

"It is dangerous, boy, so you leave it alone." Mr. Austin's voice dropped to a mumble. "But not so much because of what's in it."

"What's that supposed to mean? If nothing's dangerous in it, then it can't be dangerous."

Mr. Austin turned a sour look on him, sighed, and glanced around. Nobody else was near. "Let me tell you a little story about my Uncle Filbert," he said in a confiding tone. "He, unlike most dwarves with any sense, actually loved to swim."

Levi stifled a laugh at Mr. Austin's obvious disgust.

"One day when he was very young," Mr. Austin went on, "Filbert was bragging about what a great swimmer he was. A bunch of his cousins and brothers dared him to jump into the moat. Of course they didn't think he'd do it, but he did. Plunged straight in and never came up again."

Levi blinked. "You're kidding."

Mr. Austin pursed his lips. "No, I am not kidding." He harrumphed. "As I was saying, none of his cousins or brothers could swim at all, so they hollered for help. By the time help came and searched the bottom of the moat, there was no trace of Filbert. After a while, his folks gave him up for dead." He nodded vehemently. "And don't you know, two days later, he turned up at the south door of the castle, bruised and bedraggled, but very much alive."

Levi's mouth fell open. "But how . . . ?"

"From what they could gather, when Filbert dove into the moat, a storm was blowing on the Great Lakes. You know, in your world."

"What's that have to do with anything?"

Mr. Austin grunted. "I thought you knew how this place was situated." He placed his right hand about a foot above his left. "Let's say this is Terracaelum." He nodded toward his right hand. "And this is your Lake Superior." He indicated his left. "Terracaelum itself is suspended above the lake, but in a different realm, you might say."

"I thought the castle connected the two worlds."

"'Course it does." With an irritated headshake, he took Levi's hands and arranged them as his had been, the right about a foot over the left. He pointed at Levi's right hand. "Terracaelum." And his left hand. "Earth." He eyed Levi. "Got it?"

"Um . . . yeah, I guess."

The dwarf placed his own left hand tip-to-tip, parallel with Levi's left, then angled his right so that it arced from his left up to Levi's right. "Right here." His chin tilted toward the bridge made by his right hand, the connecting point between their hands. "This is where the worlds connect. This is the castle."

Levi nodded. He pictured the way the cliff dropped away and the invisible castle took over, Terracaelum an invisible realm suspended well above Lake Superior in his own world.

"Filbert was here." Mr. Austin nodded to a spot just at the beginning of Levi's right hand. "When he plunged into the moat, the atmospheric conditions were such in your world that a hole opened in the base of ours. And Filbert fell through."

Levi's eyes widened. Imagine falling from one world to the next. No wonder the campers were warned to stay away from the moat.

"He said it was like washing down a waterfall." Mr. Austin's voice grew eerie. "One minute he was in the calm moat, the next he was falling hard and fast into the writhing lake. If he hadn't been such a strong swimmer, he would surely have drowned in your world. His death would've forever remained a mystery."

Levi's aching arms brought him to his senses. He dropped them to his sides. "Wow."

Mr. Austin shrugged. "That was a long time ago, nearly five hundred years now." He turned stern eyes on Levi. "But it won't do to be foolish. You steer clear of that moat." He strode toward the castle, turned back, and said in a fierce voice, "That's true in other areas, boy. Don't trifle with things you don't understand. They may be dangerous. Deadly even." He turned and stomped away.

Chapter 29

Della

"Wonderful move, young man," Dr. Baldwin told Levi even as he moved his king out of danger. "You nearly put me in check that time."

"Yeah, well, you got out of it." Levi grinned at the dwarf's obvious pleasure. Though he wasn't sick or injured, the doctor had invited Levi to the infirmary for another game of chess. They sat on adjacent cots with the game on a cart between them and just enough light trickling through the drawn curtains for them to see the board.

"Of course I did," the doctor said, still beaming at him. "I've been playing this game for hundreds of years."

Levi's face scrunched in disbelief. "Hundreds of years? Seriously?"

"I'm quite serious."

Levi eyed his opponent's salt-and-pepper hair. "You can't be all that old. Mr. Dominic looks older than you."

"Appearances can be deceiving, son." Something strange glinted in the doctor's black eyes. "I'm much older than your Mr. Dominic."

Wariness crept across Levi's shoulders. He still wasn't too comfortable with all this nonhuman stuff. "Exactly how old are you?"

"Let's see." Dr. Baldwin rubbed his gray-streaked beard. "I believe I turned five hundred and sixty-three last March." He counted silently on stubby fingers. "Yes, that's right, five hundred and sixty-three."

Levi waited for the doctor to laugh. He didn't. "Okay then, how old is Mr. Dominic?"

Dr. Baldwin squeezed his eyes shut. "Hmmm . . . let's see. Tobias has a summer birthday. Late August, I believe." Opening his eyes, he nodded. "He turns one hundred and forty-two in a few weeks' time."

Levi blinked. How could a human be alive at a hundred and forty-two, much less running a summer camp full of kids? "Oh."

"Dwarves are much longer lived than humans." Dr. Baldwin's tone was matter-of-fact. "Elves, too, for that matter."

"Is Mr. Dominic's wife that old?"

The dwarf's thick brows lowered. "I presume so, but I couldn't say for certain. It isn't polite to ask a female her age." A smile twitched his lips. "I learned that long ago from my Della."

Levi's bishop slipped from his fingers. "Your Della? You mean you have a wife?" The Austins were a married couple, so it wasn't the dwarf marriage part that surprised him. It's just that he'd assumed the doctor was an old bachelor. He was certainly crusty enough.

A far-off look softened the dwarf's eyes. "Long ago I was."

"What happened to her?"

Dr. Baldwin sat in silence a long time. A variety of emotions crossed his features—joy, fear, sadness, anger. "She's dead," he whispered. "Deceptor killed her." Though they hadn't finished their game, he scooped up chess pieces and slammed them into the wooden box. "Don't ask me anymore about it."

Levi slowly gathered his pieces and set them in the box. After he replaced the box top, he looked at Dr. Baldwin, who sat motionless on the other cot, his face dark and brooding.

"I'm sorry about your wife," Levi said quietly. He left the room, easing the door shut behind him.

Chapter 30

Telling All

"The countdown is on," Mr. Dominic announced at breakfast one morning in late August. "Only ten days remain before we hold our Camp Classic Olympics and the production of *The Trojan Horse*, written and directed by our very own Mr. Austin."

The campers clapped as the Literature teacher flushed brick red.

Mr. Dominic waited for the applause to die down. "The schedule for the Olympics is posted on the wall back there." He gestured toward the wall near Levi. "You'll notice that the games will take a couple of days, followed by *The Trojan Horse* performance on the last evening at the archery range. We'll build a bonfire for our spotlight. Not to mention, to keep the sand flies at bay."

Everyone began talking at once.

Mr. Dominic raised a hand for silence. "In all your bustle to finish preparing for the Olympics and the play, don't forget to study for finals. Exams are fast approaching."

The kids moaned.

After they quieted, he continued. "Remember, although you won't receive school credit for these courses, your performance will determine whether you'll be invited back next summer. The games will also be part of that. We don't require perfection, but certainly expect improvement. Our motto is *Excelsior*! We seek to go ever higher in all things. Laziness is not tolerated."

Levi swallowed hard. In spite of the weirdness and danger, he'd be crushed if he didn't get invited back next year. The other kids' solemn faces told him they felt the same.

Mr. Dominic smiled. "You'll do fine. All you need to do is buckle down and work hard."

Levi determined to do just that.

That Saturday Levi pounded the last nail into the Trojan horse he'd helped build for the play. He and two other boys pushed the wheeled prop under the covered stone walkway where it would wait until performance day. Once it was in place, Levi gave the wooden horse one last pat and grinned. It looked good. He had done okay with some of the drawing lessons for his art class earlier that summer, but he'd really enjoyed helping create this prop. It not only looked good, but it was sturdy enough to carry three people inside.

As the others drifted off to different activities, Levi leaned against a stone pillar to watch play practice. He thought Lizzie made a pretty good Helen of Troy. She clearly liked being the center of attention. Ashley played her clarinet in the ensemble accompanying the play. Monica was in charge of hair and make-up, which Levi thought was hilarious since she was forever scolding Lizzie for her constant primping. He'd wisely kept his humor to himself, though. He didn't want to turn Monica's wrath on him. His roommates had only recently invited him to play Spades again, and the girls had stopped giving him the cold shoulder.

Levi sighed, his eyes moving to Sara, who stood in the walkway with Miss Nydia discussing the best materials for a Spartan soldier's helmet. Levi knew Sara and the hall chaperone spent countless hours in Miss Nydia's room designing and stitching all the costumes. It was no wonder they were such close friends.

As Levi's gaze drifted from one female friend to the next, his feelings of guilt overwhelmed him. Albert and his roommates were right: Levi wasn't being noble, trying to protect the girls from the truth about Terracaelum. He'd known for a while now he was wrong. He'd known he needed to talk to his friends, to apologize for acting like he was in charge of the world when he couldn't even control himself. It was just so hard.

But he couldn't wait any longer. It was time to make things right.

Despite his good intentions, finding an opportunity to speak privately with a group of seven turned out to be more of a challenge than Levi expected. When supper came and went with no chance, Levi snagged Sara's arm on the way out of the dining hall. "Would you come with me a second?"

She followed him into the foyer. "What?"

"Your room's directly under ours, right?"

She scrunched her face at the strange question. "Yeah, I think."

"After room check tonight, tap on your ceiling three times. We'll tap back when we're in the clear. Then you girls meet us at the top of the northeast tower. We need to talk."

Sara eyed him uncertainly. "Exactly what am I supposed to tap on the ceiling with? They're ten feet high, in case you hadn't noticed."

"I don't know, a bat or broom or something? Use your imagination."

The corners of her mouth drew in. "Why should we come? What if we get in trouble?"

He put on his best pitiful puppy look. "Please, Sara. It's important or I wouldn't have asked."

She studied him, her mouth still tight.

"Please."

Her eyes shifted heavenward and she sighed, "Oh, all right. We'll tap."

"You did what?" Trevor's jaw looked hard enough to crack a boulder.

Levi frowned. "I thought you wanted me to tell them."

"Yeah, but . . ." Trevor flopped onto his bed. "You're missing the point. You think you should choose when and when not to tell. It's not all about you."

Levi tossed his hands and plopped down on his own bed. "What do you want from me? I'm trying to do what you said."

Tommy rolled his eyes.

Steve shrugged. "Hey, at least we're finally telling them." He raised an eyebrow at Trevor. "Just drop it, okay?"

Albert piped up from his spot on Tommy's bed. "I agree with Steve. The boy finally wised up. Leave it at that."

Levi considered Albert, not sure whether to thank him or thump him, but Trevor snapped his mouth shut.

"By the way, I ain't gonna make your little meeting tonight." Albert popped the huge pink bubble he'd blown. "I got guard duty."

The Trojan Horse Traitor

"Guard duty?" Tommy looked at the others. "Since when is there guard duty?"

Levi shrugged. It was news to him.

"Since the past six weeks or so." Albert shook his head like they were dense. "Told you I got me a special assignment from the big boss. Haven't you noticed I'm not in here a couple times a week? We take it in turns watching day and night ever since that fire when you guys was camping."

"Where do you watch from?" Levi's shoulders tensed. "I mean, will somebody see us tonight?"

"Nah, I'll be on the northwest tower, and somebody else—Althea maybe—has the southeast." Albert gave his gum a few chomps. "Unless you plan on shooting off fireworks or something, you ought to be fine."

"You're hilarious, Albert." Levi turned his attention to Trevor. "Okay, so we wait for the girls to tap, meet them on the roof, and then tell all." He cocked his head, eyebrows raised. "Deal?"

"Yeah, okay. Deal." Trevor bumped knuckles with Levi, a tiny grin on his lips.

Chapter 31

Sara

Just before eleven, three thuds echoed through the floor. Mr. Sylvester had checked the boys' room nearly two hours before, so long ago Levi thought the girls had backed out on them. He was glad to be wrong. When he snagged a hiking boot and banged the floor three times in response, Steve snorted awake.

"Come on." Levi stuffed shoes on his feet and grabbed a flashlight. He led his roommates quietly from the room, using the moonlight to navigate the corridor.

When the tower door clanked shut behind Steve, Levi clicked on his flashlight and started climbing. What if they got caught? Would they get in trouble? They shouldn't. They wouldn't stay out long. Besides, this conversation was too important to wait. He chose to ignore the fact that he was the reason it had been postponed so long already.

As Levi reached the top step, a clatter echoed from below. Steve let out a yelp.

Tommy clapped a hand over Steve's mouth.

Trevor whispered, "It's probably the girls."

Levi nodded. Had to be the girls.

Yet as he slipped onto the tower rooftop, acid burned his stomach. The brisk night air raised chill bumps on his bare arms. Summer was almost over.

Levi waited a few paces beyond the door, far enough so he wouldn't block the girls from getting out, near enough so he could reach the stairs if escape became necessary. The fact that Mr. Dominic set up round-the-clock guard duty meant Levi and his friends should be careful, both of getting spotted by a guard and of encountering the one they guarded against.

The tower door creaked open, revealing a thin stream of light.

"Levi?" Sara's quavering voice broke the silence.

"I'm here." Her obvious anxiety made him square his shoulders. "It's okay, come on out."

She stepped through the doorway, eyes wide in the light of the three-quarter moon. The other girls followed.

Levi beckoned them to the center of the tower where he and Trevor had star-gazed an eternity ago. He sat, glad the stones still held warmth from the sunny day. The others sat in a tight circle beside him, as if closeness meant safety.

No one spoke or moved a muscle. The tension grew until Levi felt a ridiculous urge to laugh. He struggled against it but couldn't stifle the giggles. He wound up rolling uncontrollably on the tower floor, laughing until tears flowed.

"What is wrong with you?" Sara's voice trembled with fury. "You think it's funny, calling us out here in the middle of the night?" She jumped up. "I'm out of here. I'm not getting in trouble so you can have a laugh at my expense. Come on, girls."

Back rigid, Sara stalked to the door. The rest, even Levi's roommates, followed her, muttering angrily.

Levi stumbled to his feet, gasping for breath. "I'm sorry. Wait, please."

Sara whipped her head around and glared at him. The others, icy-eyed, hovered beside her. "What? You'd better make it good."

"It is good." Levi thumped his fists against his thighs. Ugh. He was only making things worse. "I mean it's bad." He huffed. "Just sit down." He motioned them back, but no one moved. He turned pleading eyes on Sara. "I'm sorry, okay? Sometimes I can't help laughing when I get nervous." His ears burned. "And I'm scared stupid right now."

Sara tilted her chin, assessing him. After a moment, she returned, took his hand, and pulled him to sit beside her. The others came back as well.

"Okay," Sara said, "tell us what we're doing out here."

Levi looked around the circle. How to explain? He glanced hopefully at Trevor, but the bigger boy simply shook his head as if to say, *you planned this thing, you do the talking*.

Levi plunged in, eyes on his shoelaces. He told of the castle's appearance where a cliff had been, of the strange ears he'd noticed, of Hunter's evil actions, of Mr. Dominic's explanation about Terracaelum, of Deceptor's attacks leading to one of the girls. When he reached the last part, he looked up. Three sets of disbelieving eyes met his.

One girl didn't look at him. Sara's head hung over her lap, her hair shielding her face.

"Sara?" Levi lifted his hand uncertainly. He wanted to move her hair so he could see what she was thinking—probably that he belonged in a nuthouse.

Before he touched her, she flung back her hair and startled him with her furious scowl. "You've known for weeks and haven't breathed a word. How dare you, Levi Prince!"

He pulled back his hand, cradling it as if she'd slapped it.

"If I'd only known you knew . . ." Unshed tears glittered in her eyes. "Things could have been so much easier for me. I wasn't allowed to tell anyone, but if you figured it out yourself—" She released a strangled sob. "But no, you—" She dropped her face into her hands and wept.

Fixing a glare on Levi, Monica wrapped her arm around Sara. The rest sat in uneasy silence.

Levi's mind scrambled to catch up. "It's you he's after? Why?"

Sara looked up, scrubbed tears from her cheeks. "Because I'm their daughter, of course."

"Whose daughter?"

"The Dominics' daughter."

He tossed his hands. "The Dominics? But they're old."

Sara hiccupped a laugh. "Is that all you can say? Yes, they're old. They didn't think they'd have children, but like Abraham and Sarah in the Bible, they had a child in their old age."

He gave a slow shake of his head. "You told me your name was Sara Christopher."

She lifted her chin. "Sarafina Christopher Dominic. Christopher is my mother's maiden name."

"So that's why Deceptor wants you?" His head hurt. "To get at Terracaelum's rulers?"

Sara nodded, her eyes filling again.

"Why didn't they introduce you as their child?" Monica asked in a quiet tone. Levi could almost see the wheels turning in her mind.

"Good question," Trevor inserted, a frown trenching his forehead. "Why make it look like you're from somewhere else?"

Sara sniffled. "I'm a pretty recent addition to a very ancient world. They've kept me a secret from all but their closest subjects, knowing Deceptor would come hunting if he found out about me—especially this late in their reign."

"Their reign?" Ashley whispered, but no one answered.

"I haven't seen you in conversation with Mr. or Mrs. Dominic . . . I mean, your parents, and I'm with you most of the time." Hurt flashed across Monica's face as she removed her arm from Sara's shoulders.

Sara touched Monica's wrist. "I couldn't exactly chat with them whenever I wanted. Anybody who knew what to watch for would've picked up on who I was."

Steve cast Sara a disbelieving look. "You haven't been able to talk to them at all?"

Sara shook her head. "Miss Nydia acts as our go-between, carrying messages back and forth. She's been my nurse since I was a baby. She's like a second mother to me." She smiled sadly. "I don't know what I would've done without her this summer. It's been so lonely not being with my parents."

Lizzie scrunched up her face. "Let me get this straight, honey. You've been hidden away here in this castle all your life with no kids to play with and nothing to do? You couldn't even go shopping?" She clucked her tongue. "You poor thing."

"It hasn't been so bad. My parents and the staff have taught me all kinds of things. That's why archery and canoeing and the rest come so easily for me. I've trained in them all my life."

Lizzie rounded her eyes at Sara. "But shopping, honey. No shopping."

"Or friends." Monica raised an eyebrow at Lizzie. "That's more important, right Lizzie?"

Lizzie flipped her hair. "I already said that."

"That's such a sad story." Trevor sniffled loudly, oblivious to the brewing catfight.

Tommy rolled his eyes and gave Trevor a light shove.

"What?" Trevor demanded.

Sara giggled. "That's part of why my folks reopened Camp Classic, so I could make friends like you." She reached for Monica's and Levi's hands. "I'm glad they did."

"Me too." Face hot, Levi squeezed her fingers.

"Same here." Trevor swiped his thick knuckles under his eyes. "You don't have to worry about anything bad getting to you, Sara." He stood up and slapped himself on the chest. "We'll protect you."

"Well, of course we will." Monica stood too, her stern eyes finding each face in the circle. "Does everyone realize we can't talk about any of this except when we're completely alone? Otherwise, we might endanger Sara."

The others rose, murmuring agreement.

Levi stood and met Sara's eyes. "None of us will do anything to put you in danger. We'll help you however we can. From here on out." He willed her to see how sorry he was. "I promise."

Levi stared at the shadowy ceiling above his bed, once again listening to his roommates' snores. He couldn't sleep, not with all Sara had told them. He flipped to his belly, hoping pressure from the mattress would settle his roiling stomach. Sara had let him off so easy. If she'd smacked him upside the head, maybe he wouldn't feel so bad now.

He sighed, rolled onto his back, sat up. How could he have failed Sara like that? How different this summer would've been if he hadn't been so intent on controlling everybody else. Maybe he should spend more time reading his Bible. He'd barely opened it at all over the past few weeks.

"I'm sorry, God," he whispered into the darkness. "Help me learn to stop trying to run everything myself. Help me make things right."

He lay back and fell into a dreamless sleep.

Levi was thankful the next morning was Sunday because his tired brain couldn't have handled Latin conjugations after the late night. Plus, he'd grown to enjoy chapel services. Mr. Dominic talked about Scripture as if it were a matter of life and death. Maybe it really was in a place like this.

That afternoon, Levi joined the large group hiking down for one last phone call home to confirm pickup times the next Saturday. When he called, he was glad his family sounded eager to have him home after a summer away. He looked forward to seeing them, too, but he hated to leave Camp Classic.

He hung up, deep in thought, and bumped into Hunter at the next telephone table.

"Sorry," Levi mumbled, bracing for the rude remark Hunter was bound to throw at him.

But Hunter didn't even look up. Relieved, Levi slipped by as Hunter said into the receiver, "Look, Mom, I'm glad you found a new property in New York but—"

A loud crack turned Levi's head in time to watch Hunter snap his pencil a second time.

"Mom, listen a minute." Hunter's face was a mask of frustration. "Will Dad be back from his business trip in time for the two of you to pick me up next week?" He paused, snapped the pencil again. "Saturday, yes." Another pause, another snap. "I know you plan to scout properties in New Hampshire but—" He sighed, hand fisted around the pencil bits. "I'll only have a week before I leave for school. Okay, fine, bye."

Hunter slammed down the receiver, chucked the pencil pieces onto the table, and his gaze fell on Levi, still gawking at him. Rage narrowed Hunter's eyes. Levi scurried out the door. He had no desire to end up like that pencil.

Once outside, Levi sat on a fallen tree within the tree line where he could stay out of sight of Hunter but still catch his friends when they finished with their calls. What was all that with Hunter anyway? Sounded like life at home wasn't as perfect as he'd pretended. Levi wished he hadn't overheard the conversation. He didn't want to feel sorry for Hunter. It was much easier to think of him as a shape-shifting demon sorcerer, or at least a really big creep.

Levi sighed, trying to relax. His gaze drifted to the trees swaying in the lake breeze as his fingers picked at the bark on his tree. A flash of yellow drew his attention. Hunter and Martin emerged from the woods nearby, heads together in whispered conversation.

Oh, no, this can't be good. Levi held very still. If they got hold of him here in the forest with no adults near . . .

Hunter's eyes snagged on Levi. His face split into a vicious grin as he elbowed Martin and gestured toward Levi. Smirking, Martin started for Levi, fists balled. Levi's pulse pounded in his throat. He was dead meat.

"Hey, Levi, where'd you go?" Trevor's call drew Martin's and Hunter's eyes in the direction of the castle trail.

"Over here!" Relief sagged Levi's spine. Thank God for friends big enough to scare away bullies.

Hunter's livid face swiveled toward Levi. "I've got plans you're not gonna like," he mouthed, then turned and strode away, Martin at his side.

Levi stared after them, his eyes on Hunter's receding back. *"I've got plans you're not gonna like."* Chills skittered across his scalp. Hunter must really be Deceptor, and that pathetic phone call must've been a fake to mislead the other campers into thinking Hunter was a normal kid with normal problems. He'd even tugged a little pity from Levi, the creep.

More importantly, though, what plans was Hunter talking about?

At a loss, Levi peered around the woods. "What am I supposed to do?" he said aloud.

A hot wind struck his cheek, making him flinch.

Watch out for Sara.

Levi spun around. Had somebody spoken? The words almost seemed part of the wind.

Some nearby bushes parted and Trevor stepped into the little clearing. "There you are. What're you doing in here? Hiding?"

Glad as he was for Trevor's appearance, Levi ignored him, preoccupied with the words he thought he'd heard. *Watch out for Sara.*

Purpose gelled in Levi's heart. "I will," he said aloud, even though Trevor looked at him like he'd lost his mind. "I promise."

Chapter 32

Plans

The cooler temperatures that afternoon called Levi and his friends outside to study for their exams. As Levi tried to cram his brain with logical fallacies and Latin verbs, his thoughts constantly returned to the same problem: what to do about Sara. He had reported Hunter's words to his friends—all of them, girls included. They'd gone round and round on what the bully meant. Tommy thought Hunter was just trying to freak Levi out. Ashley, who'd also overheard Hunter's phone conversation, suggested Hunter bullied people because his parents didn't give him enough attention. But Levi wasn't buying it. Ashley was projecting her own homesickness on Hunter, and it was making her soft. Besides, he really thought Hunter staged the whole thing: if people thought of him as a poor little rich kid, they'd never suspect him of being what he was, a demon sorcerer named Deceptor.

Levi was right, he knew it. Especially after the *watch out for Sara* bit, which he hadn't shared with the others—he didn't want them to think he'd gone off the deep end. Nope, there was no question Hunter was Deceptor in disguise.

But knowing Hunter's true identity wasn't enough unless Levi convinced Mr. Dominic of the truth. Even if Levi managed to keep Deceptor away from Sara the rest of the week, she'd still be here after camp. Then Deceptor would simply shapeshift again, and she'd be forever vulnerable. They had to act now, while they knew Deceptor's form.

That meant Levi had to prove Hunter's identity to Mr. Dominic. Immediately. Unfortunately, the plan that kept nagging at him was something he really didn't want to do. He pushed it away time and time again as he quizzed his friends on history dates, but it wouldn't leave him alone. Finally, a few minutes before suppertime, Levi set aside his notes. "Guys, I have an idea."

They all looked up from their books.

He leaned in close, glanced around for eavesdroppers, and whispered, "It's a plan to catch Deceptor before Saturday so we don't have to leave Sara here with him after camp."

Before he could elaborate, Miss Althea strode up. "It's time for supper. Into the castle." She made a shooing motion with her hands.

Levi groaned. His plan would have to wait.

Levi's exams went okay—even math, which was always sheer torture. On Wednesday, the instructors graded tests while the kids finished last-minute preparations for the Olympics and the play, but Levi was preoccupied. As they waited outside the forest for the staff member designated to canoe-sit them that day, he pulled everybody into a tight huddle.

"All right, here's what I'm thinking." He kept his voice low. "Hunter and his thugs have all signed up for tomorrow's wrestling event. When everybody goes outside, I'll sneak up and search their room. There has to be proof in Hunter's stuff that he's Deceptor."

Trevor raised a hand. "But what if he's not Deceptor?"

"He is. Trust me." Levi turned away from Trevor's curled upper lip and studied the others. "Okay, so what I need you guys to do is make sure nobody goes back to Hunter's room before I'm clear. That means I'll need a couple people to distract anybody who tries to come inside early, and I'll need one guy to stand guard at each stairwell to warn me if somebody does come up before I get out." Levi paused for volunteers. Trevor, Tommy, Monica, and Lizzie exchanged incredulous glances. Steve stared at his shoes, and Ashley played with a button on her shirt. Sara looked at Levi, her face white with horror.

Why didn't anybody answer? Levi huffed. "Listen, guys, I'm not trying to boss you around, if that's what you're thinking."

Several eyebrows shot up.

"I'm really not." Levi slapped both hands against his thighs. "I just can't stand waiting around to see if something bad's going to happen to Sara. If any of you have a better suggestion to deal with the problem, feel free to share."

He glared at each of them in turn, not moving on until each eye had met his.

Tommy cleared his throat. "Um, question: what if you're wrong?"

Trevor muttered, "That's what I'm saying."

Levi slid him a dirty look then breathed in deep. "Okay, fine. It's a fair question. Maybe, just maybe, Hunter isn't Deceptor. But what if I'm right and we do nothing? We go home and Sara's left with this evil creep, closer than ever to snatching her. If we do what I say, worst case is we've wasted a little time and energy finding out who isn't after Sara. No big deal. But if I'm right . . ."

Silence followed.

Finally, Steve spoke up, his face a blotchy pink. "I'll guard the southwest stairwell. I can do a birdcall if Hunter or anybody comes back."

Yes! Levi flashed him a huge smile.

Tommy sighed. "Yeah, okay. I've got the other end, but we'll have to think of some other signal because I couldn't imitate a bird to save my life."

Levi turned his smile on Tommy. "No problem. Just whistle instead."

"Well, I'm sticking close to Sara." Trevor tapped himself on the chest. "I'm not really comfortable with her being out near the forest with some monster on the loose—whether he's really Hunter or not."

Levi chose to ignore the doubt in Trevor's words. "Good idea."

Sara shook her head. "No way, you guys. Nobody's doing anything that might get them hurt, not on my account. It's not worth it." She turned anxious eyes on Levi. "You know how Hunter's friends are—they'll throw you off the roof if you get in their way."

Levi forced lightness into his tone. "If they don't catch me, they can't throw me off the roof." He touched her arm. "Seriously, Sara, I'll be careful. We all will. Don't worry."

She didn't look convinced.

"You boys are bound to have problems with Suzanne and Jacqueline." Monica's nose wrinkled. "I'll have to shadow them until you've finished your search. If they suspect something, they'll tattle to Hunter."

"Well, girl," Lizzie said, resting a perfectly tanned arm across Ashley's shoulders, "guess that leaves you and me to distract any of Hunter's henchmen who try to slip away early." She batted her lashes. "We'll

The Trojan Horse Traitor 183

think of something, I'm sure."

Ashley nodded, her lips a thin line.

The snap of a twig whirled Levi around.

Miss Nydia stood no more than three feet away. "Are you children canoeing today or not?"

"Sure," Sara said brightly. "Let's go, everybody."

As Levi trailed his friends, his gaze flicked to the elf hall chaperone. Had she overheard their plans?

Chapter 33

The Search

After breakfast the next morning, Levi's friends split up to take their posts. He hid in the first floor bathroom and waited for the building to clear. At exactly five after nine, he left the bathroom, scanning the corridors for any stragglers. Not spotting anyone, he darted to the northwest staircase and listened. Silence. Taking the stairs two at a time, he raced to the fourth floor and nearly ran over Tommy huddled outside the door to Hunter's hallway.

Levi stopped to catch his breath. "Any sign of trouble?"

"Nothing."

Levi eased open the door and peeked into the corridor. With a thumbs-up for Tommy, he strode down the hall, grinning. He'd done it . . . entered the lion's den without getting bit.

As he yanked open the first door, he realized he'd made a mistake—a stupid mistake.

He had no clue which room was Hunter's.

He looked from one four-poster bed to the next then stepped back into the corridor and examined the four other identical doors. A soft groan seeped from between his lips. Now he had to search five rooms, possibly twenty beds, to find Hunter's.

Wait. If he knew which room belonged to the chaperones, he could narrow things down. And maybe, like on his hall, there was an extra room not used by campers, like the one Albert was staying in. Feeling somewhat better, Levi left the first door with the plan to check out the entire hallway before deciding which rooms to give a more thorough search. He opened the second door. Dirty socks, messy beds. Definitely belonged to campers. The third was locked, which meant it must belong to the Drakes. The fourth was so spotless he figured it had to be empty, but the fifth had stuff thrown around like the first two.

Levi began a systematic search of the fifth room. He looked under the beds at all the junk and opened each wardrobe, seeking a tag or scrap of paper with a name on it. He checked in each nightstand drawer for loose papers. Nothing of Hunter's. It was the wrong room.

He scurried down the hall to the second room and began a systematic search there, only to conclude after fifteen wasted minutes that it was the wrong room also. He groaned. The door he'd opened first was the right one after all. Why hadn't he started there? With a frustrated sigh, he stomped back into the first room and to the nearest bed. Moving stuff around underneath, he spotted a suitcase tag: MARTIN SERGE.

"Finally."

He recognized the shirt wadded up on the next bed. Hunter's shirt. Hunter's bed. He tore into the wardrobe and found nothing but clothes. Rifling through the nightstand produced nothing but old homework papers and a stash of candy bars.

A glance at his watch dampened his armpits. The wrestling matches wouldn't last forever. Was there nothing here? Desperate, he dropped to his knees and shoved his hands between the mattress and box springs. His left hand brushed against something solid. He wedged his fingers around it and yanked. It was that washed-out purple book Hunter had stuffed into his backpack the first day in the cabin. Why would an old book be important enough to hide under the mattress?

Sitting back on his heels, Levi peered at the cover. Cracked gold lettering read, KRISTIANNA FAE MORGAN.

Brow furrowed, he opened the book. The spine crackled, and the pages felt like they might crumble beneath his fingertips. Dust tickled his nose. Biting back a sneeze, he squinted at the faded loopy handwriting:

June 10th, 1886
Dear Diary,
So begins my sojourn far from home. I still find it difficult to believe Mother and Father allowed me to continue my education here this summer . . .

Levi gave his head a quick shake. *1886?* Why was Hunter hiding some dead girl's diary?

Hang on, maybe it wasn't so much the diary he was hiding. Maybe he'd tucked something between the pages.

He flipped through the brittle pages. Halfway through, a shaft of sunlight illumined the words, *that Prince boy.* Levi froze, heart skipping, as he bent nearer the page. Was it talking about him? Couldn't be. It was written way before he was born.

A creak sounded behind him. Shifting the book out of sight, Levi swiveled, still crouched on the floor.

Greg closed the door behind him. "Well, well, well, if it isn't the little runt, Levi Prince." He cracked his knuckles, sending chills up Levi's spine.

Wary eyes on Greg, Levi gave the diary a quick shove toward the bed. He could only hope it was out of view.

Greg swaggered a few paces nearer.

Levi scrabbled to his feet and waited with his hands loose at his sides.

"What're you doing in here, huh? This ain't your room."

"Uh." His brain scrambled for a good excuse. "I thought you were wrestling." He bit the inside of his cheek. *Idiot!* Why not just announce he was trespassing? Now all Greg had to do was tell Mr. Dominic he'd caught him trying to steal something, and Levi would get kicked out of Camp Classic for good.

"So that's how it is, huh? When you didn't show up at the match, Hunter thought you might be up to something." Greg took another step. "That's why he had me throw my first match." His face reddened. "I don't like to lose."

Levi backed into a bedpost. Maybe Greg wouldn't turn him in after all. Maybe he'd toss Levi out the fourth floor window. *Think, Levi, or you're dead!* Levi glanced wildly around the room for an escape.

Greg the Hulk blocked the way to the door. The path to the bathroom was full of obstacles. Not that going in there would help, not unless he wanted to flush himself down the toilet. That was not an attractive option.

Levi sized up Greg's broad shoulders and meaty fists. The toilet looked easier to deal with than him. There was no way Levi could beat this guy in a fight.

Levi heaved a sigh. *Lord, help me.* His only chance was to talk his way out of this one.

"So, Greg," Levi said as casually as he could manage, "do you plan to throw all your events or just the ones Hunter tells you to?"

Greg halted mid-stomp. "What're you saying?" His furious glare reminded Levi of the angry bull with red swirling eyes in those old Bugs Bunny cartoons.

Levi widened his eyes. "I only wondered why someone so obviously superior at wrestling and other, um . . . contests of physical strength, would obey someone like Hunter." He shrugged. "It makes you wonder if he was trying to get you out of the running so he could win."

When Greg frowned, his thick eyebrows merged into one.

Levi silently thanked God that Greg was a mental midget. "Ah, well, if you don't mind playing Hunter's puppet while he gets all the glory . . ." His sigh alone should've won him an Academy Award.

"Hunter's puppet?!" Greg's voice boomed so loud a notebook from Martin's nightstand crashed to the floor. "I ain't nobody's puppet!"

Greg stormed from the room. Levi listened as his thumping footfalls ended with a door slam. Levi followed slowly, checking right and left for anybody else who might want to beat him up.

Then Levi stopped dead at a horrible thought. "Tommy!" How bad a beating had Greg given his roommate? He ran to the door and snatched it open. A bruise-free Tommy blinked at him.

"Did he come by you?" At Tommy's blank stare, Levi whirled around. "Oh, no, Steve!"

He ran back along the corridor, Tommy at his heels. Steve wasn't at his post. Levi barreled downstairs, too worried to answer Tommy's anxious questions.

Halfway between the fourth and third floors, they ran into Steve racing up. Monica halted a step behind Steve.

"I'm so sorry, I'm so sorry." Steve's sweaty face flamed. "Did he find you? Did he kill you?"

"He found me, but I'm okay."

Tommy glanced between them. "What happened?"

"I didn't chicken out, I promise." Steve wrung his hands, his eyes watering like he was about to cry. "I heard a girl calling my name from downstairs, and I thought it was Lizzie or Ashley so I went to check."

Tommy tapped Levi on the shoulder. "Hello? Guys? A little information?"

Steve didn't look away from Levi. "I saw a classroom door open on the third floor, and when I went inside to check it out, somebody slammed the door on me. I heard somebody laughing outside, then it got quiet like they left."

"It was Suzanne," Monica spoke up. "I was following her until she started up the stairs, then I hung back." Her mouth quirked into a sheepish smile. "I didn't want her to see me. By the time I got near the third floor, I heard a door slam and laughter. And I heard Steve pounding." She turned to Steve. "Sorry I didn't stop her."

Steve shook his head. "It's not your fault she tricked me. Again." He studied his oversized feet. "I'm so stupid."

Levi patted Steve's shoulder. "It's okay, really. I never thought you'd chickened out on me." He cocked his head. "Lucky for me Greg has a big ego and a small brain."

Steve half-smiled. "Find anything up there?" He pointed upstairs.

Tommy huffed. "That's what I want to know, but nobody tells me anything."

"I did, actually—" Levi smacked himself on the forehead. "Oh, no, I left the diary under Hunter's bed."

"What diary?" Tommy said.

Levi jogged up a few steps.

Monica grabbed his arm. "You can't go back. Greg's bound to have told Hunter you were trespassing in their room by now. We need to get away from here. Besides, we'll be late for the canoeing event if we don't run."

Levi cast a glance upstairs and groaned in frustration. What choice did he have? He followed Monica downstairs, shoulders drooping.

All that danger, and he had nothing to prove Hunter's true identity to Mr. Dominic.

Chapter 34

Camp Classic Olympics

Levi and the others skidded to a halt at the river as the first group climbed into their canoes. Scooping up life vests, Tommy and Monica joined their partners, Sara and Lizzie, in canoes. Levi smiled at Sara, hoping to erase the concern in her eyes so she could focus on the race. She and Tommy actually had a chance of winning this thing. Unlike Levi and his partner, Ashley.

Levi joined his friends on the riverbank to wait his turn in the second heat. Though he knew Hunter hadn't chosen this event, probably because he was still in the bad graces of the canoeing instructor after paddling off with Levi that day, Levi searched the crowd for him anyway. When he didn't see Hunter or any of his henchmen, Levi frowned. He'd been sure Hunter would be here making fun of Levi during the race.

Pushing aside worries over what Hunter might be up to, he stumbled along the bank with the crowd and cheered for his friends. Monica and Lizzie took the lead early on and easily won the race. Sara and Tommy took second, both pairs earning slots in the final race.

Trevor and Steve were in the next group, along with Levi and Ashley. When the starting whistle sounded, he and Ashley surged forward, stroking in a relatively smooth rhythm, but they soon fell behind and wound up in third. Surprisingly, the tiny kid Luke from his floor and a girl named Christine from the girls' hall came in first, with a pair of boys from Hunter's floor—Bradley and Derrick—coming in second. Steve and Trevor came in last because Steve tipped their canoe, dumping them both in the water.

Levi, Ashley, and a soaked Steve and Trevor cheered themselves hoarse for their friends in the next round. Monica and Lizzie took the gold. Luke and Christine got the silver, while Sara and Tommy took the bronze. Bradley and Derrick didn't look happy with last place.

On the way to lunch, Levi told the others about finding the diary.

"That's just disturbing, y'all." Lizzie's nose crinkled. "Why would he keep some dead girl's diary in his bed?"

Levi shrugged. "I don't know, but it has to mean he's Deceptor. There's no reason a boy from this century would hide a thing like that."

"I'm more concerned about why your name's in it." Sara lowered her voice to a whisper, her eyes trained on Levi. "You've got to go to my dad. Maybe you're in more danger than I am."

Levi shook his head. "It's got to be about some other guy named Prince, somebody who lived nearly a hundred and fifty years ago. That handwriting was so faded there's no way it was added in the last thirteen years. Besides,"—he threw up his hands—"I left the diary. I've got nothing to show him." He couldn't believe he'd been so idiotic.

They were still arguing over what to do when they reached the castle, but as they neared the dining hall, an unsettled feeling crept across Levi. "I think I'm gonna run upstairs before lunch." He turned to his wet roommates. "You going up to change?"

"I'm too hungry to climb all those stairs," Steve said. "I'll air dry."

Trevor shook his head hard, raining water droplets over everybody. "I'm good now."

Lizzie slugged him. "Neanderthal!"

"What?" Trevor demanded, earning a laugh from the others.

Rolling his eyes, Levi headed for the stairs. Before he'd climbed more than a handful of steps, he heard raised voices from the other staircase. As soon as he recognized the voices, he sat down and ducked to make sure his head wouldn't show over the banister.

"Don't ever disobey me again." Hunter's icy tones sent a shiver up Levi's spine. "If you do, you'll regret it."

"Oh, yeah, what're you gonna do about it?" a voice Levi recognized as Greg's snarled back.

"To start with, I'll have to report to the director that you copied Suzanne on every exam you took." Hunter clucked his tongue.

"But then I'll get kicked out," Greg whined, "and they won't let me come back next year."

Hunter snorted. "You must not be as stupid as you look."

"Who would do stuff for you then?"

Next came the clack of heels on the foyer floor, followed by Hunter's short bark of laughter. "Do you really think I'll have trouble getting idiots like you to help me? Maybe you are as stupid as you look."

Levi glanced over the banister in time to see Greg's neck redden. Once the two disappeared around the corner, he stood and ran up the steps to his hall, Hunter's words raising vague fears in his mind.

When Levi opened his door, he gasped. It was a complete wreck—much worse than anything his roommates had ever done. Wardrobes were thrown wide with shirts and socks dangling out. Papers littered the floor, drawers hung open, pillows and blankets lay in crumpled heaps. He picked his way through the mess and peered into the bathroom, also a disaster with strewn towels, spilled shampoo, and unraveled toilet paper. Whoever had trashed the place was gone now.

Levi turned toward his bed. Though he knew he'd left it in his bottom nightstand drawer, his Bible now lay open upside down on his bed. Stifling a groan, he crossed the room, picked it up, and smoothed the crumpled pages. As he returned it to the drawer, a breeze blew through the open window and picked up several scraps of paper from his bed, scattering them. Levi caught a few pieces.

His Camp Classic invitation. Ripped to shreds.

Levi's fist closed over the pieces. He knew just who'd done this: Hunter Jacobson, Deceptor in disguise.

A short time later, Levi whispered the news of the destroyed room to his roommates, who were inhaling pizza.

"He did what?" Trevor bellowed.

Levi shushed him, but not before half the people in the room turned and stared at them. Even Mrs. Dominic glanced down at them from the staff table. Levi shrugged and smiled. *There's nothing wrong, everybody. Eat your pizza.* When people returned their focus to their lunches, he leaned close to his friends. "Don't let Hunter know it bothers us."

"Sorry." Trevor rubbed the back of his neck. "Those people really get on my nerves, trashing our room like that."

Tommy bobbled his eyebrows at Trevor. "Yeah, 'cause you're such a neat freak."

Levi and the others laughed.

Raucous laughter a few tables over dampened the mood. Hunter pointed at Levi as Martin, Greg, Jacqueline, and Suzanne cackled hysterically.

A sour taste filled Levi's mouth. He was so sick of Hunter and his jerk friends laughing at his expense. Levi turned to his friends, a grim smile on his face. "Greg wasn't laughing a little while ago." He told about Hunter's threats, pleased at the satisfaction on their faces.

After lunch, Levi and his roommates decided to watch the javelin event with the girls instead of dealing with their room. Levi was disappointed when Martin took first place. Especially when Hunter sidled up and said, "Too bad they don't do things like they used to."

Levi frowned, confused.

"You know, back when they'd throw the javelin at their enemy, and whoever drew first blood won." Hunter grinned. "Martin could've gone up against you. Wouldn't that have been fun?" He stalked away, cackling.

Levi stared after him, still frowning. When Hunter's meaning sank in, heat seeped into his face.

But Levi didn't have time to worry about Hunter. He needed to get to the area marked off for fencing. He'd actually started understanding swordplay a little over the past couple of weeks, only because he'd started viewing it from a logical perspective. His chess games with Dr. Baldwin had helped him learn to anticipate his opponent's possible moves, and when he sparred, the dwarf's words to "see the whole board" ran like a refrain in his mind.

Today, Levi had to fight Greg the Hulk. After this morning, he knew Greg probably wouldn't be in the mood to let him off easy, but he was more worried about Trevor, who was matched against Hunter. As he and Trevor donned their protective equipment and chose blades, Levi murmured to his friend, "Watch this guy. I know you don't really believe me that he's Deceptor, but he's bad news. He'd just as soon kill you as look at you."

Trevor shook his head. "He can't." He tapped his forefinger on the buffered sword edge.

"Be careful anyway. I don't trust him to fight fair."

"You be careful too. Greg's as much of a cheater as Hunter." Trevor turned his glare on the big boy stretching on the opposite side of the arena. "If he told him to hurt you, you know he'll do it."

Levi nodded. Trevor was right, but he had no choice. It was time to fight.

Chapter 35

Fencing

Levi jerked away from yet another heavy blow. So far Greg had done nothing but stand dead center, hacking away like a deranged lumberjack trying to fell a tree with a dull ax. Greg hadn't moved his feet and had barely shifted his upper body, but he was sucking wind big-time.

At this rate, Levi just had to stay out of the way and let Greg wear himself out, so he continued his dance around the perimeter while Greg chopped and hacked. The big boy's face grew redder by the second, and his breathing came in short gasps.

Soon Levi planned to go on the offensive. Who knew? Maybe he could actually win this thing. A tiny smile touched Levi's lips at the idea.

A flash of red behind Greg pulled his attention from the sword-wielding maniac. In that split second, Greg whacked him. Pain shot from Levi's left forearm all the way up to his shoulder. His whole arm went numb. His eyes watered. He blinked hard to clear them. If he missed the next blow, he'd be done for.

Just as his vision cleared, Greg brought down his sword with all his might, this time aiming for Levi's head. Levi twisted out of the way, his paralyzed left arm swinging useless at his side. A stinging foretold the return of feeling, then a rush of excruciating pain.

Another flash of red appeared in his peripheral vision. *Focus, Levi.* Distraction hurt too much.

Striking Levi must've whetted Greg's appetite because he gave up his tree-hacker position and chased Levi around the ring, his big-toothed grin visible through the mask. The two circled and twirled for several long moments while the sunlight beat down with even more intensity than Greg's blows. Soon Greg slowed. Sweat streaked his blotchy face, and his chest heaved. Levi had to keep blinking sweat from his eyes so he could see the next blow.

A short but exhausting time later, Greg's sword came down with an earth-shattering blow that dented the ground beside Levi. The force of the blow nearly felled Greg himself. Seeing his opportunity, Levi lifted his sword high and rushed him. Greg parried the blow at the last second but stumbled backward. Levi moved in, swinging again and again. Greg's eyes widened as he tried to fend off the attack. His puffs turned to wheezes, which soon became gasps.

But Levi didn't back off until he knocked Greg's blade from his hand. With a huge grin, he lightly jabbed the padding on Greg's chest.

The crowd around him cheered.

Almost immediately, screams and boos turned his head to the girls' match going on nearby. Lizzie lay on the ground unarmed while Suzanne hit her in the face with the hilt of her sword. Mrs. Sylvester, the girls' referee, ran over and pulled Suzanne away from Lizzie, who lay sobbing. Blood seeped from beneath her face mask.

Levi ran over, shoving aside a chuckling, red-handkerchief-waving Hunter. Levi reached Lizzie at the same moment as Trevor.

"You okay, Lizzie?" Trevor's jaw clenched as he helped her sit up.

Levi squatted and gently tugged up her mask. Blood streamed from between her swelling lips.

"Why'd she h-h-hit me?" Lizzie's face was pale.

"Shh," Levi said softly. "It's okay now, she won't hit you anymore."

"I know I'm t-t-terrible at fencing." Tears dripped from the end of Lizzie's nose. "B-b-but y'all always quit fighting when it was c-c-clear you'd won."

Levi patted her shoulder and glanced at Trevor, who appeared about to pop a blood vessel.

"Let me through, please," Dr. Baldwin called as he shoved through the crowd. Levi scrambled out of the way, accidently backing into Sara.

"Sorry," he said, but she didn't answer.

She was glaring at Suzanne, who stood with Hunter. Suzanne simpered up at Hunter. Hunter whispered something that looked like *Good job*.

Levi's blood boiled.

"Suzanne, you won this match," Mr. Dominic said sternly. Suzanne jumped and turned from Hunter to the director, her smile fading instantly. "But our goal in these games is not to injure others. You had clearly defeated your opponent; to hit her when she was down was wrong."

"I'm sorry, sir," Suzanne said, eyes downcast, the picture of repentance. "I guess I got carried away in all the excitement."

"If anything of this sort happens in your next match, you'll be disqualified." Mr. Dominic's eyes slitted. "And you will jeopardize your chances of returning to Camp Classic next summer."

"Yes, sir."

As soon as the director turned away to check on Lizzie, Suzanne pointed to Sara and mouthed, *You're next*.

Chapter 36

A Final Game of Chess

After Dr. Baldwin helped Lizzie from the field, Sara beat Jacqueline, which put her into the next round against Suzanne. Though Sara was excellent at fencing, Levi wondered if Hunter told Jacqueline to let Sara win so Suzanne could fight her. If that was the case, what did they have planned for Sara?

Hunter soundly whipped Trevor in less than five minutes and probably would've punished Trevor with extra blows if the director hadn't monitored the fight extra carefully. Even so, Trevor limped away after the match.

Sara and Levi would face Suzanne and Hunter the next morning in the final round. How Levi wished he'd let Greg win their match. Because now he had to do what he'd avoided all summer: sword-fight Hunter. As he trudged to the castle for supper, dread settled in Levi's gut, though he wasn't sure if he was more worried for Sara or himself.

When they reached the dining hall, they found Lizzie seated at a table with an ice pack on her mouth. She only had a busted lip and a loose tooth, but she turned on the melodrama. "Tell me something, y'all." She pointed to her swollen lip with a pink nail that had somehow remained chip-free. "How am I supposed to play a woman so gorgeous she causes a war with this hideous face?"

Levi smiled, glad she was her usual self again.

"I'm serious, guys." Real tears flooded Lizzie's eyes, and Levi's smile vanished.

"You look fine," Tommy insisted, awkwardly patting her arm.

Not knowing what else to do, Levi tossed a scowl at Hunter's table.

Then Monica shocked them all by wrapping an arm around Lizzie.

"Don't worry, honey. When I get finished with your makeup, you'll be as beautiful as ever."

Levi's left eyebrow shot up. Honey? Since when did Monica call anybody *honey*, much less Lizzie?

Lizzie turned a watery smile on Monica. "Thanks."

Monica nodded and returned to her seat.

After supper the boys cleaned up their trashed room. Since his wardrobe and drawers had been thoroughly emptied, Levi went ahead and packed. Steve and Tommy headed downstairs for a final dress rehearsal of *The Trojan Horse*. Ignoring the pile of clothes on his bed, Trevor played War with Albert.

After a while, Levi got tired of watching the game and slipped downstairs to Dr. Baldwin's room for what might be his last visit of the summer. If he got invited back next year. Otherwise, it could be his last visit ever. His throat tightened at the thought.

When Levi arrived at the infirmary, he found the door ajar and the doctor staring out the open window at the dark forest beyond.

"Dr. Baldwin?" Levi said softly. Why was he by the window he usually avoided? "You okay?"

The doctor started then turned to face him, his dark eyes recessed in his craggy face. "Leviticus Prince, why have you come?"

Levi took an involuntary step back—away from the darkened room and the shadows cast by the clouds crossing the nearly full moon. Away from the creature he'd come to view as a friend, but who now seemed like a beast disturbed in its lair. "I can come back another time, uh . . . sir." Levi took another backward step.

"No." The doctor flicked on a battery-powered lantern beside him. The light made him look more like the mentor Levi knew. Pale, but less . . . bestial. "There's no need for you to leave." Dr. Baldwin's lips curved into what he probably meant for a smile.

Levi hesitated. Was it safe?

"You'll be doing me a favor," Dr. Baldwin said, holding out a hairy hand, "taking an old dwarf's mind off his sorrows."

Levi studied Dr. Baldwin's eyes a moment longer before nodding. "If you're sure I'm not bothering you." He moved into the room as his pulse settled into its normal rhythm.

Levi sat in his usual spot on the bunk next to the wall. The doctor sat opposite him and gestured toward the chess box on the nearby rolling cart. "Shall we?"

Levi nodded and opened the box.

They played several moments before Levi dared say, "I was surprised to see the window open."

The doctor grunted then took his bishop. Levi sighed. He'd better focus on the game.

A little later, Dr. Baldwin said, "Got stuffy in here."

Levi's eyes narrowed. He'd never known stuffiness to make the doctor open the window before. Even in July.

The dwarf shot him a disgusted look. "Okay, so I was feeling depressed." He sniffed, swiped a hand across his face. "It was a hundred and twelve years ago tonight my Della died."

"Oh." Levi wasn't sure whether to respond to the length of years or the fact that the doctor was clearly still in mourning. "I'm sorry." He returned his stare to the chess board.

Several moves later, Levi glanced up at the doctor, whose head was bowed. "Why did Deceptor kill her?" he asked, then tensed. He shouldn't have brought it up.

Dr. Baldwin sighed. "I won't tell you that now, young Master Prince, but I fear the day will come when I have to tell you for your own sake."

What was that supposed to mean? Levi opened his mouth to ask, but snapped it shut at the old dwarf's uplifted hand.

"No more questions." Shoulders slumped, Dr. Baldwin looked at the board. "You'll forgive me for wanting to think of other things tonight."

Levi tried to focus on the game, but he couldn't keep his mind on his opponent's moves.

"Checkmate." Dr. Baldwin harrumphed. "You're not paying attention this evening." He peered at Levi. "I don't think it's only my Della distracting you. Could it be tomorrow's fencing match against that wily snake Hunter?"

Levi's eyes widened. Was a staff member allowed to call a camper a wily snake?

"What?" Dr. Baldwin cracked a grin. "You don't think I see the attitude on that one, smug and sneering but forever fawning around the adults? Well, I see it. And you'd best be more observant tomorrow during your match or he'll hurt you." The grin disappeared. "Use the skills I've taught you. Think of all you know about your enemy. Be constantly vigilant. Never let your concentration waver as you did today against Greg."

Levi's face heated. So the doctor saw his failure during his first fight.

"Yes, I noticed your distraction. And I noticed who caused it."

Forehead crinkled, Levi thought back to the match. A flash of red behind Greg is what distracted him, he remembered that much. His mind jumped to the seconds after the fight, of his rush past Hunter, his irritation at the boy's laughter. And Hunter's red hankie.

"The cheater." The tips of his ears burned.

Dr. Baldwin inclined his head. "That may well be true. In fact, it probably is, but we can't prove it." He met Levi's eyes. "You must be wary. Today's trickery won't be the last. He'll have plenty up his sleeve tomorrow. And his friends aren't above foul-play either, as your friend Lizzie discovered today." His lips puckered with disgust.

Levi thought back to the sneer on Suzanne's face that afternoon. Then his mind shifted to Lizzie's battered face and on to Hunter's satisfied smirk. Finally, an image of Sara's face filled his mind, her warm eyes suddenly turning cold with terror.

Levi straightened his back. He'd do whatever he could to protect her. And that meant paying constant attention—starting with an early-morning fencing match.

Chapter 37

Fencing Finals

The night's clouds were a mere memory in the next morning's blazing sunlight. The air was humid from the damp night, frizzing Levi's hair into a big orange puffball. He put on a hat.

At breakfast, Hunter kept talking about all the people who had died in fencing accidents. The glint in Hunter's eyes made it clear they were threats, not reports. The thing that bothered Levi most, though, was Sara's pale face and red eyes. She looked like she'd spent the whole night crying.

Halfway through the meal, he leaned near her and whispered, "What's wrong? Are you worried about fighting Suzanne?"

She shook her head, tears swimming in her eyes. "No, I can beat Suzanne easy. It's just that . . ." She swallowed back a sob. "My parents sent a message through Miss Nydia last night that they're sending me to boarding school with Monica next week. They're afraid it'll be too dangerous here for me now that Deceptor knows about me."

Levi felt like she'd just kicked him in both shins. He was such a failure. He had known most of the summer that this world was different and for weeks that one of his female friends was in danger. If only he hadn't been so stubborn—if only he'd told all of his friends what he knew, maybe they could have caught Hunter sooner so Sara wouldn't have to leave her home.

Then Sara wouldn't be heartbroken.

He was actually relieved a few minutes later when Mr. Dominic announced, "Back to the games!"

Levi stood abruptly and snagged Sara's arm. Together, they marched out of the castle. Levi had a duel to fight. And, much as he hated the thought, so did Sara.

Levi stood in the boys' fencing area with his nerves zinging. Staff lined both the girls' and boys' arenas, probably to watch for cheating. He was glad they were there, but he wished the matches weren't at the same time. He really wanted to watch Sara's. At least Trevor and others were there, positioned between the two matches, so they could watch both.

Levi closed his eyes tightly, willing himself to focus. He knew Sara was more than a match for Suzanne. That is, if Sara didn't get distracted with thoughts of boarding school. Levi, on the other hand, had no chance at all against Hunter. He'd need all his wits about him just to survive.

He sized up his opponent. Even with the protective webbing on Hunter's facemask, Levi could see the hatred in his steely glare. Definitely David and Goliath. Too bad Levi didn't have a slingshot handy.

Levi's eyes darted. He still had time to make a run for it. He blew out a slow breath, praying his stomach would settle. Then again, puking all over Hunter might give him an advantage.

Levi shook his head. Throwing up on your opponent was definitely an unfair tactic.

As soon as the match began, Levi knew he was in serious trouble. Hunter followed him around the ring swinging his sword relentlessly, like a weed whacker after a blade of grass. It was all Levi could do to keep from getting whacked.

"Bet you wish you'd stayed out of my room now, don't you," Hunter hissed with a perfectly timed thrust.

Levi ducked and weaved just in time to avoid the blunted blade.

"Or that Greg had killed you when he caught you." Hunter sliced at his chest.

Levi dove aside, scooted to the far side of the ring. He was already sweating. A stitch seared his side. Hunter hadn't even broken a sweat. How was Levi ever going to survive? Maybe he should try a little trash talk too—ask Hunter why he had a dead girl's pretty purple diary under his mattress.

Before he could say anything, a burst of applause from the girls' match distracted Hunter. Levi took advantage of the moment and attacked, his sword weaving and swiping. Hunter's blade struck the ground, and

Levi's pulse surged. Maybe he had half a chance after all.

A second later, Levi realized Hunter had played him. When Hunter raised his sword from the ground, its bare blade flashed like its wielder's malicious eyes. Hunter sliced at Levi's head, and Levi knew: Hunter planned to kill him and blame a faulty blade buffer.

Fear fueled Levi's weary muscles. He fought, too focused on survival to even cry out for help from the crowd that must've been preoccupied with the girls' match. Swirling and dancing, thrusting and parrying, the two boys battled. Levi knew a mistake would mean his death.

See the whole board! See the whole board! Dr. Baldwin's admonition ran like a mantra through Levi's desperate mind. His world shrank into narrow focus: Hunter's eyes, taut muscles, blade, rhythm. Levi's actions, reactions, fervent prayers for deliverance from this sword-wielding Goliath. After several long moments, Levi began to see a pattern in Hunter's movements. If he could just anticipate . . .

Finally his chance came. As Hunter began a downward slash, Levi shoved his padded sword upward, forcing Hunter's sword high above his head. The bare blade caught and reflected the sunlight.

"Halt!" Mr. Dominic commanded.

Levi and Hunter froze, blades crossed in the air. Only the sound of their heavy breathing broke the sudden silence.

"Hunter Jacobson." The fury in the director's voice made the hair on Levi's neck stand up. "What do you mean dueling bare-bladed? You might've killed him."

"Sorry," Hunter mumbled. He lowered his sword to the side, but his cold eyes remained fixed on Levi, reminding Levi of a cat waiting for the dog to leave so he could pounce on the mouse.

Levi lowered his sword as well, but his muscles stayed coiled as he watched Hunter's every twitch. He didn't want to be a skewered mouse.

Hunter tossed the director a hard look. "Levi must've knocked the buffer off my sword."

Levi sputtered an incoherent protest, but Mr. Dominic simply glared at them both, motioned for Mr. Drake and Mr. Sylvester to join him, took the boys' swords, and commanded them to stand still. Then he ordered the girls' fight to resume.

Levi did as he was told but strained to see over the shoulders of the crowd around the girls' match. When Trevor cast Levi a questioning glance, Levi nodded toward the girls, wordlessly telling Trevor to watch out for Sara.

After a few moments' huddled discussion, the director, mouth tight and eyes bulging, strode to him and Hunter. "We've decided it isn't worthwhile to continue this match." He turned furious eyes on Hunter. "While I can't prove that any wrongdoing has occurred, I am unwilling to chance anyone becoming injured." At this, he turned to Levi. "Therefore, we have chosen to award two gold medals. You tie for first place."

Levi blinked. Was he disappointed or relieved? On the one hand, he knew Hunter deserved punishment. On the other, he was glad not to have to fight anymore. Plus, there was the added—and truly bizarre—bonus of winning the gold, for fencing of all things.

He settled for offering Mr. Dominic a smile to show he knew the director had no way of proving Hunter meant to kill him. Hunter didn't smile, though. With a kick at the grass, he yanked off his gear, slammed it to the ground, and stormed away. Greg, Jacqueline, and Martin surrounded him. Hunter shoved them away and stomped into the forest alone.

Chapter 38

Terracaelum

Levi ran over to watch the rest of Sara's fight, squeezing through the crowd in time to see Suzanne strike Sara's sword and knock it from her grasp. With a smirk, Suzanne struck Sara's chest protector. Levi groaned. The outcome of his fight had probably cost Sara hers.

He knew he was right when she whipped off her mask and searched the crowd. When her eyes met his, she smiled in apparent relief.

She jogged to his side. "Are you okay?" She looked him over. "Did he cut you?"

"I'm fine," he told her. "Really," he told his other friends as they rushed up tossing questions at him. He looked back at Sara. "Your dad stopped him in time."

She smiled. "I'm glad."

"Yeah. Me, too."

After the rest of the Olympic events, the eight friends returned to the castle, excited over Sara's gold in archery. They went to the tower roof for an hour before dinner and final play preparations. As Levi followed his friends onto the roof, something like homesickness clogged his throat, though he couldn't place the feeling. He understood missing his family, but this was new.

It wasn't like missing grandparents or cousins between visits or being sad to leave a favorite vacation spot. The closest thing he'd experienced was when his family moved from the town where he was born. He'd felt torn, like he did now, as if his heart didn't know which way to turn—toward home and family or toward castle and friends.

Shoulders low, he crossed to the wall and gazed out across Terracaelum. Trees swaying in a light breeze, sunlight shimmering over the green grass, hazy peaks just in view—while nothing shouted that this was a different world, there was an indefinable shimmer to its beauty. No wonder the thought of leaving here upset Sara. Then there was the fact that she'd be leaving her parents for the first time ever.

He turned his head and spotted her peering through another opening in the wall, her eyes sad. Levi glanced over to where the others sat laughing and joking. Trevor congratulated Monica on her silver in archery. Ashley congratulated Trevor on his bronze in fencing. Tommy teased Steve for the bullseye he'd shot into Hunter's target.

"I couldn't help it." A sheepish grin crossed Steve's face. "He was insulting me when I was trying to shoot. He got my aim off."

"I'll say." Tommy jabbed Steve lightly in the ribs. "But, hey, it was your first bullseye of the summer."

A smile touched Levi's lips. Yeah, he'd miss these guys. With a sigh, he turned and walked to Sara. "Thinking about next week?"

She nodded, tears in her eyes. "I'm scared. I don't know how to exist outside of Terracaelum—in your world."

Levi touched her hand. "You'll be fine. You fooled everybody here, didn't you?"

She shrugged even as she allowed a tiny smile.

"You'll be with Monica. That's gotta make it easier." His eyes drifted to Trevor. Would they see each other at all during the school year?

"You'll miss it too, won't you?"

He nodded, swallowing hard. "Come on." He gestured toward the others. "Let's enjoy it while we can."

Chapter 39

The Trojan Horse

That evening the campers had an early supper, a feast of lake perch and cod.

As Levi and his friends finished their strawberry shortcake, a wide-eyed Miss Nydia ran into the room and grabbed Sara's hand. "A couple of the Spartan soldiers were rough-housing in their costumes and ripped them. I need you to help me make repairs. It's nearly call time, and I have so much to do."

"Of course." Sara jumped up.

"I'll help, too," Monica said, pushing back her chair.

"No." Miss Nydia blushed. "I mean, no thank you, Monica." She offered a tight smile. "Isn't it nearly time for you to help Lizzie and the others with their makeup?" She turned toward Levi and Trevor. "And you two, Althea's busy setting up for the musicians, so I'll need you to help me move the horse. Get the other props out to the archery range, and meet me in the courtyard in . . ." She consulted her pocket watch. "Twenty minutes."

Levi nodded. Sara followed the elf from the room.

Monica glanced at the grandfather clock in the corner. "Come on, Lizzie, we really do need to start your makeup."

As the girls hurried out, Levi looked at the others. "Guess we'd best get moving."

Tommy and Steve headed upstairs to put on their soldier costumes, while Ashley went to warm up on her clarinet. Levi and Trevor went to the storage area off the courtyard and filled their arms with wooden swords and spears.

It took two trips to move everything into the wings—really the woods behind the archery mound, their makeshift stage. The boys returned to the courtyard as Miss Nydia emerged from the shadows behind the wooden horse. Her eyes looked strange, sort of frantic and definitely teary. Levi started to ask what was wrong but doubted she'd appreciate his concern. With a mental note that elfish women didn't handle stress well, he joined Trevor by the Trojan horse.

Even with both boys shoving from behind and Miss Nydia pulling from the front, it was hard work getting the horse out of the castle. When they paused for breath on the drawbridge, Levi looked at Trevor. "Wonder where Sara is."

Trevor wiped sweat from his forehead. "Maybe finishing up the repairs. Wonder who was stupid enough to horse around in their costume." He let out a guffaw. "Get it? Horse around!"

Levi groaned. "Enough with the bad jokes. Let's get this thing moved."

Moving the massive prop across the field was no easy task, even without the load of soldiers who would hide inside during the performance. Both boys were red-faced and panting by the time they reached the woods behind the archery mound.

Miss Nydia, on the other hand, seemed to cool down during the trip. Her eyes no longer looked wild and frantic. Her face didn't look at all red, more pale than anything. But it was growing dusky under the trees as sunset neared, so Levi couldn't see clearly. Once the horse felt stable on the uneven ground, he plopped onto the grass to rest. Trevor plunked down beside him.

"Get up." Miss Nydia stood over them, hands on hips, eyes hidden by shadows.

"We just need a minute." Levi nodded toward the horse. "That thing's heavy."

"There's no time." She pointed an imperious finger toward the castle. "Go make sure we didn't leave any props behind."

"Yes, ma'am." Trevor pushed to his feet and raised both eyebrows at Levi as if to ask, *What's her problem?*

With a shrug, Levi stood and trailed Trevor from the forest. After a few steps, Levi glanced back.

Miss Nydia still stood next to the Trojan horse. She waved him on.

"It's fine." Her voice was gentler, more normal. "I'll be there soon. I just want to be sure things are ready here."

Levi nodded and turned away. As he and Trevor crossed the field, they passed Albert and a couple of his cousins feeding wood to the bonfire.

After they'd washed up, changed their shorts for jeans, and gulped down much-needed glasses of water, they trooped back out of the castle with the rest of the campers and staff, everybody talking and laughing as they walked. The evening's activities, along with the events from the day, created a carnival atmosphere. Levi's heartbeat was erratic, though, and his palms were sweating. At first he thought he might've had bad fish for supper, but his stomach didn't hurt. He just had the jitters.

Levi flinched when Greg, dressed as a soldier, ran into him. The hulking boy said something about ramming the Trojan walls then cackled stupidly. Levi rolled his eyes and turned away to scan the field. What felt wrong? Was there something he'd forgotten to do? They'd checked for props like Miss Nydia said. Everything was in place. But something definitely had him on edge.

He spotted Monica near the stage and nudged Trevor. They shoved through the crowd toward her.

"Is everybody in costume?" Trevor asked her.

"Yeah, I left Lizzie with Tommy and Steve backstage." She pointed toward the woods where they'd left the horse.

Levi heard the sound of warm-up scales and spotted Ashley playing her clarinet in the ensemble left of the mound. Levi did a mental count of his friends, barely registering Monica's comment that she was glad Hunter and Martin didn't have parts in the play because Greg and Suzanne had caused enough trouble as Spartan soldiers.

Sudden fear squeezed Levi's heart as his count came up one short. "Where's Sara?"

Monica stared blankly at him. "I don't know." She scanned the field where the audience was settling down on the grass.

Trevor's eyes turned to the field as well. "Did you see her after supper?"

She shook her head. "Last time I saw her was when she left with Miss Nydia to repair those costumes."

The Trojan Horse Traitor

"Without you." Trevor's voice was flat.

Trying not to give in to his rising fear, Levi rose on tiptoe, eyes scouring the crowd for Sara's golden-blonde hair. She had to be there. If she wasn't . . . His mind flitted to Miss Nydia's strange behavior that afternoon. He turned to Monica, his pulse skipping. "Did you ever hear who tore their costumes?"

Monica's eyes widened in dawning realization. "No. Everyone was ready by the time I finished helping Lizzie. Nobody mentioned torn costumes."

"Nobody? You're sure?"

Monica nodded, her lips trembling. "You don't suppose . . ."

"She was acting really weird tonight," Trevor said quietly.

"She wouldn't betray Sara." Tears surged into Monica's eyes. "Would she?"

"It has to be her." Levi rubbed both hands across his face. "Why didn't I see it before? She has access to Sara all the time." He smacked his fist into his palm. "Sara and her parents trust her completely."

Trevor's eyes blazed. "Sara said she was like a second mom to her."

"But why would she do it?" Tears traced Monica's cheeks.

"I don't know, maybe we're wrong and Sara's fine, but we still have to find her. Come on." Levi led the others backstage, waving off Mr. Austin's irritated hisses that they shouldn't be there.

They questioned Lizzie, Tommy, and Steve, none of whom had seen Sara since supper. They interrupted Ashley's clarinet playing, but she hadn't seen her either. Leaving their worried friends behind, they ran to search the castle. Monica checked the girls' rooms while the boys did a quick search of the common areas.

As they met in the great hall with no clue to Sara's whereabouts, the truth clicked in Levi's mind. He knew exactly where she was—or, at least, where she had been not long before. Throat burning with bile, he grabbed each of his friends by the arm. "The Trojan horse! We helped Miss Nydia kidnap Sara!"

Chapter 40

Tricked

"What're you talking about?" Trevor's eyes narrowed then rounded with realization. "Oh, no! You're right!"

Monica glared between them. "What? Explain."

"We helped Miss Nydia push the Trojan horse to the woods for the play," Levi said flatly. "And she sent us back to the castle without her."

Monica's mouth formed a perfect O. "You believe Sara was inside the horse?"

Levi started pacing. "She reversed it, the whole Trojan horse story. Mr. Austin warned us that day in class. He said not to let go of the truth ever, to be careful who you trust. But she didn't use the horse to bring the enemy inside the castle." He stopped pacing, yanked off his hat, pulled his hair. "The traitor tricked us! She used the horse to sneak Sara out for Deceptor." With a low groan, he slapped the hat back on his head. "And like an absolute idiot, I helped her!"

Trevor yanked two fistfuls of his own hair. "Stupid, Trevor, stupid!"

Levi clamped his teeth tight. He had no time to beat himself up over the past. If he didn't think logically about all of this now, Sara might not survive. What should they do next? Try to find Mr. Dominic? Stop the play? Every fiber of Levi's being longed to run into the woods and tear every leaf from every tree until he found her, but he couldn't seem to move his feet until—

"Maybe she's still in there!" Levi yanked his two friends through the castle doorway and across the field, pitch dark because the stars and moon could no longer pierce the thick clouds. Despite Mrs. Sylvester's scolding for them to sit down, he and the others slunk behind the audience now involved in the play and slipped into the forest. They moved quickly between the trees, bypassing the kids waiting their turn on stage. When they reached the horse, Levi shoved aside the canvas door and strained to see into the dark interior.

It was empty.

Hopeless, he whispered, "Sara?" and felt around on the dark floor. At first he found nothing but a splinter, which stuck in his pinky. Then he ran his hand over something cold and metallic in the back corner.

He grabbed it and turned to his friends. "She's not here, but I found this on the floor." He held the object closer to his eyes. It was a gold necklace.

Monica snatched it from him. "It's Sara's. I helped her put it on this afternoon. She told me it was a gift from her mother she only wears on special occasions."

Levi swallowed the fear in his throat. "That's it then, I'm going after her." He pulled a flashlight from his pocket. Why hadn't he thought to use it when searching the horse? *Come on, brain, wake up.*

With the light, he searched the forest floor for some sign of Sara's passage. Too bad he hadn't paid more attention in woodcraft classes.

Another flashlight beam crossed his. Trevor tossed him a grim smile then turned to scour the ground. "Did you think you were the only one who planned ahead?"

Levi returned his focus to the matted ground. With so many footprints, how could they find the right ones?

After several agonizing minutes, Trevor whispered, "Here."

Levi hurried to his side. Two pairs of small footprints separated from the trampled mass and extended several paces north of the wooden horse, then disappeared into the dark forest.

Levi nodded, mouth tight. "Thanks. I'll be okay now." He started forward.

Trevor grabbed his arm. "You're not going alone."

"Am too."

"Uh-uh." Trevor glared at him. "Don't forget you're not the boss, Levi Prince."

Levi sighed. "I'm not trying to boss you. I just have a feeling this could get dangerous."

"It's a good thing I got these then."

Both boys turned. Monica held three scabbards. She unsheathed a sword. Its unprotected blade glinted in the dim light. A burlap bag lay on the ground at her feet.

"How did you—?" Trevor began.

At the same time, Levi said, "You're not going."

"Oh, yes I am. And there's no time to argue. Who knows where that lunatic has taken Sara."

"Listen." Levi snatched a scabbard and buckled it around his waist. "Somebody has to scout around here for Hunter's buddies and distract them. I don't know how many of them know who he is or would actually be willing to kidnap Sara with him. But he got to Miss Nydia, so who knows—"

Monica and Trevor gaped at him, the other two swords still on the ground at their feet.

Levi frowned. "What? I only meant you two could keep them busy while I go after Hunter and Miss Nydia."

"Levi." Trevor sounded like he was talking to a slow two-year-old. "You can't possibly still think Hunter is behind all this. I mean, this has gone way beyond some stupid rivalry. It's serious."

"Of course it's serious! What do I look like, an idiot? Deceptor is a shape-shifter. I still say the best way to get into the castle is to pose as a student. No telling what form Hunter—or should I say, Deceptor—has taken by now."

"I just saw him, Levi," Monica said softly.

"You just saw Deceptor? Right."

"No, not Deceptor. Hunter." She got in his face, fists on her hips. "He and all of his buddies are heckling the actors up near the stage."

"I don't believe it." Hunter was guilty. He had to be.

"Come see for yourself." Monica tugged him to an opening in the trees.

He leaned forward and scanned the crowd seated on the ground. It was so dark he couldn't tell who anybody was. Near the stage, though, in the light of the bonfire and torches, he recognized Hunter and his friends.

Levi turned back to Trevor and Monica. "Okay, so he hasn't gone yet. You two keep an eye on him, follow him when he leaves. I'll follow Nydia's trail and hopefully get Sara away before he shows up."

Trevor and Monica exchanged a look that plainly said, *can you believe this moron?*

Levi scowled. He wasn't about to waste more time arguing with these two. They could believe what they wanted. He had to go.

The sounds of Hunter and his buddies insulting the actors tugged Levi's attention. He glanced at the adults stationed behind the audience. Why wasn't the staff closer to keep the kids under control?

Then it hit him. They were acting as guards—with no idea the crime had already been committed.

Mr. Dominic. Levi scanned the adults, hoping for some real help. Because Monica and Trevor just didn't get it. But there was no sign of the director. Or any of the men, for that matter. He turned to Monica and Trevor, his voice firm. "Here's what's going to happen. You two are gonna find Mr. Dominic and tell him what happened. He can follow Deceptor when he leaves to meet Miss Nydia." He cocked his head toward the campers. "I'm going after Sara."

Without waiting for a reply, he trudged into the woods with his flashlight trained on the scuffmarks he hoped would lead him to his friend.

Soft footfalls whirled him around. Trevor and Monica marched after him, their faces stone.

Why wouldn't they listen? "I told you two to stay there." Irritation steeled Levi's voice. He chose to ignore the tiny surge of joy that welled in his chest at not having to follow a maniac all by himself.

"Look, man." Trevor's shoulders bunched in anger. "You're an absolute fool thinking Hunter is Deceptor because he's not. But we can't let you traipse off through the woods alone at night, thinking the worst you'll face is some frail elf lady."

Monica's lips pinched. "I'm sure Miss Nydia is perfectly capable of trouncing Levi in a duel, lady or not."

Levi shook his head as if he hadn't heard her right. "Excuse me?"

Monica ignored him. "However, Trevor is right. Your tracking them alone isn't going to help Sara, especially if you have to battle two adults. You need help."

"How is Mr. Dominic supposed to know where to find us if we all go? You should stay here, Monica." Levi pointed back the way they'd come.

"No." She perched a fist on her hip. "I left a note on the Trojan horse, explaining to Mr. Dominic where we'd gone. Somebody will find it soon, but we have to go after Sara now. Besides, you'll need me. Especially when you meet up with the real Deceptor." She indicated the waiting path. "Now go. We don't have time to waste on a debate."

Levi whipped around and stomped into the darkness. She was right. They didn't have time to argue.

That didn't mean he had to like it.

Chapter 41

The Search

Levi and his friends hiked for so long he wondered if they'd taken a wrong path somewhere. His anxiety mounted by the minute. No telling what they'd meet in these woods. At best, a lunatic elf. Worst, some horrific creature—maybe that basilisk Albert mentioned. Or one of the bad dragons. What did a good dragon look like anyway?

Levi shook his head. Who was he kidding? The worst they'd face was Deceptor, in the form of Hunter. Hunter was definitely scary, but Levi had fought him before.

But what if Levi was wrong about Hunter, as his friends insisted? What if Deceptor was something much worse than the bully who'd tormented him all summer? The thought wormed a hole in Levi's confidence. He shoved it away.

He was right about Hunter. He had to be. But what if Deceptor took a different form—maybe some creature so terrifying it made Levi bolt, leaving his friends to deal with the demon alone?

A new thought stopped Levi in his tracks. Deceptor, no matter his form, wasn't actually the worst they might face. Satan himself was. Levi swallowed hard. They couldn't possibly be expected to stand up to the Prince of Darkness himself, could they?

Don't borrow trouble, Levi. His grandma's pet saying weighed his heart with homesickness.

He forced his focus back to the trail. Which way now? He couldn't tell. The scuffmarks that had been so clear were now faded . . . or else a figment of his imagination.

He glanced into the undergrowth. Were those yellow eyes reflected in his flashlight beam? Pulse pumping, he blinked hard and looked again.

Nothing.

Control yourself, Levi. This is no time to freak.

"Ouch!"

At Monica's soft scream, Levi whirled around and attempted to yank out his sword, but he somehow managed to get it hung up in the sheath. Some hero he was. Thankfully, by the time he wrenched it free, he didn't see anything scarier than trees and brush. "What's wrong?"

"Thorns." She held up her blood-streaked arm.

"Be careful." Levi sheathed his sword.

"Thanks for the warning."

"At least we wore jeans," Trevor pointed out.

"True." Levi looked down at his dirty pant legs. Briars stuck to the hems.

"I'll bet Sara didn't," Monica said quietly. "That woman probably dragged her through the woods in her shorts."

Trevor kicked at some undergrowth. "Evil witch."

"Come on." Teeth clenched, Levi led the way along the faint trail, which he was beginning to fear was nothing more than a deer path. They stopped several times to argue over which way to go, and an hour later, Levi knew they were lost. He had no idea where he'd led his friends. He'd never been this deep into Terracaelum. He didn't even know which direction they were headed because he couldn't see the sky. He kept trying to visualize the map he'd seen on his one visit to the director's office—he knew there were mountains to the north with tunnels and caves beneath them. They'd crossed the river awhile back—it ran in a roughly east-west direction. But, try as he might, he couldn't figure out where they were in the tightly packed trees.

He heard nothing in the dead air, not even the rustling of night animals or the hoot of hunting owls. Nor did he hear the sounds he dreaded most: the crashing of a werewolf on the attack or the hiss of Deceptor in the underbrush. Every few minutes the silence would get to him, and he'd halt and raise his hand for the others to stop. Then all three would stare into the woods, moving only their eyes, not making a single sound. But each time they stopped, he heard only their rapid breathing.

It was much later before Levi thought of God. What was the matter with him? Why hadn't he prayed at the first sign of trouble? "God?"

He kept his voice low so his friends wouldn't hear. "Do you see what's going on? Sara's in trouble and there're just us three kids to save her. We're gonna need a little help." This was no time for pride. "Actually, we're gonna need a lot of help. So if you could send a legion of angels or something, that would be great."

A legion of angels. Mr. Dominic had told him things were different here—that the spirit world took on a more physical form. That meant a shape-shifting demon sorcerer would be a very real opponent and so would ghosts and ghouls. But it should also mean God's servants were more real, too, that angels could appear as physical warriors to protect Sara and his friends. A memory jostled for attention. Hadn't Mr. Dominic told him Terracaelum had an angelic protector? Levi was almost sure he had.

The thought of a big, burly angel fighting Deceptor comforted him nearly as much as the gentle breeze on his face, giving him the courage to keep searching for Sara. And for whatever unspeakable evil had captured her.

Because giving up wasn't an option.

Chapter 42

Lucien

"Levi..."

At Monica's whimper, Levi turned her direction. Her hands trembled as she groped for the hilt of her sword. A wide-eyed Trevor pulled his sword from the scabbard strapped across his back and made a squeaking sound. Levi pivoted slowly, examining the dark trees, searching for whatever had them so scared.

A huge gust of wind forced him back a few paces as a warning rang in his mind. *Flee.*

Not seeing anything scarier than the gloom itself, he braced himself against the wind. "What's wrong now, Monica?"

"Over there," Trevor squeaked, pointing a shaky finger to their left.

Levi looked. Dread traced cold fingers down his spine. With one hand, he gripped his flashlight. With the other, he whipped his sword from its sheath. At least it didn't get stuck this time. His mouth dropped open to release a scream. He couldn't make a sound.

He raised his light higher, aiming the trembling beam at the huge figure mere feet away. The light revealed a creature unlike anything he'd ever seen: two large shining blue wings furled behind a white body that shimmered iridescent silver. He—the creature looked male to Levi—hovered above the forest floor, bare except for loose pants and a long scabbard belted at the waist. As Levi raised the beam to light his chiseled face, so bright it seemed to glow on its own, Monica let out a whispered shriek and Trevor gasped. Again Levi wanted to scream, but something held him back.

The creature's marble-like lips parted. A deep voice reverberated through the forest. "Leviticus Isaiah Prince, kindly lower your light."

Too startled to do anything but obey, Levi lowered his arm so the beam didn't glare in the brilliant blue eyes. With the light on the being's bare chest, his bulky pectoral muscles were thrown into relief. Levi shivered at the sheer power implied by those muscles. He could easily rip them to pieces if he chose.

Levi's ankles trembled. What was this thing? Could it be an angel? Hope raised goose bumps on his arms. Could this be Terracaelum's resident angel Mr. Dominic had mentioned? Levi gulped. "Um, excuse me . . . how do you know my name?"

"You called on the Ruler of the Universe for aid." The creature's voice was so rich and melodious it sent a surge of excitement through Levi's belly. "I came."

The words hung in the air. Levi shivered. He wanted to see his friends' reactions to the announcement, but his prickling neck hairs told him not to turn his back on the creature. He didn't even consider trying to wield his sword because, somehow, he felt sure the creature spoke the truth. The Great Emperor had sent help—very physical, very terrifying, very big help. Terracaelum's protector.

"What should we call you?" he asked after a moment. "The creature" seemed disrespectful, even in his thoughts.

"You may call me Lucien." He gave a slight bow.

Lucien? Latin for light. The perfect name for an angel.

Levi sheathed his sword. What was the proper thing to say to an angel? "Uh . . . nice to meet you, Lucien." He offered his hand.

Lucien smiled, one eyebrow lifted. Feeling silly, Levi dropped his hand. He darted a glance at his friends staring slack-jawed at Lucien. "These are my friends, Monica and Trevor."

"Yes." Lucien nodded once. "Monica Marie Jefferson. Trevor Barnabas Patterson. I know much of you both."

Monica shrank behind Trevor. Trevor's face was so white he looked like he might pass out. Obviously, Lucien's knowing them did nothing to ease their fears.

But Levi was pleased that his flashlight beam, still trained on Lucien's chest, no longer trembled. "No disrespect intended, Lucien, but how do you know so much about us?"

"I am a servant of the Great King. When he bids me, I go out from his presence to do his will." Lucien's eyes flashed. "And as for how I know of you three—well, you are among the redeemed, among those for whom the Prince of Peace shed his blood. Do you not think he speaks of you?"

Levi could only stare. He knew Jesus had died to save him, knew he'd been rescued from his sin through Christ's death on the cross. But God himself talking with Jesus about runty Levi Prince . . . he couldn't imagine it.

"But why?" Trevor's husky whisper drew Levi's gaze. His friend's face was wet with tears, but all Levi could think of was that Trevor's voice hadn't squeaked.

Trevor took a single step nearer Lucien, pain stark in his face. "Why would God talk about me? My own dad doesn't even give a rip about me."

The creature watched Trevor for several moments. "Your unrepentant earthly father is not a mirror of your Heavenly Father. The God of Heaven and Earth loves you more completely than even the best earthly father could. He loves to speak of you." Lucien's mouth tightened, Levi figured in disapproval of Trevor's dad.

"What about my parents? Does he speak of them?" Monica's voice was a strained whisper. She stepped out from behind Trevor and inched nearer Lucien.

Levi glanced back at Lucien in time to see a look he couldn't read on the marble-like features. The angel dipped his head. "Certainly."

Monica stretched out her hand. "What does he say? Will they be safe? Will they come home to us soon?" Her forehead wrinkled. "Or will they stay on the mission field without us?"

Levi's throat burned at the longing in her voice.

"You poor child." Lucien shook his head. "I cannot read the future. I am only a servant in his Majesty's court, nothing more. He has not seen fit to inform me of his plans for your parents or for you and your sisters." Again an odd look crossed his face. "I know only that he loves you deeply. Your family holds a special place in his heart, torn and uprooted as you are by your parents' service. He knows your pain. He speaks often of you."

Monica's hand dropped to her side. She breathed out, offered a sad smile, and wiped a tear from her cheek. "That'll have to do then."

"Yes." Lucien returned her smile. "It will have to do."

Rustling sounds and vague mutters came from a thicket on Levi's right. He glanced from Monica and Trevor to Lucien and pulled out his sword. He wove quietly through the trees until he could peek through low branches into a small clearing. In the middle stood Sara, hair disheveled, bare knees bloodied, and tears on her face. She had a gag in her mouth and a rope leading from her bound wrists to Nydia Sylvester's hand.

Levi's blood boiled.

The muttering elf paced in front of her victim. By the patchy moonlight, Levi could just make out her blotchy face and swollen eyes. As Sara's whimpers drew his focus, his muscles coiled, poised to jump out and rescue her.

A vice grip yanked him back.

Chapter 43

The Elf

Levi glared back over his shoulder at Lucien, kneeling on the ground. "Wait, Leviticus Prince." Lucien nodded toward the clearing. "Look carefully before you expose yourself and your friends. You have the element of surprise for the moment, but you must see all before acting."

Levi froze, the words a sharp reminder of Dr. Baldwin's instruction to see the whole board. Levi turned his head and scanned the area, this time paying close attention to every detail. He was glad he did. In the deepest shadows beyond Sara and Miss Nydia was a darker blot, a black hole in the middle of the forest.

"What is that?" He pointed toward the dark patch.

Monica moved closer. "It appears to be some sort of cave."

"Why would there be a cave in the woods?" Levi's eyes skimmed the surrounding trees. "We haven't gotten to the mountains yet."

"We may have," Trevor said from Monica's other side. "The ground's been rising for a while now, but it's so dark we couldn't see past the trees."

Levi didn't admit he hadn't noticed the rising terrain. "Well, if it is a cave, what do we do? We don't know what's inside."

"It could be where Deceptor is waiting for Miss Nydia to bring Sara." Monica's voice trembled.

"Then we'd better get her now." Trevor started to rise.

"Hold on." Levi pulled him back down and turned to Lucien. "What should we do? Is Deceptor watching for us? Should we get Sara now?"

"I do not know." Lucien's smile twisted. "I told you I am not all-knowing. I am mercy here to lend you a comforting presence from the Almighty. You must choose your own course of action." He leaned closer to Levi, the smile vanishing. "Think. What ought you to do?"

Levi scowled. What good was an angel sent to lend a comforting presence? They needed real help.

His eyes shot to the clearing as Miss Nydia gave Sara a vicious yank toward the dark hole. Sobbing through her gag, Sara stumbled. Rage bubbled in Levi's stomach. He couldn't wait any longer. He couldn't let Miss Nydia drag Sara into that black hole.

Sword high, he shoved through the trees. "Stop!"

Both females turned at his bellow. Sara let out a muffled yelp. Nydia snarled like an angry cat.

"What are you doing here, boy?" Nydia drew a long knife from her belt. "You should've stayed at camp."

Levi sensed movement on either side and knew his friends had joined him. He didn't look away from his opponent though, even when it was clear from Miss Nydia's startled, upraised eyes that Lucien stood behind him.

"Why are you doing this, Miss Nydia?" Monica pleaded from Levi's right. "We trusted you. Sara trusted you. How can you betray her?"

The elf's eyes shifted to Monica. "You don't understand. I have no choice."

"But, why?" Trevor's harsh voice cut in from Levi's left. "Think about your parents. You're shaming them." The elf shot Trevor a stricken look, at least until he continued. "What about Sara's parents? They'll be crushed if something happens to her."

At the mention of the Dominics, Miss Nydia's jaw jutted. "I hope they are. He deserves the pain, and I hope it kills her!"

Sara's head shot up.

"How can you say that?" Levi demanded. "They treated you like family." The insanity in Miss Nydia's eyes made his skin clammy.

Miss Nydia released a cold laugh. "Family? I was supposed to marry Tobias, not her. He loved me and she stole him. But now . . ." She glanced over her shoulder at the yawning cave. "Now I will get the desires of my heart, desires I've been denied for over a century."

Panic rippled through Levi's veins, but he kept his voice rational. "If you're mad at Sara's parents, how can you take it out on her?" He darted glances around the area. He had to keep the crazy woman talking, buy some time. He inched nearer Sara, eased between her and the cave.

"Oh, but Sara won't be hurt. He promised." Nydia patted the weeping girl's head. "I know she'll be sad over her mother's death for a time, but soon she'll get over her grief." The elf's smile turned sappy. "She'll have her father and me, after all. We'll be the family we always should've been."

Levi drew back a step. This woman was a nutcase—one who was again pulling Sara toward that black hole. "Wait a minute," he said, fighting panic. "Let's talk about this."

"Enough talk! Get out of my way." Nydia shoved past him.

Sara dug in her heels, straining the rope taut.

Levi leapt forward and slashed the rope. He snatched Sara's arm and flung her behind him, hoping Trevor or Monica would catch her.

Whirling, Miss Nydia raised her arm. The cut rope dangled. Rabid fury blazed through her eyes. Though someone moved behind him, Levi didn't dare look away from the elf.

"You shouldn't have done that," she purred even as her nostrils flared. She raised her knife and advanced slowly on him.

Levi spread his legs and raised his sword. Why did his first real battle have to be against a girl?

Miss Nydia flung herself at him, her knife leveled at his chest. He swiped wildly with his sword, deflecting at the last second. As the ring of metal filled his ears, Levi whirled and steadied himself. She was stronger than she looked. When she came at him again, this time swinging for his head, his attempt to parry failed. If her aim had been better, she'd have slit his throat.

Rage burned away his last bit of hesitancy. Who cared if she was a woman? She was trying to kill him. He swung at her.

Miss Nydia easily blocked Levi's strike. "You irritating boy. Always interfering—just like your namesake."

Distracted by her words, he faltered.

But she didn't attack. Her feral eyes moved to something beyond his left shoulder. "Never try to outwit Deceptor or his servants." A slow smile spread across Miss Nydia's face, a smile that made cold sweat dribble down Levi's back. "Because it never works."

Scalp prickling, Levi glanced back. What he saw felt like a physical blow.

Eyes glittering with malice, Lucien squeezed Sara in a grip so tight it made her eyes bulge. When she finally stopped struggling, he stroked her cheek with a single white forefinger. One of her tears coursed down his finger and dropped to the ground where Trevor and Monica lay face-down, bound and gagged.

"Lucien?" Levi's sword drooped. "What're you doing? You told us you were an angel sent to help us. You're . . . you're . . ."

A cold smile lit upon Lucien's lips. "Deceptor?" He shrugged a massive shoulder, amusement in his icy gaze. "I lied to you. That's what I do."

A deranged giggle whirled Levi around. He'd forgotten the elf. Her knife sliced into his left shoulder.

Levi gasped as numbness trickled down his arm. A sharp stinging soon replaced the numbness. He managed to hang on to his sword with his right hand, but he wasn't sure he could fight. He bit his tongue against the pain. His eyes darted between Miss Nydia and Deceptor.

He couldn't think of a single move that would get them out of this alive.

Chapter 44

Weakness

"We have them, master," Miss Nydia said in an oily tone. "Now we can take Sara to the castle and trade her for her mother. Then I can take my rightful place as its mistress."

Deceptor sneered. "No, elf, now I can kill her and her friends, and when the Dominics come looking for their child, I'll kill them and take my rightful place as Prince of Terracaelum."

Levi's heart froze. How could he have ever believed a schoolyard bully like Hunter was this . . . monster? His friends and Mr. Dominic had tried to tell him. Why hadn't he listened? Why had he led his friends straight into a trap, thinking he, a stupid, undersized kid, could rescue Sara? Now they were all going to die, and it was all his fault.

"You promised!" Miss Nydia's eyes bugged. A nerve twitched in her right lid. "You said if I helped you, you'd give me what I want."

"You'll be grateful if I let you live." Deceptor's lip curled. "Now deal with the boy." He turned and set Sara on the ground with the others.

God, please, I'm an idiot. I don't deserve it, but please help!

The elf closed in on Levi. Before she reached him, an idea rose in his mind.

"He lied to you, Miss Nydia," Levi breathed.

She hesitated, eyes flitting to his, and his heart skittered. "Now he's going to destroy Sara," he whispered. "You know you love her more than anything else." He glanced at Deceptor, who was binding Sara's ankles. He had maybe a few seconds. His eyes flicked back to Miss Nydia. "He plans to kill Mr. Dominic. Probably you too."

Miss Nydia speared Deceptor with a look of pure hatred. Hope surged through Levi. Maybe this would work. But then the elf pressed her lips into a hard line and reached for Levi's sword. "Shut up, boy."

His hopes crashed.

No, he couldn't give up. "If you both survive," Levi breathed, talking fast, "you know Sara's dad will never forgive you. It won't matter that you did all of this out of love for him. He'll despise you."

Tears flooded her eyes, and her hand drifted back to her side. Without his sword. She again turned hard eyes on Deceptor.

"Why haven't you killed him, elf?" Deceptor's words stabbed like icicles.

The ring of metal warned Levi the sorcerer had drawn his sword from its scabbard. He whirled around. Deceptor lunged, his blade a blinding flash of silver. At the last possible second, Levi feinted left and swiped with his sword. It clanged against Deceptor's blade, jarring Levi's arm so hard he thought his shoulder might be dislocated.

With a desperate prayer, Levi twirled right and struck again. This time Deceptor's laughter rang out louder than the clank of his blocked strike. Both arms shaking from the pressure of blade on blade, Levi stared into the laughing face above him. A drop of sweat trickled into one eye. He didn't dare blink.

He'd thought fighting Hunter was horrible. This was David and Goliath for real. Except this time Mr. Dominic wasn't around to rescue Levi from the giant. Levi's left arm burned in agony. His right arm trembled. With the utmost casualness, Deceptor pressed Levi's blade backward inch by inch, making it clear he could crush him with ease whenever he chose.

He should just give up and die. He deserved it. He was such a weak fool. *I'm sorry, God.*

A muffled moan from one of his friends brought tears to his eyes. *God, they'll die too. Forgive me! Help us!*

The tiniest breeze touched his face. *My strength is made perfect in weakness* echoed through his mind.

With all of his might, Levi pressed his sword against Deceptor's. But it was like trying to push the entire island. His last vestiges of strength drained away. *I'm weak, God. I can't beat Deceptor. Please . . .*

Just as his trembling arms gave way, something shoved him from the side. His sword separated from the shape-shifter's with a clank. As he fell, Levi watched Miss Nydia run full-force into Deceptor, burying her knife to the hilt in his exposed belly. Deceptor's laughter ended in a shriek. He doubled over but didn't fall.

"You will not harm my Sara." Nydia's face shone with the fierceness of an eagle protecting her eaglets.

"Fool." Deceptor rose to full height and sliced his blade across Nydia's throat. She crumpled to the dirt.

Levi scrambled between his friends and Deceptor, shoved himself upright on wobbly legs. He could barely raise his sword. Deceptor hobbled toward Sara with a hungry look in his eyes. A silvery substance oozed from his wound.

"You can't have her!" Levi surprised himself with his forceful bellow. No way could he defeat Deceptor, even with the wound. "God, please, you have to stop him."

Deceptor lifted hate-filled eyes. "I am lord of Terracaelum." His sword quivered, poised for attack.

A fierce wind blasted the forest, leaving a perfect circle of calm around Levi and his friends. Trees swayed as if battered by a hurricane. Deceptor sank to his knees under the blast. He tried to rise, tried to lurch toward Levi with sword raised. But the wind flung him to the dirt and pressed him flat. In slow motion, Deceptor crawled toward the cave on his belly like a half-frozen snake.

With a final, high-pitched howl, the demon disappeared into the black pit.

The wind died instantly.

My strength is made perfect in weakness hung in the silent air.

Chapter 45

Journey's End

For a second, Levi stood there blinking. Had that really just happened?

As his astonishment faded, his gaze roved the clearing. What should he do now? Follow Deceptor into that terrifying cave and try to finish him off? He sure didn't want to, but was it the right thing to do? Someone whimpered in the huddle of bodies on the ground, and he let out a relieved breath. He couldn't go after Deceptor. His friends needed him.

He bent and cut their bonds. While they removed their gags, he hurried to the fallen elf, yanking off his shirt as he went. Maybe it wasn't too late to stop her bleeding and save her life.

When Levi knelt beside her, he saw she was dead. His throat closed and tears pricked his eyes. Even though Miss Nydia had tricked them, she'd been tricked as well—first, apparently, by Sara's parents, then by her own mind, and finally by Deceptor.

A soft thump pulled his eyes from the elf. Beside him, Sara huddled over Miss Nydia, weeping in silence. He put his arm around her shoulders and felt her tremble. Her skin was so cold. Why hadn't he brought along a jacket?

A sense of failure weighed on him. How could anything he might say console Sara in this horrible situation? He finally murmured the only thing he could come up with. "She died protecting you, Sara."

Trevor stood rigid near Miss Nydia's head, fists jammed into his hips, face livid. "Yeah, after she dragged Sara out here in the first place! It's her fault Sara—and all of us—almost died."

Levi sighed. He was too tired to feel angry. "I think she regretted it in the end."

Trevor made a sound in his throat, almost a growl. Was he going to kick her dead body?

Levi met Trevor's eyes. "We should forgive her. She paid with her life."

Monica came up on Sara's other side and hugged her, gently rocking and quietly shushing. The act reminded Levi so much of his mom that his stomach ached. With a sigh, he pulled his shirt back over his head.

His gaze drifted toward the cave where Deceptor had disappeared. He shook his head, blinked, squinted. "The cave's gone." Hefting his sword, he moved cautiously to the spot he'd last seen it.

Trevor followed. "It was there a minute ago. I saw that foul creature go inside."

"Yeah, me too." He shook his head. "It's definitely gone. Did you see—" He wanted to ask Trevor if he'd seen the whole windstorm thing, but Trevor had already started back to the girls.

"We have to get them back to the castle," he said to Levi over his shoulder. "Everybody's probably going crazy trying to find us."

Levi nodded. He'd think about the windstorm later. For now he was simply thankful they'd all survived. Well, almost all. He cocked his chin toward Miss Nydia's body. "We have to figure out a way to get her back."

"Why bother?" Trevor's voice turned brittle. "Let the animals have her."

Levi frowned. He understood Trevor's anger to a degree, but how could they just leave her? Her parents deserved a chance to say goodbye. "No. We'll take her home."

Though clearly not happy, Trevor carried Miss Nydia's upper body while Levi carried her feet. Monica led the way, helping Sara while trying to follow their trail from earlier. Before long, Levi felt sure they were walking in circles. Every tree looked the same, every bit of underbrush dark and shadowy. Miss Nydia, although light, weighed heavier and heavier as the night passed. Levi's body ached. The congealed cut on his left shoulder ripped open and seeped hot blood. Still, he didn't complain. Monica was doing her best.

As dawn poked tiny holes in the darkness, he heard voices calling their names.

"Here!" His voice came out a croak.

The sound of tramping feet neared, and a lump formed in Levi's gut. He stared down at the small ankles he clasped, ankles now cold and stiff, and thought of how devastated his parents would've been if the dead body had been his. What if the person approaching was one of the Sylvesters? Would he have to watch Miss Nydia's mom or dad cry over her?

The mere idea made him want to hide.

But it wouldn't be right to let Sara and Monica face whoever it was first. What if Deceptor had somehow healed himself and was even now tricking them? Not likely, but . . .

"Trevor." Levi jutted his chin toward the girls, who'd paused ahead of them on the trail. "We need to get in front."

Trevor nodded. The two moved up the trail, and the girls stepped back into the shadows. As the bushes in front of him quivered, Levi angled his body to better hide the elf's. He'd break the news gently, the way he'd want someone to do for his own parents.

When Mr. Dominic appeared between the branches, Levi blew out a relieved breath. As the director strode into the clearing, a scabbard strapped to his back, his eyes locked on Levi's. Levi watched the man's gaze flick to the body. The blood drained from the director's face, and he pushed past Levi. Only then did Levi realize Mr. Dominic thought he and Trevor carried Sara. As Mr. Dominic caught sight of Miss Nydia's face, his fearful expression shifted to one of relief, then to deep sorrow.

The undergrowth rustled as Dr. Baldwin joined them. "Who is it?" The doctor's voice quavered as he stopped beside Levi.

"Nydia Sylvester," Levi said hoarsely. Now that adults had arrived to take the burden, exhaustion threatened to press him into the ground.

"Daddy?" Sara's quiet voice came from the shadows.

"Sara!" Face crumpling, Mr. Dominic rushed over and scooped her into his arms. "My baby girl, are you all right?"

"It was Miss Nydia, Daddy." Sara pulled back and looked into his eyes. "She tricked me." Tears streaked her dirty face. "How could she do that?"

Mr. Dominic's face was gray as he patted her back. He squeezed his eyes shut tight. A moment later, he opened them. "I should've realized."

"She saved us in the end though, sir." Somehow this fact was crucial to Levi. Bad as Miss Nydia's actions had been, he didn't want anyone to think the worst of her. "She stabbed Deceptor to help us escape." His voice dropped to a whisper. "Then he killed her."

Dr. Baldwin squeezed Levi's shoulder.

Mr. Dominic scrubbed a hand over his face. "We should get back to the castle and signal that you're found." He kissed Sara's brow. "Your mother's frantic for you, little one. Let's get you home to her so she can fuss over you."

Sara gave him a tiny smile. He set her on her feet and turned to Levi and Trevor. Drawing in a pained breath, Mr. Dominic took the elf's body. Levi felt strange without the burden, relieved to have it lifted, but guilty too, as if he should take it back and carry it to the castle himself.

They were a silent group—Sara walking close to her father, Monica and Trevor following hand-in-hand, Levi bringing up the rear with Dr. Baldwin. When they emerged from the dank, dark forest into the bright early morning sunshine, Levi sucked in a huge mouthful of air. He felt almost like he'd been underwater too long, like now his body could get the oxygen it so desperately needed.

Then he saw the castle looming before them and almost ran back into the forest. The Sylvesters were inside. Did he have the strength to face them?

A strong yet gentle breeze caressed his face. He drew in another lungful of fresh air. He could do this. The journey was almost over.

As they neared the lowered drawbridge, a trumpet blare pierced the stillness. Levi's head jerked up. Albert leaned between the ramparts on the tower roof, the instrument at his lips.

"The signal that our lost have been found," Dr. Baldwin explained.

When they entered the north foyer, a swarm of staff persons descended on them. Mrs. Dominic, looking old and frail, shoved through the crowd. When she saw Sara, she burst into tears and gathered her child into her arms. When her gaze fell on the burden her husband carried, she bowed her head and wept into her daughter's hair.

A second later, Mrs. Sylvester ran into the room. She searched until her frantic eyes caught on Mr. Dominic. With obvious dread, she lowered her gaze to her daughter's body in his arms. "No!" The color drained from her already-pale face. She swayed.

Levi lurched forward as if to catch her. But her husband, who had entered the room behind her, caught her before she hit the floor. With his wife in his arms, Mr. Sylvester staggered across the room to reclaim his child.

Chapter 46

Monica and Trevor

Under Dr. Baldwin's orders, Levi, Trevor, and Monica waited for Mr. Dominic on the infirmary cots sipping hot tea. They'd washed up, changed their blood-stained clothes, and had their cuts and bruises cared for. A few minutes earlier, Dr. Baldwin had gone to his room to rest. Levi's body demanded he lie down and sleep, but his heart wanted nothing more than to climb the stairs to his room, gather his things, and walk down to the southern tip of Castle Island to wait for his family. He wanted to go home.

It was much too early, though. He'd heard the buzz from the dining hall as the other campers ate breakfast, oblivious to the previous night's events. The ferry wouldn't arrive at the island until noon when they'd have the awards ceremony and a feast. Along with a second performance of *The Trojan Horse*. Levi's fuzzy brain told him he needed to help move the horse down to camp, so he stood and set down his cup.

"Levi?" Monica called as he opened the door.

He didn't get far because Mr. Dominic stood poised to open the door, Mr. and Mrs. Sylvester behind him. Levi peered into the couple's ashen, tear-streaked faces and didn't know what to do. He opened his mouth to tell them how sorry he was, how he wished he'd been able to save their daughter, how everything was his fault because he'd been so blind and stubborn . . . but before he could speak, Mr. Sylvester stepped forward.

"We"—he gestured between himself and his weeping wife—"wanted to thank you children for bringing our daughter back." A sob escaped him. "After all she's done . . . it still means so much to be able to say goodbye."

Levi stood in wide-eyed silence. He looked back at his friends as the Sylvesters walked away. Monica wept into her hands, and even Trevor, who hadn't spoken since they'd picked up Miss Nydia's body, looked shaken.

Mr. Dominic moved into the room and guided Levi back to his cot. "Please rest and drink your tea. There's nothing you can do right now."

"But the Trojan horse—" Levi said stupidly, an image of the wooden prop imprinted in his mind.

"Yes." The director sat down and patted the cot. Levi sat beside him. "Sara told us how Nydia hid her in the horse and sneaked her from the building." He looked pointedly at both Levi and Trevor. "I know the two of you pushed it out of the castle for her."

Levi gulped, suddenly alert. He deserved whatever Mr. Dominic was about to yell at him.

But Mr. Dominic said, "You bear no blame for that. You had no idea she was inside, so release any guilt you might be harboring right now."

Levi blew out a breath, and Trevor's shoulders sagged.

"And you, young lady." The director turned to Monica, who stared at the teacup gripped in her hands. "You're a good friend to my daughter, the best she's ever had, and I want to thank you for it."

Monica's eyes flew to Mr. Dominic's as a tear slipped down her cheek.

"In fact," Mr. Dominic went on, "she wanted me to ask you to join her as soon as you could."

"I'll go now." Monica jumped up and set down her mug, sloshing her tea onto the table.

Mr. Dominic smiled. "Before you go, I'd like to ask you to keep the events of the night to yourselves. Most of the campers are blissfully unaware of the danger and tragedy the past few hours held for you four." His eyes squeezed shut. "As well as for the staff and inhabitants of Terracaelum."

He opened his eyes and peered out the window, his thoughts clearly on his kingdom's grief. After a moment, he looked back at them. "I will release you to speak of these events with your parents. And with your other friends, if you feel they can be trusted to remain discreet."

The three exchanged questioning looks then nodded. No one in their group would betray a confidence.

"It's not that I want to hide important information from the other campers," Mr. Dominic continued. "It's simply that the danger is past and, since Nydia always distanced herself from others, the grief is not theirs. They should be free to go home from summer camp without the burden of these heartbreaking events."

"We understand, sir." Monica's fingers knotted. "If I weren't involved last night, I really don't think I'd want to know myself."

With a sad smile, Mr. Dominic inclined his head. "I know you're anxious to see Sara and your other roommates. Please feel free to go now."

She moved to the door but turned back before opening it. "Sir, I don't know what your plans are for Sara now, and I'd love to have her join me at boarding school." She twisted the knob back and forth as if uncertain whether she should continue. Finally, she sighed. "But I really think she'd be better off here with you this year."

"Thank you, child. You truly are the best kind of friend."

Monica smiled through her tears.

The door clicked shut. Trevor stood and set his cup on the table next to Monica's. "Guess I should go pack my stuff. I've still got a lot to do."

"Trevor," the director said softly, drawing Trevor's troubled gaze. "Did anything happen last night you want to talk about?"

Trevor picked at his fingernail. Levi pretended to study a poster of the circulatory system on the wall.

"Did Deceptor say anything to you? Anything that bothered you in particular?" Mr. Dominic waited. "That's his specialty, you know. Using words to hurt others."

Levi sneaked a peek at his friend.

Trevor glared at his hiking boots as if he'd like to strangle them. "He pretended to be an angel when we first met him."

The director's eyes widened.

Trevor ground the toe of his boot against the floor. "Called himself Lucien and told us God loved us and talked about us a lot and stuff. Monica asked him about her parents, you know, if God had mentioned about whether they'd survive wherever they're at and all—"

Mr. Dominic released a quiet, "Poor girl."

"And I asked him"—Trevor's voice broke—"I asked him how he

could say God cared so much about me when my dad's hated me since my mom died." His glare cut to the director. "Deceptor told me God loves me even if my dad doesn't. But how can what he said be true? Since he's a nothing but a liar." Trevor's anger turned to silent sobs.

Levi twisted his fingers into the sheet. Should he say something?

Mr. Dominic moved to Trevor and wrapped an arm around his shoulders. Levi tried not to breathe too loudly.

After Trevor released a final noisy sniffle, he said, "Then there's Miss Nydia. She was supposed to be like a second mother to Sara, and she betrayed her." Pain flashed in his eyes. "Moms aren't supposed to hurt their children."

"First of all," Mr. Dominic said in a soothing tone, "Nydia's betrayal isn't the same as your mother dying. Your mom didn't want to leave you. She loved you."

As Trevor nodded, Levi's mouth fell open. So that's why Trevor had gotten so mad at the elf the night before.

Mr. Dominic raised both eyebrows at Trevor. "As for what Deceptor said to you as Lucien, that's one of the cruelest things he does, and he learned it from the Father of Lies himself. He says a true thing—in this case that your Heavenly Father loves you, even if your earthly father doesn't seem to—but he says it under false pretenses. And his deception makes you fear his words were a lie as well." He bent his head until Trevor met his gaze. "His words to you on that point were true, son. God the Father, Ruler of the Universe, loves you completely. Enough to send his Son to save you for all eternity. Do you understand?"

"Yes, sir, I understand." Trevor scrubbed his knuckles beneath his eyes. "My mom taught me about God. Jesus saved me before she died. I've kept going to church with my neighbor, even though my dad and brother make fun of me for it." He looked down. "But when Deceptor lied, I wasn't sure all of a sudden." He met the director's eyes again. "He threw me for a while there."

"I understand, son. As I said, that's his specialty." With a gentle smile, Mr. Dominic stood, his hand on Trevor's shoulder. "Now off with you. Get that mess of a room in order and pack up your stuff. We'll need to head down for lunch before too long. I'm getting hungry."

Trevor grinned and smacked a palm to his belly. "Me too."

Chapter 47

Keep Fighting

After Trevor left, Levi and Mr. Dominic sat in silence.

Levi finally broke it to ask the question that had bothered him throughout the night's journey, weighing heavier and heavier like the elf they carried. "Why did she do it?"

Mr. Dominic shook his head, though Levi could tell he understood the question.

"She said Mrs. Dominic stole you from her." Levi bit his lip. He shouldn't press the question when it was clear the director didn't want to answer. And yet, he really wanted to understand the reasons behind what happened.

Mr. Dominic blew out a long breath. "I guess you deserve to know. You almost died because of my foolishness."

"Never mind, sir. I don't want to know." And he didn't really. A vague queasiness had suddenly replaced his need to know.

The director offered a sad smile. "I need to tell you, Levi, so maybe you won't fall into the same sinful attitude I did." He paused. "Long ago when I was a camper here—along with your Papa Levi—I fell in love. Well, not really in love." He grimaced, his gaze sliding to the window. "When I was sixteen, I was taken with a girl from a different species, a girl most of the others had no idea wasn't human. But I knew. Like you, I discovered Terracaelum early on and quickly learned one of the campers was an elf."

"Miss Nydia?"

"Yes, Nydia Sylvester." Mr. Dominic met Levi's eyes. "Being an elf, she was much older than I was, but she looked like a human teenager. I'm sure you've noticed how young she still appears . . . appeared." He sighed. "Anyway, she was my friend from the time I started coming here when I was your age. She'd always loved to learn, so she was allowed to attend camp with the humans. I convinced myself I loved her and told her as much."

Mr. Dominic's mouth twisted in self-disgust. "Her parents, in agreement with Terracaelum's rulers at the time, made it clear we couldn't be together. They told us to marry across species was against God's law." He shook his head. "But I was so headstrong, so sure I could handle the situation, so certain I knew best."

Levi's gaze slithered away at the *headstrong* description. It sounded too much like himself.

"I made Nydia promises of marriage I had no business making," Mr. Dominic continued, seemingly unaware of Levi's discomfort. "And spent a miserable school year until the next summer when I discovered her parents had sent her off to relatives. I got over her quickly and fell in love with Sophia a couple of summers later." He smiled at Levi. "Mrs. Dominic to you."

Levi's ears burned. Did he really have to hear all this?

But Mr. Dominic kept talking. "To make a long story short, I married Sophia and we became Terracaelum's rulers. When Nydia returned to her parents several years later, I told myself she was as over our foolish relationship as I was and never spoke of it. I should have asked her forgiveness, but, once again, I thought I knew best." He shook his head and again drifted into silence.

A little later, he went on, "If I had only swallowed my pride and spoken to her as I should, she might've let the whole sorry relationship die. Then Deceptor never would've tricked her into helping him. But I didn't and thought all was well. We didn't see much of her until we had Sara decades later. When Nydia came to us and offered to act as nurse for our infant, we accepted. I thought it would be a way to finally smooth over the past. How wrong I was."

For several quiet moments, Levi stared at the top of Mr. Dominic's bowed head.

After a while, the old man looked up. "I can't change the past." He gave Levi's leg a quick pat. "I want to thank you for bringing Sara home. My wife asked me to offer her thanks as well." His face shadowed. "I'm afraid all the excitement has left her feeling unwell. We're both feeling our age today."

"At least Sara's safe now," Levi said as much for himself as the director.

Mr. Dominic pressed his lips together.

Levi frowned. "I mean with Miss Nydia and Deceptor both dead." He waited for the director to agree.

Mr. Dominic touched his whiskered chin and flicked his eyes around the room.

Levi's stomach bubbled. "What's wrong? Miss Nydia stabbed Deceptor, and he crawled into a cave to die, right?"

Mr. Dominic shook his head. "I hate to tell you this, son, but Deceptor likely isn't dead."

Levi opened his mouth to argue. Deceptor had to be dead.

Mr. Dominic raised a hand. "Such creatures don't die easily. He was wounded, and that bought you enough time to get back here safely. But he'll be back once he's had time to heal."

Levi shut his mouth hard. How could Levi even think about coming back next summer if Deceptor wasn't dead?

"Time and time again we've battled him, and he always returns." The lines in the director's face etched deep. "We never know what he'll try next. This time he infiltrated from within the castle and took on the appearance of an angel. In times past he's appeared in any number of disguises, both monstrous and beautiful." He released a heavy sigh. "He always comes back to fight another day."

Levi knotted his hands in his lap. "What will you do?"

Mr. Dominic met his eyes. "What we've always done in the past. We'll keep fighting."

Chapter 48

Going Home

Levi plodded through the castle doorway and onto the drawbridge, baggage weighing down his weary body, feet aching from last night's journey, shoulder wound throbbing despite the doctor's care. Everyone else had already gone down to camp for the play. He hoped if he moved slowly enough he'd miss *The Trojan Horse* performance. He couldn't deal with seeing that horse again. He didn't want to face Hunter either. He knew he'd been wrong about the bully all along, but he just couldn't shake the fear of Deceptor that was all mixed up in his mind with Hunter.

"Leviticus Prince!"

Levi turned to see Dr. Baldwin clinging to the frame of the infirmary window.

"Wait a second," the doctor called, "I'm coming down."

A minute passed before Dr. Baldwin appeared, huffing, in the doorway. "Didn't want to miss you. Wanted to say goodbye."

"You're not going down?"

"No, too tired." Dr. Baldwin pressed a hand to his chest. "If anybody needs a doctor, they know where to find me."

"Yeah, I guess they do." Levi offered his hand. "Thanks for everything, sir. The time you spent with me . . . it meant a lot."

The doctor gave his hand a firm shake. "I enjoyed it, too. Keep working on your chess game." He slapped Levi's back. "I expect you to be a real contender by next summer."

Levi smiled. "Yes, sir." Yet as his gaze shifted to the castle, his smile faded. Was he ready to leave this place? Would he ever return?

"Get going now. You're late." Though Dr. Baldwin's voice was gruff, moisture shimmered in his eyes.

Levi nodded but didn't move. "Can I ask you something?"

Dr. Baldwin's eyebrows pulled together. "I suppose."

"It's about Hunter."

"I thought you'd figured out that boy is not Deceptor."

"No, I know. It's about something I overheard you and Mr. Dominic saying one day." Levi flushed at the doctor's stern look. "What you said made me think you knew Hunter's ancestors somehow. Like maybe he had family here at one time."

The doctor worried his lower lip, his eyes piercing Levi. "You shouldn't listen to other people's conversations."

"I know. Sorry."

"You should be." Dr. Baldwin considered him another long moment. "I'll tell you this much: many long years ago, Hunter's great-great-aunt was here at camp with the Dominics and your great-great-grandfather."

Levi's jaw dropped.

"Now get on with you," the doctor said, his eyes gleaming. "I'm going to bed."

Levi sank into the back row as the Trojan horse was wheeled onto the stage. He avoided looking at it, his gaze instead skimming the audience in search of his family. There they were, in the front row. The sight of them only added to his confused emotions until he felt stuck, like a clogged drain, smelly and rank. He wanted to go home, yes. But what about his friends? What about Sara? With Deceptor alive, she'd still have to leave her home.

Tommy, Steve, and another kid burst from the Trojan horse's canvas door, snagging Levi's eyes. Then he couldn't tear his attention away from the prop.

He sensed someone slipping into the seat beside him, but his focus stayed on that horse.

"She's not in there," Trevor whispered.

Levi glanced at Trevor then settled his eyes back on the horse. "I know that."

"It's empty."

Levi frowned. "Yeah, I got it."

"We did right."

Levi turned his head, focusing his attention fully on his friend.

"We did right to bring Miss Nydia's body back to her parents." A fragile peace shone in Trevor's eyes.

A tiny portion of the weight lifted from Levi's spirits. "Yeah, we did right."

After the play, Mr. Dominic awarded gold, silver, and bronze medals for the winners of the Camp Classics Olympics, though he was careful to point out that the ancients used laurel wreathes instead. Levi clapped for each of his friends as they received their awards, but Trevor had to push him forward when Mr. Dominic announced his first place fencing award. He'd forgotten all about tying for the gold with Hunter.

As Levi passed the front row, he gave his family a quick wave. His sister Abby shrieked, "Yay, Levi!" When his mom snatched him into a hug, he gave her a quick return squeeze and pulled away. While he longed for the comfort of his parents, the weight of more than a hundred eyes, not all friendly, spurred him to keep moving.

But when his dad squeezed his shoulder and whispered, "You've grown a lot, son. I'm proud of you," tears stung Levi's eyes.

Blinking them away, he crossed in front of his little brothers Zeke and Jer just as Jer shrieked, "Levi won a medal?" and Zeke hollered back, "No way. There's gotta be a mistake."

Levi couldn't help grinning at his little brothers as he climbed onto the stage. Those two hadn't changed any. But they were right, really. He didn't deserve a medal. He hadn't defeated Hunter in the Olympics. And he'd failed Sara.

As Mr. Dominic slipped a gold medal over Levi's head, Hunter shot Levi a hate-filled look he knew he deserved. Nasty as Hunter acted, it was wrong for Levi to accuse him of being a shape-shifting demon sorcerer intent on destroying Terracaelum's rulers. Levi should apologize somehow.

Before they left the stage, Levi forced himself to congratulate Hunter.

Hunter turned his back and went to sit beside Martin. Levi scanned the nearby seats. An oversized couple he figured were Martin's parents sat on the big boy's right. No one sat near Hunter. Apparently, his parents hadn't made the trip to pick him up.

After a lunch Levi could barely eat, it was time to go home. He stopped on the way to the ferry and told Mr. Dominic goodbye.

"Farewell, young man." Mr. Dominic pressed a piece of thick paper into his hand.

"Um . . . goodbye, sir," Levi said, wondering vaguely if the director had replaced the invitation letter Hunter had shredded.

When Levi found a seat on the ferry, he noticed others holding similar papers. Some looked pleased with what they read, and others, like Greg, did not.

Trevor plopped onto the bench by him. "How'd you do?" He flapped his paper in Levi's face.

Confused, Levi unfolded his paper. A grade report. His shoulders relaxed as he skimmed it. "Good. Even passed in Math. You?"

Grinning, Trevor gave him a double thumbs-up.

The engines rumbled and the boat lurched out onto the open lake. Levi glanced around the deck at his family and friends talking together. He rose and crossed to Sara, alone with her elbows propped on the railing, her gaze on Castle Island.

"I'm sorry."

She scrunched her eyes at him. "What're you talking about?"

"If I'd gone into that cave after Deceptor, maybe you could've stayed in Terracaelum with your parents." Guilt pressed the air from his lungs.

Sara's giggle felt like a slap, but she immediately rested her hand on his wrist, her expression soft. "I don't have to leave Terracaelum."

"Then what're you doing here?" He gestured toward the packed ferry deck.

"You guys are the only ones who know who I am. Don't you think it'd be a little suspicious if I stayed on Castle Island when everyone else left?"

"Oh. Yeah." His neck heated. "But will you be safe . . . you know, back there?" He jutted his chin toward the island.

"I'll be okay. I just have to be careful." She shrugged. "Daddy says it always takes Deceptor a long time to recover after he's defeated." Her hand tightened around his wrist, her eyes serious. "And don't ever apologize for last night. You rescued me, and if you'd followed Deceptor into that black hole, you'd be dead now. What you did was very brave."

Levi's cheeks burned at the heat of her hand and the warmth of her words. "I didn't do much." Besides make a mess of everything trying to control his friends. "Trevor and Monica were great." And that whirlwind thing, had Sara seen that? It almost seemed like a dream to Levi now, but it must have happened. He sure couldn't have driven Deceptor away on his own. He was way too weak. He knew that now.

Sara smiled. "I know the others helped. You were all wonderful. Thank you."

"You're welcome."

Sara's smile faded. "I'll miss everybody so much." She looked out across the lake.

"Me too." Levi followed her gaze to Castle Island, the familiar pang clutching his throat.

Sara was silent a moment before facing him. "You will come back next summer, won't you?"

He looked at her. Would he come back? He honestly didn't know. With Deceptor around, not to mention Levi's own control-freak self . . . His gaze drifted to his friends and his shoulders sagged. What if next summer was like this one? What if he endangered his friends with his stupidity? His eyes dropped to the ferry's wake.

He couldn't come back.

A gust of wind blew into Levi's face. His eyes lifted to the horizon as he recalled Mr. Dominic's words about how God sometimes interacted in Terracaelum through wind and whispers. Cocking his head, Levi let the now-gentle breeze caress his cheeks.

His gaze moved to Sara. A line formed between her brows, probably because he hadn't answered her question. But he felt a smile blossom on his own face because he'd just made a connection—one that made everything all right.

That wind had visited him at every important moment this summer—when he'd needed comfort, encouragement, direction, even warning, which he had unfortunately ignored more than once. Then there was last night in the battle against Deceptor when the hurricane had saved Levi and his friends. And that victorious whisper, *My strength is made perfect in weakness*, words straight from Scripture. Levi suddenly understood it was God's Spirit that had comforted, directed, warned, and protected him every step of the way, all summer long.

And that was the most important thing of all because it meant God would be with Levi no matter where he went. Sara, the others, even Levi himself, none of them were dependent on Levi's ability to get everything right. Because God would always be strong, no matter how weak Levi was.

Over Castle Island's northern cliffs, a thousand rainbows suddenly shimmered, drawing Levi's eyes. A huge iridescent bubble blew from the tiny castle and out over the lake beyond. As both bubble and castle disappeared, Levi turned a joyful smile on Sara.

"Oh, yeah," he said, "I'll definitely be back next summer."

ABOUT THE AUTHOR

Author Amy C. Blake has appeared in many publications, both Christian-based and secular. With a Masters in English from Mississippi College, her work has consistently won praise and awards throughout her writing career, which has included everything from contributing articles to the publication of her full-length novels *Whitewashed* and *Colorblind*. Amy is a pastor's wife and homeschooling mother of four who resides in beautiful Ohio.

CPSIA information can be obtained at www.ICGtesting.com
Printed in the USA
BVOW05s0805030316

438788BV00002B/4/P